Demonic Summoning for the Modern Woman

Woman

Rifton Chronicles: Book 1

By Robinne Weiss

Published by Sandfly Books

ISBN-13: 978-0-473-67150-1

Cover design by Jenn Rackham

This book is also available in electronic formats.

Discover my other books and stories at https://robinneweiss.com

Prologue

1892: Death of the Witch

Isabella carefully set out the candles around the pentagram filling the floor of her one-room cottage. The illustration in the book showed rosemary scattered within the pentagram. Was there a pattern to it? Peering at the book in the flickering light, she frowned and then pushed some herbs around with her toe. How exact did the placement need to be?

The summoning was long, but Isabella had done other spells, so the rhythm of the words was familiar. She'd decided years ago that if she was going to be accused of witchcraft, she might as well become a witch. She'd mastered the simple household spells early on, but these summonings were trickier than a simple laundry blueing spell. It didn't stop her trying. If she could summon a demon, she could take revenge for the persecution her neighbours had subjected her to in the years since her abusive husband had died.

The accusation of murder hadn't bothered her—

the only thing she regretted about his death was that she hadn't caused it. What rankled was being accused of witchcraft after she discovered she was with child to Mr Taylor, who claimed he'd had nothing to do with her. Ensorcelled, he'd claimed. Ha! She'd been an easy mark, high on freedom after Robert's death. If she knew where Mr Taylor had vanished to, he'd be the first victim for her demon once she summoned it.

As it was, there were plenty of other people in the village she wanted the demon to terrorise. Nearly everyone had jumped on the 'ostracise Isabella the witch' bandwagon. She shut her eyes and took a deep breath to begin the incantation.

Men's voices on the road. Her eyes flew open. She snapped the book shut and hurriedly tucked it back into the metal box she kept her few treasures in. Then she slipped the box under the loose floorboard. She flipped the rug over the board and snuffed out all but one of the candles. She was sweeping the floor when a fist pounded on her door.

"Mrs Deacon, open the door." Ted Watson, head of the town council.

Light flickered against the curtains. Isabella resisted the urge to peek out. How many men were with Mr Watson? The whole council?

"Mrs Deacon, we know you're here. Open the door." That was William Grey, town council secretary.

If only she'd managed her summoning before they'd shown up. She'd fling open the door and welcome them in.

The banging continued. Isabella glanced around the room. Nothing incriminating was visible. She swept the last of the herbs into the fireplace where they smoked briefly and then sparked to flame.

She hesitated—she was alone, vulnerable. The idea of opening the door to Mr Watson and Mr Grey made her nervous. Could she simply refuse? This was exactly the sort of situation her daughter, Catherine, had warned her of when she begged her to move out of her cottage, to join Catherine and the grandchildren in their large villa. Maybe she should have accepted the offer.

The thought was extinguished with the next voice.

"Isabella, please." Ah, there he was—Thomas, her son-in-law. At least here she could choose not to open the door to him. Had she been living under his roof, that would be impossible. If he was here, the whole town council must have come. "It's about Phoebe Baker. We want to ask you some questions."

Phoebe? Isabella's heart sank. "Has she had the baby yet?" she called through the door.

Phoebe lived on a sheep station in the foothills. She'd come from Wellington with her much older husband, who had more money than sense. He loved station life, surrounded by farmworkers and freed from the necessary manners of city life. Phoebe, on the other hand, was distraught. The only woman for miles, she was lonely and fearful. When she found herself pregnant, she threatened to move back to

Wellington alone.

"I will not raise children in this godforsaken wasteland!" she'd protested.

But her husband wouldn't hear of it, and more importantly, wouldn't pay for her stagecoach and ferry tickets.

Every time she came into town, she looked more haggard. Isabella had pulled her aside once and grilled her, suspecting her husband might be beating her, as her own had done.

"No. He has never harmed me. He barely looks at me, and never talks to me." She'd burst into tears, and Isabella had taken pity on her and invited her to have tea. After that, Phoebe visited Isabella whenever she came to town. She was still worn down, but at least she looked a little happier whenever she left Isabella's place. Last week when she visited, she complained of heartburn. Isabella fixed her some herbal tea.

"This is what I drank when I was pregnant—did wonders in the last month."

It worked for Phoebe as well, so Isabella sent her home with a small packet to see her through to the birth. They parted with a hug, and Isabella promised to visit her after the baby was born.

"There was trouble with the baby." The voice jolted Isabella out of her thoughts. In her concern for Phoebe, she didn't stop to consider why the entire town council might be visiting her in the middle of the night to tell her about Phoebe's baby. She opened the door.

A mistake.

Six men tumbled into her small house, boots clomping on the floor, beards bristling. *Wolves.* She swallowed. *And I'm the deer. Dear God, what has happened to Phoebe?*

While her brain recoiled in terror, her body stood its ground—years of facing down her husband followed by the harsh slurs of her neighbours made the reaction instinctive.

"What has happened to Phoebe? And quit shining that lantern into my eyes!" She batted at Mr Grey's arm, and he lowered it.

"Mrs Baker's baby was stillborn."

Isabella's heart went out to Phoebe. Her first child—poor girl! Then she narrowed her eyes at the men. There had to be something more, if they were all here in her house in the middle of the night. "And?"

"And the child was missing half its skull."

"Dear God!" Isabella sucked in a breath. Her first thought—*Oh Phoebe!*—was followed instantly by fear.

Mr Watson cleared his throat. "Mr Baker says his wife visited you weekly during her pregnancy." The accusation was clear.

"Yes. She was lonely and frightened, all alone out there on the station. We sat and had a cup of tea whenever she was in town."

"And you provided her with a special tea of your own making?" Mr Watson slipped a hand into his breast pocket and pulled out the paper packet she'd made up for Phoebe. He dropped it on the table as though it were a snake.

"The same tea I took when I was pregnant and suffering from indigestion. I daresay half the women in town have taken it while pregnant. The recipe is common knowledge—mint, ginger and lemon verbena."

"And yet Mrs Baker couldn't make it herself?"

"She's from Wellington—no doubt the women there simply buy tea. She can't be expected to know our country remedies. And how would she hear about them, isolated as she is?" Her worry for Phoebe pushed aside her fear. She reached for her cloak. "I should go to her. She must be beside herself with grief." She looked at Thomas. "I won't trouble you to drive me there, but if I can borrow one of your horses—"

"You will go nowhere near that poor girl, after what you've done to her," Mr Watson barked.

"After what I've done? Is offering friendship to a young woman a crime now?"

"You poisoned her baby with your witch's brew."

"I did no such thing!" Isabella wrapped her cloak tightly around her at the word witch and surreptitiously glanced at the rug to ensure the loose floorboard was properly hidden.

"Mr Baker claims he's seen this before—a relative of his was similarly poisoned by a witch—"

"Mr Baker can go to the devil!" Anger burned in Isabella's chest now, and the men's shocked looks gave her a grim satisfaction. "He ignores his wife, refused to let her return to Wellington where she would have had family and friends nearby for her during her pregnancy, and then has the gall to accuse an old woman of poisoning her child? I offered her friendship and the motherly care she needed. He can burn in hell with my husband, as far as I'm concerned. And you can get out of my house. All of you!" She waved them out like flies.

"I'm afraid we can't do that," Mr Grey said. "You've been charged with murder. We'll need to restrain you until we can transport you to Christchurch for trial."

If only she'd gotten that summoning spell to work.

"I did not murder Phoebe's child. And you will not restrain me or take me to Christchurch." She gripped the chair beside her, not sure if the tremors running through her were fear or anger.

Mr Watson stepped toward her, and she let anger get the upper hand. She lifted the chair and swung it at his face. But the chair was heavy, and her reflexes slow. Mr Watson caught the chair and ripped it out of her hands, throwing her to the floor. Her hip struck the corner of the stone hearth and a deep, searing pain shot through her whole body.

She tried to rise, but the pain lanced through her again. She couldn't move, and her breath came in shallow pants. "Fetch my daughter."

"You will not drag Catherine into your evil schemes," Thomas growled.

"I'm not dragging her into any schemes. I've been

injured. I need her help."

"Only God can help you now. I suggest you pray for his forgiveness." Mr Watson nodded to the other men, and they turned and left. Mr Watson strode to the fireplace, grabbed the blackened poker, and scattered burning brands across the wooden floor.

Chapter One

Grandma

Alex glanced at the clock—4:55 pm—thank God. She was only halfway through the draft policy document her boss had emailed to her this morning. He couldn't be bothered reading it himself—Alex was tasked with pulling out important points and creating a one-page summary for him to read so he could go to his meeting on Thursday and pretend he'd read the whole thing. Maybe she could call in sick tomorrow and someone else would finish it for her.

At five o'clock on the dot, Alex bolted out the door. Free at last.

The late afternoon sun was still warm as she walked to the bus stop. It was one of Wellington's good days—the kind that came so rarely. Blue sky, not too windy, not too cold. She'd wasted it indoors, sitting at a desk. It wasn't what she'd imagined she'd be doing when she got a degree in biology.

But she was in Wellington, doing important work, keeping invasive organisms out of Aotearoa New Zealand. She was protecting the natural world she loved, while living in a city where there was plenty to do. Beaches, forests, museums and restaurants, all within a walk or a bus ride. What more could she ask for?

A better flat, housemates who actually washed dishes, a job that didn't involve sitting at a desk all day, and a salary that did more than barely cover rent and food? Okay, there was a lot more she could ask for.

No. She wasn't going to complain. She'd move on eventually. Get a new job, a new flat. Nothing was permanent. She'd learned that the hard way. But she'd also learned she could manage whatever life threw at her.

Managing required a lot of time alone, preferably outdoors. Bypassing the bus stop, Alex took the City to Sea Walkway to the Mount Street Cemetery. She'd been haunting cemeteries since she was thirteen. That was the year her parents had been killed by a drunk driver. She didn't want anything to do with Mum and Dad's graves—visiting them was too painful—but after she was sent to live with her grandmother on the South Island, she'd felt drawn to historic cemeteries. Maybe it was the solitude—no one bothered you when you were strolling through a cemetery. Maybe it was a roundabout way to visit with her parents without actually confronting the set-in-stone finality of their gravestones. Either way, she found them peaceful.

While she strolled among the graves, her phone rang—probably her boss wondering where his summary was. She glanced at the screen—unknown number. She ignored it. No one ever rang her except her boss and Gran.

Two minutes later, the phone rang again.

Maybe she should answer.

"Hello, this is Alex."

"Alex! I'm so glad I found you." The woman's voice was vaguely familiar, but Alex couldn't place it. "This is Linda

Dickinson, your grandmother's next-door neighbour."

"Oh! Mrs Dickinson. Hi." Unease skittered down Alex's spine.

"I'm afraid I have to tell you that your grandmother passed away this morning."

"What?" Alex's peaceful summer evening shattered.

"I'm taking care of things for the moment—you know, feeding the dog and the cats—but you'll be needed. I'm not sure if she had a will or not, but since you're next of kin …"

Alex turned, picking up her pace. "I'll catch the soonest flight I can. Thanks for ringing, Linda."

She jogged out of the cemetery and crossed the street to catch the next bus to her flat, her mind in a whirl and emotions roiling. Gran was dead? When had they last spoken? Christmas Day? Only a month ago, but they didn't talk often. Gran rang her on Christmas and her birthday, and that was about it. They hadn't parted on the best of terms.

When Gran took her in, she was a sad and angry teenager, mourning the loss of her parents. Alex resented being torn from her friends and the excitement of Auckland to live with an old lady in a little town out in the wop-wops where the biggest excitement was the occasional late-night fire alarm at the local primary school.

She had bussed to the high school in Darfield, where half the students were farm kids and all of them thought Christchurch was the Big Smoke. She despised them all. At thirteen, she was a city kid through and through. At least that's what she told herself. In retrospect, it was a defence mechanism—clinging to what she knew as her whole world flipped on its head.

Gran had gotten the brunt of her anger and resentment. She hadn't deserved it, and Alex knew that—she just couldn't help herself. When she stormed out of the house on her seventeenth birthday and hitchhiked to Christchurch, it was merely the culmination of a thousand smaller acts of defiance she'd committed during the previous four years. She couldn't remember what the argument had been about but she did remember the words she'd slung at her grandmother before slamming the door. "I don't need your mothering. I don't *have* a mother. I don't have to listen to anybody! Especially not an old bitch like you!"

She regretted those words now, eight years later, but was never brave enough to talk to Gran about it. She didn't regret leaving Gran's care at seventeen. She'd proven in the past eight years that she could take care of herself. She'd finished her senior year of schooling via correspondence while working at a grocery store. Then she'd gone on to get a biology degree, paying for university by working nights and picking up a few scholarships.

She was proud of all she'd done and who she'd become since she left Gran. She didn't regret any of it. Still, her heart twisted with the knowledge that she would never be able to apologise for the pain she must have caused her grandmother. She could have at least picked up the phone more often and talked to her.

She shut her eyes for a moment. Something squeezed her chest, and her eyes prickled. *Take a deep breath. Don't fall apart on the bus.*

Dealing with logistics instead of emotions would help. She opened her eyes and texted her boss—at least she wouldn't have to finish reading that boring policy document.

"You don't have anything smaller?" Alex didn't drive much, and the ageing white station wagon the rental agency offered her was twice the size of her Mini. Could she even park that thing?

"We'll give it to you for the price of a compact, since it's the only thing we have available." The rental agent glanced over Alex's shoulder at the queue of customers behind her.

"Fine." She wouldn't have to parallel park it. This was Christchurch—there'd be no crazy traffic—and she'd be out on the open road most of the way to Gran's.

Forty-five minutes later, Alex pulled up in front of Gran's cottage, relieved to step out of the vehicle. A wave of nostalgia brought tears to her eyes. The colourful zinnias lining the path, the nodding pink columbines sprawling through the fence palings, the stupid garden gnome tucked under a broad-leaved hosta—nothing had changed in eight years.

She retrieved her bags and then stood on the footpath gazing at the house, unable to move forward.

"Alex? Is that you? My goodness, you've grown!" Linda called over the fence from next door. "You'll be wanting the key." She vanished into her house and returned a moment later, holding the key over the fence. "Now, Alice is at Rolleston Funeral Services—I had to choose somebody, I hope that's okay. And here's her lawyer's number." She handed Alex a business card. "I'd ring him first thing tomorrow. Oh, and the cats refused to move out—they've been going in and out the animal flap and I've been feeding them in the kitchen like Alice always did. David just took Benji for a walk—I'll have him bring him over when they return. Here's what's left of the dog food. You'll need to pick up more soon. And the pastor was by earlier; you should ring him tomorrow morning. I don't have his number, but just ring Trinity Church. And—"

"Thank you, Linda." Alex was going to scream if she had to listen to Linda for another moment. "I'm going to go in

13

and get settled. I've taken two weeks off work, so I'll be here a while. If I need you I'll give you a ring." Linda brought out the angry teenager in Alex, and she hoped she'd infused her voice with enough weariness and sadness to hide the irritation.

"Oh. Well. Of course." Linda opened her mouth, as if to say more, closed it, nodded, and then returned to her house.

Free of Linda, Alex took a deep breath and entered the place she'd lived for the four most difficult years of her life.

The door echoed in the empty house as she shut it behind her. Or maybe that was her imagination, because the house was every bit as stuffed with junk as it had been when she'd lived here. It was far from empty. Really, Gran? Couldn't you have had a clear-out *before* you died?

A tall stack of magazines teetered on the coffee table, Gran's wool basket perched next to it. A low bookcase bent under the weight of the mystery novels lined up on it. Knick-knacks crowded together on the fireplace mantel and lined the windowsills. Crystal glasses and colourful teacups jostled for space in a tallboy with glass-fronted shelves. A stack of plastic storage boxes held dried herbs, candle wax, ancient tin moulds, bundles of candle wick, bottles of aromatic oils—all of Gran's supplies for making the scented candles she loved. Candles Alex couldn't stand.

Two sleek cats—one midnight black and the other steel grey—blinked at her from the top of a cat tree where they had clearly been sleeping.

"You must be Thor and Thunder, but I have no idea which of you is which." They were the latest in her Gran's long string of feline companions. Zig had been the cat of the day when Alex lived with Gran. He'd been a decrepit old beast when Alex arrived, and he'd died shortly before she left. "I suppose it doesn't matter what I call you, I doubt you'll answer to your names." The cats regarded her for a moment longer, clearly decided she was uninteresting, and then resumed their nap.

She passed through the hallway into the bedroom that had once been hers. Pushing open the door, she sucked in a breath. The room was exactly how she'd left it, aside from the bed being made and the lack of dirty ice cream bowls on the bedside table. That was part of the argument that had sent her storming out on her birthday—whether the birthday girl had to tidy her room on her special day.

She gave a rueful laugh and shook her head at her teenaged self. Once she'd left Gran's she'd kept her bedroom spotless. She liked a clean and tidy room. She'd just enjoyed rebelling more.

"I'm sorry, Gran." The words, finally spoken aloud when it was too late, crushed every last scrap of rebelliousness. She dropped her bags and sank down on the bed, tears tracking down her cheeks. She mourned not only the loss of her grandmother, who had loved her steadily through all her anger, but also her parents, because she'd never told them how much she appreciated them. In truth, she hadn't *known* how much she appreciated them until they were gone, but still … they were all gone, and she was truly on her own, like she always wanted to be. Except it didn't feel as good as she imagined it would.

Chapter Two

Cleaning Out

Alex stood and stretched her back. After hours of going through Gran's bills, bank statements, and other documents, searching for the information the lawyer needed to settle Gran's estate, she needed a break.

"Come on Benji. Walk?"

Benji's ears perked up and the little terrier leapt to his feet, claws clicking on the wooden floor. Alex snapped a lead on him and they headed out.

It had been years since she'd walked around Rifton. The little village had grown, with new subdivisions almost doubling the size of the township. The houses in the new subdivisions were cookie-cutter monstrosities with no character. She steered clear of the new streets, opting for the well-worn paths of her teenage years. Little houses, narrow footpaths, tiny petrol station—the places that had loomed so large in her mind as a teen had shrunk in stature. A car motored past—the first she'd seen in five minutes. Rifton was a world away from busy Wellington. There, you couldn't hear yourself think. Here? No surprise she'd bolted to the city as soon as she could. Too much thinking as a teen had always led to brooding.

Benji trotted happily beside her as she made her way past the showgrounds to the rugby field. Ignoring the *no dogs* sign, she slipped Benji's leash off and let him race in circles around the field.

As always, she was drawn to the cemetery. Her progress slowed as she revisited familiar graves. She'd never known anyone buried here, but the tombstones felt like old friends.

Catherine Parker nee Deacon, 1 April 1861 – 23 October 1934, Loose thyself from the bands of thy neck, O captive daughter of Zion — Isaiah 52:2

What bands had been on Catherine's neck? Alex felt a particular bond with Catherine Parker. She'd sat with her back against this tombstone many days as a teen, feeling the bands on her own neck tighten.

Catherine's tombstone was flanked by four others—a husband and three children, the oldest of which had been born when Catherine was seventeen. Alex's bands as a teenager had clearly been nothing compared to Catherine's.

She moved on through the cemetery, soaking in the peace. She reached the end of a row and stopped. Gran's plot. In a few days there would be a new grave here. Someone she actually knew. She blinked back tears. There was no point in crying.

Looking up from the bare patch that would soon bear her grandmother's body, she noticed a small fenced-in area at the edge of the cemetery. The fence was old—paint peeling off half-rotted wooden posts, a rusted chain sagging between them. How had she never noticed it before? Who merited their own separate space in this unassuming cemetery?

Apparently no one. The rank grass within the fence was unbroken by tombstone or plaque. How strange.

Passing through the cemetery gate a few minutes later, she examined the map, which hadn't been there when she was a teen. It showed the locations of all the graves. The fenced-off area was labelled *Unmarked Grave.* That was it. No date, no indication of who might be buried there. Surely in a community this small, there wouldn't be unknown people buried, would there?

Pondering the mystery, she headed back to Gran's house.

This house had once been home. Alex hadn't appreciated the fact before. Now she listened to the echoes of her arguments with Gran over the colour of her bedroom walls, smelled Gran's lavender sachets in the bathroom, and ran her fingers over the familiar nick in the dining table from the time Gran had asked her to cut up a swede for dinner. Alex hated swedes. Maybe she'd been a bit too aggressive with the knife. The house hummed with memories. Whenever she touched one, it stung like a zap of static electricity.

In the first couple of days at Gran's place, Alex focused on the immediately important details—talking to the lawyer, arranging the funeral. The idea of diving into Gran's personal possessions, of throwing away and getting rid of what made the house Gran's, paralysed her. How could it be that difficult? She'd always been at odds with Gran—why did it make her chest hurt to close out this part of her life?

She tackled the easy things first—thirty years of local newspapers stacked in the cupboard, an overflowing jar of rubber bands and bread tags, dozens of expired tins of peaches and green beans in the pantry, the boxes full of herbs and candle making supplies—they all went straight into the bin. The items that required thought, the things that most reminded her of Gran, would have to wait until after the funeral. Maybe once she'd farewelled Gran, she could face the rest.

Linda brought over meals accompanied by incessant chatter. She was clucky and overprotective, like Gran had been, and Alex struggled to appreciate it. She could manage by herself—she didn't need anyone's mothering. Her regret over how she'd treated Gran was the only thing that prevented her from telling Linda to shut up.

On the second day, Alex felt she was making progress clearing out the easy items. Then she opened a small cupboard in the laundry room and groaned. "What is all this?" She pulled down one of the dozens of glass jars and bottles crammed into the space. *Feverfew*, read the label. The second bottle, filled with a gritty looking slurry, read *For pustules*. She grabbed an empty box and started loading it—*bloodwort, mouse-ear, fumitory, foxglove* … Had this stuff been here when Alex lived with Gran? Maybe. Alex barely set foot in the laundry room back then.

As she carried the full box out of the laundry, a knock sounded at the door. She shifted the box to her hip and opened the door. "Mrs Walker?"

The elderly woman smiled—something she had never done when she was Alex's high school English teacher. Not that she could blame the woman—Alex had been a terrible student.

"Please call me Jane. I'm so sorry to hear about Alice. Linda mentioned you'd come home to handle things, so I thought I'd bring over a meal for you." She presented a foil-covered dish that smelled of potato and cheese. "Oh. You've got your hands full. I can set it on the bench if you'd—" She peered at the contents of the box Alex balanced on her hip.

"You're not throwing those away are you?"

"Um. Yeah. I was just taking them to the rubbish bin."

"Oh. You can't do that. Those are Alice's—" She cut herself off and raised her eyes to Alex's. "I'd be happy to take them. I know a few people who would want to have them. I mean, if you're just going to toss them out."

Alex held out the box to her. "By all means. If you want this stuff, you can have it."

Mrs Walker set the dinner she'd brought in the kitchen, and then gently lifted the box out of Alex's hands, cradling it like it was some precious cargo.

Whatever. Gran and her friends had always been weird. "Thanks for the meal. It smells delicious."

Another smile. "My pleasure. I'll see you at the funeral on Thursday."

Getting through Gran's funeral was harder than Alex expected. The crowd was surprisingly large—apparently Gran had still been active in her church, in addition to being part of a Thursday morning coffee club, a gardening group, and the local Wednesday night bowls. Alex was overwhelmed as they introduced themselves and gave their condolences. Every time someone told her what a lovely woman Gran had been, she had to blink back tears. She kept her hands clasped over her stomach, willing her churning insides to settle. No luck. Tears streamed down her face through the whole service. Thank God she hadn't planned to speak.

It was almost worse than her parents' funeral—then she'd had Gran at her side. Today she was alone. Who would arrange *her* funeral? Who would stand and receive everyone's condolences? Dark thoughts dogged her, and she barely heard the service.

When everyone filed out of the funeral home, she breathed a sigh of relief. Just the burial to get through now.

Three cars followed the hearse, and only eight people attended the burial itself. Alex couldn't help thinking that at least one of the elderly attendees was taking notes—planning his own funeral as he closely examined the hole, the hearse, and the nearby headstones.

Five members of the garden group made up the bulk of those gathered in the cemetery. They were an odd bunch of ladies. The only one of them Alex knew was Jane Walker. The others she recognised by sight, but didn't know. One looked like she'd come directly from the farm, in faded jeans and gumboots. Had she been wearing the boots at the funeral?

As the coffin was unloaded from the hearse, the small group gathered near the pre-dug pit.

"Nice to see you went for the basket casket," said one of them. Margaret maybe? Alex couldn't remember her name.

"I figured it would have been her choice," Alex replied.

Gumboot Lady chuckled. "Alice probably would have opted to be buried in her compost pile if it was legal."

This made Alex smile. "Yeah, I could see Gran doing that. She did like her compost."

"She had the best darned compost," said a stocky woman with short curly hair and a wide-brimmed straw hat. "Remember when I was trying to get that French tarragon to strike, and every time I planted the cuttings out, they died? Alice gave me a sack of her compost. I put a little in each hole and just like that those cuttings were away."

"And she made the best elderflower cordial," Mrs Walker added. "That elder grew right next to her compost bin."

Alex had never been fond of Gran's elderflower cordial. Of course, that might have been a case of sour grapes, because Gran never bought her fizzy drinks, insisting that elderflower cordial was the only soft drink anyone needed.

The casket was lowered into the ground, and the minister said a prayer. Alex blinked back tears as she tossed a handful of soil onto the casket. It pattered lightly against the rattan before sifting down inside. *Earthy*. That had been Gran to a T. As an angry teen, Alex hated it, but the years had mellowed her memories of funny-smelling teas, herbs hanging in bunches in the garage, and jars of home-made pickles in the pantry.

Gumboot Lady broke into her reverie with a hand on her arm. She pressed a small paper bag into Alex's hand. "You look tired. I know how hard it can be to sleep after the death of a loved one. This is valerian. Just a wee bit in boiling water. Maybe add some lemon verbena. You'll sleep like a rock for ten hours."

Mrs Walker leaned in. "And if you find any more … herbs and things … of Alice's we'd be happy to take them." The other members of the garden group nodded.

"Or books," Gumboot Lady added. "She had some … unusual books."

Alex took the packet and thanked the woman for coming. She said farewell to the others, and then, with one last glance back at the grave, returned to her car. As she drove out, a digger droned—covering Gran's casket.

Benji met Alex at the door when she got back to the house. His whole body wiggled as his tail thrashed a greeting.

"Well, that's over." She dropped the bag of valerian onto the dining table and fell into a chair. Benji propped his front paws on her knee, and she gave him a scratch behind the ears. The tightness in her chest eased. One hurdle surmounted. On to the next. "I suppose I need to start tackling this mess now."

She began with Gran's 'office', wheeling the rubbish and recycling bins right into the room. She might regret how she treated Gran, but she wasn't nostalgic about the woman's stuff, and had no intention of saving anything.

Gran's organising system was haphazard at best. When Alex had gone through her desk to sort out her important papers, she found bills, to-do lists, grocery receipts, and recipes clipped from magazines all shoved together into drawers, pigeon holes and envelopes. They were stratified largely by date—she'd obviously kept piling things in until the drawer was full. Then what had she done with them?

Alex opened the closet door and found her answer. The stack of cardboard boxes was as tall as she was, and paper spilled out of several, drifting to the floor.

"Jeeze, Gran. Did you throw anything away?"

With a sigh, she lifted the first box down, sat cross-legged on the floor beside it, and began to sift through the contents. Bills, advertising flyers, old newspapers, receipts … Alex was beginning to think she could just biff the whole box when she came across a personal letter in a pale green envelope with pink roses twining up the side. The return address was a Mrs G. Hadstock in Ashburton. Who sent letters anymore? And who would bother to send a letter from Ashburton, just an hour's drive away? She slipped several sheets of matching paper from the envelope.

23 April 2020

Dear Alice,

I hope you are managing during lockdown. No doubt you're eating well out of your garden, even this late in the season. My son has been a great help, bringing me groceries every week. I do miss my knitting club and trips to the library. I've read all the books I had out of the library when lockdown started, and I'm nearly out of wool! I think I have enough for one more pair of socks, and then I'll have to resort to

George's confounded book of crossword puzzles for entertainment.

But here I am complaining, when I've no reason to. I think of you often, with no children to look after you. Have you heard anything from young Alex lately? I don't suppose she's gotten any better at staying in touch, has she? Try not to let it bother you so much. She'll come round one of these days. At least she's focused her grief on proving herself, rather than turning to drugs or alcohol. That's something you can be proud of.

The letter continued, with news of Mrs Hadstock's grandchildren, local gossip about a woman fined for going for a long bike ride to Rakaia to see her boyfriend during lockdown, and a question about proper rose pruning.

Alex replaced the letter in its envelope and set it aside. *She'll come round one of these days.* Her heart felt like lead in her chest. She did *come round.* Just not soon enough. "I'm so sorry, Gran."

As she worked her way through the stack of boxes, the documents got older. Alex felt like an archaeologist uncovering some ancient civilisation, digging down through the strata of a midden. But instead of revealing the daily life of a forgotten people, she was peeking back into her grandmother's life, and her own.

There were regular letters from Mrs Hadstock—Betty, as she signed them—the women had obviously been friends in high school, based on the reminiscing and recounting of anecdotes from their teen years. Alex cringed when Mrs Hadstock compared Alex's teenaged rebellion to a boy they'd apparently both had a crush on who developed a habit of punching walls in his late teens. Had her anger been that bad?

Her stomach growled, and she glanced at the time. "Three-thirty! No wonder I'm starving." She lifted an armload of paper and dumped it into the recycling bin before heading to the kitchen for a sandwich.

Benji, who had been sprawled next to her since the funeral, trotted to the kitchen after her and sat by the door whining as she ate. "Yes, a walk is a good idea," she told the dog. "I feel like I've been tied into a knot, sitting on the floor for so long."

Chapter Three

A Secret Lover

As afternoon gave way to evening, Alex worked through the boxes. Moving further into her grandmother's past with each layer proved more interesting than she'd expected.

The first letter she found from Dex Saunders was dated 3 January 1995, two years before Alex was born. It was in an envelope without a stamp. Across the front was written *Alice*.

My Dearest Alice,

Your news about Daniel was shocking, to say the least. I am sorry for your loss. And I'm also thankful we no longer need to hide.

I know you will be mourning him. How could you not, in spite of the situation between us? I will ask nothing of you until you are ready.

I look forward to seeing you soon, my darling. Ring me when you are ready—we'll take a weekend and fly to Golden Bay to talk about our future together.

Love,

Dex

"What?" Alex sat on the floor with her jaw hanging open. Gran had a lover? Wait! She pawed back through the pile of papers she'd discarded a few minutes ago.

There it was—an obituary for Dexter Saunders, local pilot, whose crop duster had hit a power line and gone down in a barley field near Dunsandel. The obituary was dated 20 January 1995.

"Well holy shit." Gran had had a lover who died shortly after Grandpa had.

Alex wanted to know everything. There must be more letters. She began sifting through the papers more quickly, pulling out dozens of envelopes addressed in the same manner. They went back two decades, to the early 1970s. She stacked them, unread, in the order she found them. The towering pile of illicit correspondence made Alex laugh out loud. "Gran! And you called *me* a troublemaker?"

Her joints were stiff after hours on the floor. One more armload of discarded papers, and the recycling bin was full. She shut the lid and hauled it back outside. What day was recycling pick up? The night was dark and quiet, and the rumble of the bin as it bounced down the path to the garage sounded overly loud. What time was it anyway? She glanced at her phone. Ten o'clock already! No wonder she was tired.

The letters would have to wait. It was time for bed.

Gran had been having an affair for at least twenty years. A woman who was so proper, demanding and stern! Alex was dying to know what was in the letters. How had they met? Why were the letters not sent via the post? Why did Gran cheat on her husband? Alex had never met her grandfather, and Mum had never talked about him, except when they pulled out the old photo albums from her childhood. Had those photo albums ended up with Gran when Mum died? They must have. Where would Gran have stashed them?

Still lying in bed awake at two-thirty in the morning, her mind whirling with questions, Alex remembered the valerian Gumboot Lady had given her at the funeral. It was sitting on the dining room table. Maybe it was time to take some action against this insomnia. She padded to the dining room and flicked on the light. Blinking in the sudden brightness, she grabbed the bag of valerian and unrolled the top. She peered inside. "Ugh!" The vile smell of dirty gym socks assaulted her nose, and she whipped her head back. "What the fuck? You're supposed to make tea from that stuff?" No wonder Gumboot Lady had suggested adding a little lemon verbena. It would take more than that, however, to disguise the smell of foot rot coming from the valerian. She tossed the bag into the rubbish bin, then made herself a cup of mint tea to get the smell out of her nose.

Keeping the lights low, she curled up on the couch in the living room to sip her tea. The animal flap squeaked, and a moment later Thor and Thunder prowled into the room looking wide awake. "What have you two been up to? Eating mice in the garage, I hope." The grey one—she'd decided he was Thunder—leapt deftly to the back of the couch and padded behind her. Leaning over her shoulder, he sniffed at her tea, then jerked back. "You think this is bad? You should have smelled the valerian." Thor jumped to her lap and began kneading her legs through the dressing gown. Thunder gingerly stepped down her shoulder and arm to join Thor. Soon both cats were curled up, purring. She set the remainder of her tea on the coffee table and lay back, shutting her eyes.

Alex groaned as she tumbled off the couch in the morning. Mint tea and cats. Much better than valerian, but maybe she'd take the tea back to bed rather than sleep on the couch. She rolled her shoulders to ease the kinks out.

She would much rather stumble back to bed, but there was work to be done. With the funeral behind her, Alex needed to focus on sorting out Gran's stuff.

But coffee came first. And breakfast. Sweeping hogsback clouds across the sky promised a windy day, but the breeze wasn't too bad yet. Alex took her toast and coffee out to the deck—Benji needed to go out anyway, and the deck was sheltered from the wind.

She reclined in a chair, admiring the clouds as Benji sniffed around the yard and peed on the compost pile. A rustle under a sprawling feijoa caught his attention and he rushed over, barking furiously.

"Benji! Shush!"

He ignored her, poking his nose under the branches and yapping. A blackbird burst out from the bush, and Benji barked after it until it flew over the fence into the neighbour's yard.

"Okay you, enough of that." Alex stood and brushed toast crumbs off her shirt. "Come on. We have a house full of Gran's shit left to go through."

Benji bounded onto the deck and followed her indoors.

The stack of letters beckoned from Gran's office. She wanted to sit down and read every single one, but there was so much else to dispose of. She only had two weeks off. The letters would keep.

Still … Maybe she'd read just one, and then get to work. She reached for the oldest one—best to start at the beginning.

23 December 1971

Dear Alice,

Merry Christmas! I don't know if you'll find this before the holi-

day, but I hope you know I'll be thinking of you. It was good to see you Thursday night at the church committee meeting, even if Mrs Evans did nearly discover our secret. I like what you've done with your hair. Perhaps we might find a time to meet before the new year? Surely you could 'visit your sister' in Christchurch? Let me know.

Love,

Dex

Well! Sneaking around at the church committee meeting? Making fake plans to visit her sister? Obviously this thing had been going on for a while already by the time they started writing. Where had they hidden their letters? In the church somewhere? Imagine conducting an affair at church!

Alex laughed, but it was tinged with a sick horror at what her grandmother had done. It was so not right to cheat on a spouse. Her grandmother was clearly not as lovely a person as the mourners at her funeral believed.

In high school, a boy Alex dated for a while was caught snogging some bitch from the year below her. Her friend Katelyn had snapped a picture and showed it to Alex. She'd been humiliated—sure, they'd only been together for a month, but *what the fuck*? If he didn't want to date her, he should have just broken it off, not lied to her about it.

What Gran had done was so much worse.

She shook herself out of her daydreams. She had to finish this job and get back to Wellington.

By late afternoon, she'd cleared out the office, having uncovered no more bombshells about Gran. The nor'westerly winds had risen to a gale that hummed in the chimney and rattled the windows. When she took Benji for a pre-dinner walk, Linda was out tying up a bunch of cosmos that looked like they'd been run over by an elephant.

"It's a windy one, isn't it?" Alex commented.

"I think it may be the strongest we've had this year," Linda replied, pounding a garden stake into the soil next to her flattened flowers. "You know there must be a doozy of a southerly pushing this. Metservice is saying we might get thunderstorms and hail tonight."

"Really?" Alex hadn't even checked the weather forecast, since it wouldn't change her plans, regardless.

"Yes. You'll want to batten down the hatches here, if you haven't already done so. I brought in my porch furniture this morning—it was blowing all over the garden. And my red bin tipped over—rubbish everywhere! That was a real mess to clean up, I'll tell you. I heard that—"

"Well, I'd best take Benji for his walk, so I can get back and get ready for the weather," Alex interrupted, not caring what Linda had heard. "Good luck with those flowers. See you later." She hurried after Benji, who tugged eagerly on his leash.

Alex leaned into the wind. The mountains were obscured by heavy rain, spilling over from the west coast. To the south, the distant ripples of cumulus clouds marked the storm front on its way across the plains. Linda was right—it looked like a doozy of a storm coming. She shivered.

Chapter Four

The Book

The southerly hit around eight o'clock, announcing its arrival with a gust of wind and smattering of rain that spat on the windows. A moment later, both cats shot in through the animal flap, shaking water off their backs. Alex had finished dinner and was in the living room going through Gran's stacks of books and magazines. The magazines were predictable—*NZ Gardener*, *NZ Lifestyle Block*, and *Organic NZ*. Her book collection, however, was more varied.

Alex remembered browsing these books as a teenager and rolling her eyes at the selection. Hardbacks of the classics like *David Copperfield* and *The Count of Monte Cristo* vied for space with Agatha Christie novels, gardening books, and *The Hitchhiker's Guide to the Galaxy*.

She pulled off a book titled *The Joy of Compost* and snorted, tossing it into the *for the garden group* pile. Maybe they could learn Gran's compost secrets. She tucked *Hitchhiker's Guide* into the much smaller *keep* pile. Musty classics all went into the *sell* pile. In the unlikely event Alex ever wanted to read them, she'd pick up a new copy.

A rumble of thunder pulled Alex's gaze to the window. The trees across the street were bent and thrashing in the wind. Rain sheeted down now. She stood and flicked on the lights against the gloom that had descended on the room.

She hefted a box of books and set it on the stack by the door. It could wait until morning to go to the garage—she wasn't going to run it out there through the rain.

A cup of tea later, she was back at the bookshelves. Twelve mystery novels went into a new *sell* box. There was a loud peal of thunder and the lights flickered. Another flash of lightning and roll of thunder followed soon after. Did Gran still keep candles and matches in the bottom drawer in the kitchen? Small hail pinged off the window. She'd better see about the candles.

She dropped *A Gardener's Guide to Herbs* into the *garden group* box just as a brilliant flash lit the room. It was followed almost instantly by a deafening crack, and the lights went out. Benji, wedged under the couch, howled.

"Aw, poor Benji." Alex knelt down and felt her way to his quivering body. She gave him a reassuring scratch. "Let's see if we can find those candles. Then maybe we can sit together and read about organic loofah growing or something."

She still knew her way around the house in the dark—those years of sneaking out at night to irritate Gran came in handy right now. In the kitchen, she pulled open the bottom drawer and heard the familiar rolling clink of candles. A couple of tapers, a pair of squat glass candle holders—good thing Gran hadn't changed anything. A bit of scrabbling around among what she was afraid were mouse droppings produced a box of matches, and soon she had both candles lit. The flames wavered a bit from the draft seeping in through the old windows and under the doors. Lightning flashed again, and the ground shook with the thunder that rolled in its wake. Benji's howling rose in volume.

The candles cast a cosy glow around the room, enabling her to find two more. She stuck one of them into the wine bottle she'd emptied at dinner, then scanned the room for something else she could use as a candle holder. Of course! She opened Gran's highboy, where the items of porcelain and crystal too precious to use were displayed. She felt positively wicked as she selected a tall cut-crystal candle holder that had obviously never been used, and shoved the candle into it.

She brought all the candles into the living room, arranging them on the coffee table and side tables to provide a warm glow around the couch. She grabbed a small stack of books at random from the shelves and set them on the coffee table. Then she crouched down to coax Benji out.

"Come on boy. It's alright. You're safe in here. How about we sit together? I bet Gran never let you on the furniture, did she?" She stroked his ears. The lightning and thunder continued outside, and rain and hail pounded on the window. But Benji stopped howling at the sound of Alex's voice, and after a few minutes, he stopped shaking. She gently hauled him out from under the couch and sat down with him, covering her lap and most of his body with a throw.

Her voice was clearly soothing him, so she picked up one of the books from the coffee table and began to read aloud at a random page.

"*A freshly turned compost pile inspires fecundity in all living things, not least of all the gardener herself. Indeed, a sprinkle of compost in the marital bed—*What the hell is this?" Alex flipped back to the cover—*Compost Porn: Maximise Your Pleasure in Rotten Beds*. "What were you reading, Gran?" The women *did* say she had some unusual books.

She tossed the book aside and picked up another. Wising up, she read the title first—*A Hundred Years of Solitude*. She'd at least heard of this book. She opened the front cover and was surprised to find another book inside—a slim, dark volume. The embossed, cracked leather invited her fingers to stroke it. She pulled it out and angled it toward the light so she could see it better.

"*Formulae for the Summoning of Minor Angels and Daemons*," she read aloud. "What the heck?" Setting aside *A Hundred Years of Solitude*, she opened the book. Pages crackled as she turned them. This book was old. *Really* old. Should she even be handling it? She turned a page, reading aloud as Benji cocked his head to listen. "*The summoning of Spirits is best praktised by those highly experienced in Magick. Woe befalleth the inexperienced Witch who summons a Being more powerful than Herself, whereupon she be unable to control or banish it upon completion of its alloted Task.*" She raised her eyebrows at Benji. "Okay, this is weird. Why does Gran have this book?" Intrigued, she flipped a few pages and read more. "*Materpoda be multi-leggd Daemons the bodys of wich hath the appearance of Centipedes. A member of that classe of Lesser Spirits, they be easily summond by een Witchs of little power. Much to the supris of the inexperiensed Witch, control of a Materpoda once summond be more difficult than the Summoning, and attain only by those naturally born unto Magick.*"

A flash and boom interrupted her reading, and Benji whimpered. She gave the little dog a pat and continued, not worrying whether she picked up where she left off or not—reading only to calm the dog. "*Gone be Firelight 'twixt Dusk and Dawn. Materpod loveth Fox and Fawn. Find me now, and witness my call. Wish my Voyc command and thrall.*" A gust of wind shook the house, and Alex felt the draft around her ankles as the candles guttered. The lights flickered on and off rapidly, and then died again, just as the flash and crack of a lightning strike tore through the air.

Benji yelped and dove under the couch again. Alex screamed. She blinked her eyes, the afterimage of the lightning nearly blinding her. For a moment, she swore she saw a leggy creature in the middle of the room, armoured plates covering its long back. Then she blinked and the vision was gone.

Maybe reading strange books about demons on a stormy night was a bad idea. "Damn, that one was close." She bent down to check on Benji, keening from his hideaway again. "You've got the right idea, mate. Can I crawl under there with you?"

Lightning flashed again and Alex flinched, but the rumble that followed was distant and rolling. Rain still lashed the windows. The animal flap creaked and a moment later Thor shot across the living room and squeezed himself under the bookshelf. "Did you go back outside? Silly cat. What were you thinking? You must be soaked."

She moved to the window, peering out. "Where do you think that big strike hit?" She spoke aloud to calm the animals—she certainly wasn't spooked by a thunderstorm and a weird book. That would be silly. "Must have been that big gum tree across the street. It's taller than all the other trees around it. I'm surprised it hasn't been struck by lightning before."

A flicker of movement in the rain-drenched yard caught her eye. Thor leapt to the windowsill, his tail twitching, eyes fixed beyond the glass.

There, near the compost pile. A dark shape. Long and leggy. No. That was ridiculous. It must be a possum, or a branch torn off a tree during the storm. Thor let out a low growl. Alex stroked his back.

"Relax, you. It's a branch." It had to be.

At the feel of his fur, she looked down.

"You're dry." Hadn't he bolted in through the cat flap a minute ago? He should be soaked. Her hair stood on end. What was going on?

Alex shook these irrational thoughts from her head—exhaustion was messing with her brain. She hadn't slept enough last night.

She turned from the window and wrapped herself in the throw. While the storm rolled away to the northeast, she kept up a patter of inane comments, soothing herself along with the animals. The lightning mellowed and the thunder rolled gently from a comfortable distance. Wind continued to buffet Gran's old house and send chilly tendrils through the cracks. Alex thought of the creature she'd imagined and shuddered. She wasn't going to sleep much tonight, was she?

Interlude One

1893: The Witch's Daughter

Catherine closed the book as she heard Thomas' footsteps in the front hall and slipped it to the bottom of her knitting basket. By the time he entered the room, she had a needle in hand and was stitching a patch onto a pair of his trousers. She glanced up from her work. "Dinner's on the table. How was your day?"

Thomas focused on the buttons of his jacket. "Better than a sharp stick in the eye." His standard response. Never anything more, at least not in the past six months.

Since Mother's death, Thomas had been evasive. He avoided conversation and never looked her in the eye. He always came in late—they hadn't shared a family meal since the day Mother's cottage burned down.

Mr Watson had told her Mother's body was found

on her bed—she must have been asleep when the fire started. But Catherine had seen her less than an hour before, and Isabella had always been a night owl. Mother hadn't been asleep.

The circumstances of her death gnawed at Catherine. It distressed her to know she hadn't been able to protect Mother, as her mother had protected her. The whole reason she married Thomas was so she could protect Mother with Thomas' name and standing in the community. The plan had failed. Thomas had been there with the town council. Instead of protecting his mother-in-law, he'd joined the fearmongers accusing her of harming Phoebe and her baby.

Oh, he denied he went with the council that evening. But he wouldn't look her in the face now. Wouldn't talk to her about it. Didn't lift a finger when the council and the church refused to allow her to bury Mother in the cemetery. Refused to pay for a headstone.

He believed that Isabella was a witch.

That it was true was irrelevant—she'd only turned to witchcraft after being accused of it.

Catherine was the only one who had known about Mother's box of treasures underneath the floorboards. The men who sifted through the wreckage of her house, confiscating anything not burnt to cinders, didn't find it.

Catherine had snuck out in the dead of night, while the embers of the fire were still warm, to retrieve the box. Along with some gold and jewellery, two strange books, and letters from Grandmother back in England, was a letter in a sealed envelope addressed to Catherine herself.

My Dearest Daughter,

I assume that by the time you read this, I will be gone. And if I know you at all, you will blame yourself for my death, regardless of how it has come about.

You are not to blame for any of my misfortune, nor for any of your own. At this point in my life, I have stopped even blaming myself for our misfortune. I did the best I could with the cards I was dealt.

You know what your father was like. I never mourned him. The only thing he ever did for me was to give me you, and I cannot regret marrying him because of that gift of your life. My only regret was that I never got the chance to shove him down the stairs or shoot him with his own rifle. I would have liked to punish him for hurting you.

Was I blinded by Mr Taylor's kind treatment of both of us after your father's death? Yes. Was I reckless, thinking I could snare him by bearing his child? Most certainly. But we both needed his kindness. Had I known I would lose the baby and gain a reputation as a witch, I might have hesitated, but how could I have known that the rabid fear of witchcraft was so prevalent in Rifton in the modern day?

Of course, once I was treated as a witch, I saw no reason not to explore the possibilities it offered. It is surprising how much one can learn about witchcraft when one searches with an open mind.

I will not call out those who aided me in my pur-

suit of knowledge. Most were driven to the practice by desperation of one sort or another, and I would not want to add to their troubles.

I don't know what you will think of me once you know I have dabbled in witchcraft. Rest assured that I have only used it to ease our own lives. I did entertain the idea of revenge upon the neighbours who were particularly abusive to us, but I was never good enough at witchcraft to accomplish any real mischief.

It is probably unwise to put all this on paper. I wouldn't put it past the cursed town council to read this if they find it, but I feel I owe you an explanation.

The gold (if the council hasn't confiscated it) is yours—given by Mr Taylor to buy my silence or ease his own conscience. Use it wisely, for yourself. Though I never made use of it, it was a comfort to know it was always there, should we need to flee.

Do what you wish with the books. I will understand if you destroy them, but I encourage you to consider all your options first.

After all, you are still the witch's daughter.

Be well, my dearest child. Know that I loved you with every fibre of my being, and everything I have done has been for your sake. I am proud of the strong woman you have become.

Your loving mother,

Isabella

Catherine had burnt the letter, lest Thomas find it. And she'd nearly tossed the books into the fire as well, but curiosity stayed her hand.

Household Spells for Busy Women was the newer

of the two books. It was bound in dark blue cloth with gold tooling and colourful stamped images of herbs and flowers. The beauty of the cover invited her to open the book.

There were recipes for laundry blueing, stain removers, and wrinkle creams. There were spells for calming babies, taming unruly boys, and increasing a man's stamina in bed. The book was a treasure trove of useful information.

Catherine had resisted the urge to try any of the spells in the book until today. But the book called to her. Once Thomas was in bed, Catherine planned to try her first spell—one that prevented silver from tarnishing. Polishing the silver was a task she hated, and Thomas insisted it be kept gleaming at all times.

Thomas ate his dinner alone in silence, as he had for months, while Catherine finished the mending. When his plate was clean, he pushed his chair back and stood.

"I'm off to bed. I've got an early morning tomorrow—need to yard up the sheep for shearing by mid-morning," he said flatly, touching her shoulder as he passed.

She watched his back as he climbed the stairs, wondering if there were actually marriages in which the woman considered her husband's stamina in bed. She turned back to her mending with a sigh. She'd never been in love with Thomas, and he never liked Mother, but he was kind to the children and provided well for them all. She supposed she couldn't ask for more.

The clock on the mantel ticked away the minutes. Thomas' trousers slumped to the floor, belt buckle thumping on the wood as it did every night. The bed creaked—once when he lay down, again when he turned to his left side. Five minutes, ten minutes … it rarely took Thomas long to fall asleep. After fifteen minutes, Catherine set down her mending and fished the book from underneath the balls of wool in her basket.

She took the book into the kitchen, opened it to the spell labeled *Silverbright,* and laid it on the table in the centre of the room.

"A tablespoon of soda, five crushed mint leaves …" The spells in the book read a lot like cooking recipes, except they ended with an incantation to increase their potency. Catherine mixed the ingredients in a wooden bowl with a wooden spoon, as the spell instructed.

"Three turns widdershins and then—"

"What are you doing?"

Catherine gasped and snatched at the book as Thomas stepped into the pool of light cast by the lamp on the kitchen table. "I'm … I'm just making …"

Thomas strode to her and pulled the book from her grasp, turning the cover to the light. Catherine's fingers trembled as he read the title.

"*Household Spells*?" He looked at her—actually met her eyes—for the first time in weeks. The anger flaring in them made Catherine take a step back.

"It's a … figure of speech. They're recipes for

cleaning." She reached for the book. "I was making silver polish. You know how you like the silver to sparkle."

He held the book out of her reach. "You expect me to believe that a book called *Household Spells* is a recipe book?" He flipped it open and scanned a page, eyes narrowing. "She gave this to you, didn't she? That witch?"

Catherine's fear turned to anger. "That witch was my mother. Your mother-in-law. You were there, weren't you? That night? Did you light the fire yourself? Or did you just stand back and watch the flames with the others?"

Thomas slammed the book shut and waved it at Catherine's face. "This is exactly what the council was fighting against. This sort of ... devil worship." He laughed bitterly. "I was coming down to apologise. I had convinced myself I'd acted wrongly, not stepping in to save your mother. I know my actions hurt you." He waved the book again. "But seeing this. Seeing my wife brewing some ... some devil's potion in my own home? We should have dealt with your mother years ago."

He swept up the bowl and stomped into the living room, hurling the bowl, and then the book into the fire, following them up with an extra log to stoke the flames.

"What else did that witch give you? What other sorcery are you hiding from me?"

A vision of the second book flashed into Catherine's mind. *Formulae for the Summoning of Minor*

Angels and Daemons. It nestled alongside the pouch of gold nuggets underneath the neatly folded rags she used for her monthly courses—a place even Thomas wouldn't dare search. "Nothing. That book is all I had to remember her by." She let a sob escape, not sure it was entirely fake, as she intended it to be. She had loved Mother, and the loss of the beautiful household spells book was like losing another piece of her.

"Good. Maybe now you'll forget the hag and re-member what it means to be a proper wife and mother to our children."

As though she'd forgotten. Despite her grief, she'd put meals on the table three times a day, washed the clothes, scrubbed the floors, all without even a day's break when Mother died. When Mother was murdered. Anger flared at her husband.

But growing up with an abusive father had taught her well. Head to head, she would lose in a fight with Thomas. Subterfuge was more effective. She still had the second book. She still had the gold. Drawing her fury into a tight hot ball in her chest, she willed her voice quiet and steady. "Well then. I'll just go check on the children, like a proper mother." She stepped carefully up the stairs, wrapped in fortifying anger. She would try a summoning. Angel or demon? Which would best serve her needs?

Chapter Five

Shelby Saunders

The air was crisp the morning following the storm—washed clean by the rain. Alex saw no sign of the lightning strike the night before—the tree across the street was unscathed.

She read letters while she ate breakfast.

4 June 1974

My Dear Alice,

How rude of Daniel to postpone his trip! I was so looking forward to some extra time with you. It has been so long, Darling, since we were properly alone. Do you think he suspects something? Ha! That's a funny thought. The man is truly oblivious. You are far too good for him. You say you stay with him for the children's sake, but if he ignores you, how is that good for the children?

I know, I know. We've talked about this before. I respect your decision, I just ... wish it were different.

Be well, Love. I'll see you at the committee meeting on Thursday.

Love,

Dex

What would her grandfather have done if he'd found out

about Gran's affair? Was he oblivious because he didn't care? Because he was busy? Because he trusted Gran? Did he ever find out? Alex had to know more.

17 August 1976

My Dear Alice,

I didn't want to mention it at the church committee meeting the other day, but the grave they were discussing—the unmarked one they wanted to run sheep over—was supposedly my great-grandmother's. It's always been hush-hush within the family—she was accused of witch-craft and died in suspicious circumstances. My grandmother refused to talk about it, but I remember the old ladies whispering that her husband (my grandfather) was among the mob that burned her mother's house down. Can you imagine?

I always assumed the accusation of witchcraft was false, but when grandmother died, we uncovered this little book, with a note in it saying it had been her mother's and had been recovered underneath her house after her death. (I included it in my letter because I thought you'd find it amusing, since some of the ladies on the committee seem to think your herbal teas are somehow pagan in nature.) The book is utter rubbish, of course, but it makes me wonder what the woman was up to!

I look forward to seeing you on Saturday at the picnic.

Love,

Dex

Alex straightened in her chair. "That's the book!" She snatched it off the coffee table and flipped through the pages. Whatever note had been left in it was missing, but she had no doubt this was the book Dex referred to.

It sounded like the book was something of a family heirloom. But not *her* family's heirloom. Did Dexter Saunders have family still living in the area? She didn't remember any Saunders kids in high school, but that didn't mean much—they might not have the same last name.

Linda would probably know. She finished her breakfast,

drank an extra fortifying cup of coffee, and walked next door.

"Alex! Good to see you! How is the clearing out going? Are you sure you don't need help? Do you need someone to help with the furniture? I could ask David to pop over in the afternoon."

"No. It's fine," Alex broke in as Linda took a breath. "I've got a second-hand dealer coming to look at the furniture and give me a quote—I don't have to move it at all, he'll haul it all out."

"Oh, good. Look, I was going to come over to ask if you could take a look at one of my chickens. Loretta. She's off her feed today, and hobbling around on one leg."

"I'm not a vet, Linda."

"Yes, but you're so good with animals. Remember that bird I brought you?"

When Alex had first come to Gran's—surly and resentful, bursting with anger—Linda had brought her a bird that had gotten tangled in the fine black netting she'd draped over her strawberries. Its legs were encased in a snarl of netting. Alex had cradled the bird in her lap and spent over an hour gently teasing and cutting the plastic away. By the time she'd finished, the fog of rage in her brain had cleared, and she gently stroked the bird's soft feathers and massaged its misshapen legs. It had taken another thirty minutes for the bird to recover enough to scramble to its feet. When it pecked at her finger as if to say, 'Stop petting me, I'm fine,' she had laughed—her first laugh in days.

Had Linda given her the bird on purpose to take her mind off feeling sorry for herself? The thought gave her a twinge of remorse—she'd always treated Linda with disdain. Maybe it was time to grow up.

So she followed Linda around to the chicken coop at the

back of the house. Linda kept a flock of geriatric chickens, well beyond their laying years. She doted on her chooks. They occasionally blessed her with an egg, which she would show off to the neighbours. "See! And their previous owners were going to kill them because they were no longer laying." Alex respected her for her devotion to her pets, but she also understood commercial operators' need to cull birds that didn't produce eggs.

Loretta was an Orpington who must have once been a magnificent bird, but now felt thin and bony under Alex's fingers. Except for her left leg, which was puffy and swollen. Loretta squirmed as Alex manipulated the swollen appendage—it was obviously tender.

Parting the feathers high on the leg, she found the problem—a festering puncture wound. Alex pointed it out to Linda. "Something must have bitten her—a cat or a stoat? It's clearly gotten infected."

"So she'll need antibiotics?"

Alex shrugged. "You'll have to take her to the vet. I'm sure they'll know what to do."

"Yes. I'll give them a call. I wonder if they'll be able to see her today. Do you think I should separate her from the others? Do you think she'll be alright if they can't get her in until tomorrow?"

Alex had no answers for Linda. "You'll need to ring the vet and ask. I'm sure they're open by now."

Linda agreed and turned, but Alex stopped her. "I actually had a question for you, which is why I came over. It looks like Gran had ... borrowed a book from a neighbour years ago. I was hoping to get it back to their family, because it seems like something of a family heirloom."

"Like a family Bible?"

"Something like that. Anyway, she borrowed it from a

guy named Dexter Saunders. Does that name ring a bell?"

Linda frowned, then her brow cleared. "Yes! Dex Saunders. He was a local pilot, did crop dusting and whatnot. He died back in the mid-nineties I think, not too long after his wife did. Belle was her name. She sang in the church choir, though to be honest she didn't have much of a voice. Their son took over the crop dusting business and moved into Dex and Belle's house after Dex passed. His son's name is Peter. Peter's wife is a teacher somewhere in Christchurch. Teaches English, I think. They've got a son. What's his name now? He's about your age, but they sent him into town for high school, so you wouldn't have known him. Apparently he does computer stuff now—game design or something." She rolled her eyes. "Shelby! That's his name. Peter doesn't fly anymore—"

"Do they still live nearby?" Alex had no interest in hearing about Peter's aviation career.

"Oh, yes! They live in the brick house right next to that lovely two-storey place—the one that used to be a bakery? My grandmother remembered when—"

"Thanks, Linda." She checked her phone as though she was worried about the time. "Sorry, I need to run. Good luck with Loretta. Sorry I couldn't do anything for her." Alex tried not to sprint away. That would be rude. But she definitely didn't want to hear what Linda's grandmother remembered. That might go on for hours.

The idea of knocking on a stranger's door freaked her out, so instead of walking over to Peter Saunders' house, Alex sat down with her laptop and did what any reasonable person would do—she googled him. First, she typed *Saunders crop spraying*, hoping something would pop up and give her an email address or phone number.

The only Saunders crop spraying that came up was an

Australian company. She tried a few more searches to find Peter Saunders. No joy. What was the son's name? Shelby. He was in IT or something. Surely he'd have a web presence. She typed in the name.

Bingo! Facebook, Instagram, Twitter, LinkedIn ... the guy was everywhere. She clicked on his Facebook profile to do a little stalking before she messaged him. His profile picture was some anime character, and he apparently worked as a game designer for a company called Scarlet Pimpernel. His posts—at least the public ones—were all about new games, upgrades to old games, and advances in computing technology. A real computer geek. Out of curiosity, she clicked to Scarlet Pimpernel's website. Well! Interesting. She wasn't a gamer—she'd always rather be outdoors—but Scarlet Pimpernel's games were based on real-life humanitarian crises around the world. The players had to rescue people, fix the problem, and restore peace or order or public health, depending on the nature of the crisis. No zombies, no car chases, no stealing, killing or mining. She could admire a guy who made games like that, even if gaming in general was a waste of time. Even if he did still live with his parents.

She snorted. She'd been on her own for so long now, she couldn't imagine how it would chafe to still live with Gran. She knew lots of people her age lived with their parents, and maybe if her parents had still been alive she would still be living with them. But with Gran? She shuddered at the thought of dating under Gran's watchful eye. Then she remembered Dex's letters. Maybe Gran's eye wouldn't have been all that watchful. She'd certainly understand what it meant to sneak around in order to see someone.

Curiosity piqued, knowing she was stalking him way more than she needed to, she flicked over to Tinder, where she half-heartedly looked for dates once in a while. She typed in his name and laughed when she found him—of course he was on Tinder. She read his bio—not surprisingly, it didn't mention living with his parents. Who wanted to admit that? His profile photo was a surprise. A socially conscious game designer who was also good-looking—who would have thought someone like that existed? Dark, slightly curly hair, a neatly trimmed beard and moustache, and gorgeous hazel eyes in a nicely tanned face. She imagined he spent the weekends surfing to get that tan, although he hadn't listed any outdoor hobbies on his profile.

Focus. She wasn't looking for a date; she was just returning a book to the family. She logged out of Tinder without swiping left or right on his image. Back in Facebook, she messaged him.

> **Kia ora Shelby. I'm Alice Blackburn's granddaughter. Gran lived around the corner from you and recently passed away. Going through her things, I found a book that I'm pretty sure came from your grandfather, Dexter Saunders. I thought your family might want it back. Is there a good time to bring it round?**

A response came back almost immediately.

> **Hi Alex. Nice to meet you. I take it the book isn't just a mass-market paperback, but something interesting? Feel free to drop it by anytime—I work from home, so I'm here most of the time.**

> **You around now? I'll pop on over.**

> **Sure. You know where we are?**

> **Yeah. Linda Dickinson told me.**

> **Oh. Linda. Of course.**

He added an eye roll emoji. Alex chuckled.

Be there soon.

Alex picked up the book, clipped a leash on Benji, and headed out the door. Rifton was a small place. The Saunders' house was two short blocks away, past the primary school and around the corner, along a street composed mostly of old villas. The Saunders' place was newer—a brick house, probably built in the sixties.

She mounted the steps to the front door, admiring the tidy lawn and flower border before knocking.

When the door opened, Alex's first thought was *oops, wrong house*. The man at the door could only be described as frumpy. He was dressed in a T-shirt and saggy track pants that looked like he'd slept in them, and his face was pasty white. Surely this wasn't the gorgeous man in the Tinder profile. Then he smiled, and she saw it—the eyes, hair, and tidy beard. Yep. This was Shelby Saunders. A bit more the stereotypical computer geek when you saw him in person. How many Tinder dates went south when they actually met him?

She pushed her thoughts aside and smiled back. "Shelby?"

"Shel. And you're Alex?"

"Yeah." Benji barked. "And this is Benji."

"Yours?"

"Gran's dog. Not sure what I'm going to do with him. I live in Wellington in a flat that doesn't allow pets." She grinned cheekily at him. "You don't happen to want a dog, do you? Or two cats?"

He laughed. "Nah. Mum's allergic. So, what's this about a book?"

"Oh yeah." Alex held out the book to him. "I can tell you a little about it, but it's kind of a long story. And to be honest, it's not a particularly nice story."

His eyebrows rose. "Wanna come in for a cuppa and tell

me about it? Too bad my folks aren't home. They'd be interested in hearing this."

"I would, but …" She gestured toward Benji. "I don't want to bring him inside if your mum's allergic."

He jerked his head to the side. "Come around to the deck at the back. Tea or coffee?"

"Coffee please." Alex followed a path of stepping stones to the back of the house and stepped up to the deck. Shelby was visible through the kitchen window, and he gave her a little wave.

"Have a seat," he called out the window. "Milk? Sugar?"

"Just black. Thanks." She lowered herself into a director's chair, and Benji plopped down beside her with a sigh, as though he'd just run twenty kilometres.

The back yard was small, with a little vegetable garden and a wind vane in the shape of an airplane. When Shelby came out with two steaming mugs, she nodded toward the wind vane. "Your dad flies?"

He handed her one of the mugs. "Not any more. He had a stroke a couple of years ago, and after that Mum wouldn't let him go up again."

"Do you fly?"

"Nah. Dad took me up a few times—I think he hoped I'd catch the bug—but it freaked me out." He pulled the book out from under his arm as he sat down in the chair beside her. "So tell me about this book. It's not exactly what I expected when you messaged."

Alex laughed. "Yeah, it surprised me to run across it in Gran's things." She took a deep breath. May as well just blurt it out. Everyone involved was dead. Hopefully it wouldn't cause too much trouble to let the secret out. "In fact there were a fair few surprises among Gran's papers. There were dozens of letters from your grandfather to her. They apparently were having an affair … for over twenty years."

"No way!" Shel's eyebrows rose. "And your Gran was married at the time?"

Alex nodded. "And I assume your grandfather was too."

"He must have been." Shelby laughed—the same sort of unbelieving, semi-scandalised laugh Alex had made when she first learned about Gran's affair. "So how does this book figure into that?"

"One of the letters mentions it." She recounted what the letter said about its origin. "Gran was totally into herbal teas and folk remedies—apparently some of the local women considered her a pagan. He thought she'd get a kick out of reading a book on witchcraft, I guess."

Shelby paged through the book. "Weird. This is total crackpot bullshit—who would have saved it?"

"Apparently your grandfather … and a couple of generations before him, too. I thought it should maybe go back to your family. I don't know if you or your folks want it, but it's part of your family's history."

"Huh." He scanned the pages of the book. "And you say it's my grandfather's great-grandmother in that unmarked grave?"

"That's what the letter said. You didn't know that?"

"Nope. I don't think Dad knows either—that would be his great-great-grandmother." He laughed again. "A witch in the family—or at least someone who thought she was a witch. That's pretty sick. She must have been one crazy old bat."

"Yeah. Weird, eh? I had no idea witchcraft was even a thing in New Zealand. You know, you hear about it in Europe and America, but … I guess I figured all that witch burning stuff was over by the time Europeans settled here."

They talked for a few minutes longer. Alex related what

she knew of Gran's affair with Dexter. Shelby didn't seem particularly bothered by the news. Of course, he would have never met his grandfather. Hopefully he'd break the news gently to his dad.

His phone buzzed, and he pulled it out of his pocket. "Damn. That's my boss. I've got to take this. Thanks for dropping the book off."

"No worries. Thanks for the cuppa." She tossed back the last drop and picked up Benji's leash, waving a farewell as Shelby pressed his phone to his ear.

Well, one item disposed of. Shelby seemed like a nice guy, but she hoped Gran's other possessions were more quickly dealt with. And she'd rather not have to tell anyone else that their grandfather had had an affair.

Chapter Six

Materpoda

When Alex returned to Gran's, Thor and Thunder greeted her at the door.

"Are you finally going to be friendly to me?" she asked. They meowed in reply. Thor jumped to the kitchen bench and Alex shooed him off. Both cats circled her, but not in the friendly way cats sometimes do, rubbing your ankles. Instead, they paced and meowed. "What's up with you two? Did I forget to feed you?"

She checked their food dishes—they were still mostly full.

Suddenly both cats froze, tails twitching. A faint ticking sound, like someone tapping a pencil on a desk, wafted through the open kitchen window. As one, the cats galloped toward the door and leapt out the cat flap, leaving it rattling in their wake.

What was that all about? Alex shook her head. Peering out the kitchen window, she saw no sign of the cats or what had made the noise they were so interested in.

Whatever. She had work to do. She'd already filled Gran's rubbish bin, along with six extra rubbish bags. She rolled up the filthy, threadbare rug in the laundry and hauled it to the garage, tossing it beside the growing pile of rubbish bags.

She'd need to make a trip to the rubbish tip today—she couldn't put all this on the kerb. Were there any big things that needed to go? She should load those into the car first.

A walk through the house uncovered a bent ironing board, a side table that had clearly been chewed on by Benji, and a 1950s-era floor lamp in the living room that had a frayed cord. It was lucky Gran hadn't burnt her house down with that lamp.

As she lifted the lamp into the back of the car, a cat hissed nearby.

She straightened and turned toward the sound. What had gotten into those cats? Thunder's butt stuck out from under a bush at the side of the house, tail twitching. There must be something under there—no doubt another cat; the neighbourhood was crawling with them.

"Thunder!" she called.

The cat ignored her. Another cat growled from within the foliage.

"Come on Thunder. No fighting. I don't want to have to make a trip to the vet." She walked toward the cat and clapped her hands. Something rustled in the leaves, and then Thunder scooted backwards until he was free of the branches.

Still intent on the object of his quarrel, he slunk around the edge of the bush.

"No you don't." Alex wasn't foolish enough to try to pick up an agitated cat, but she stepped in front of him to try to distract him. He wiggled around her feet, following the sound of the other cat, still hidden.

A hiss sounded from within the foliage, and then there was a scuffle and a snarl. A moment later, Thor trotted out from under the bush.

"Who were you two ganging up on under there?" She shook her head. "Come on, let's go inside. Dinnertime!" She walked toward the door. Both cats scampered along with her, leaping through the cat flap before she could even open the door. Hopefully the cat they'd been fighting would slink off while Thor and Thunder were distracted.

While the cats ate their extra meal, Alex loaded the rubbish bags into the car. Looking around the garage, she figured there was at least another carload of junk in here to go to the tip, but the car was full, so it would have to wait.

She slammed the hatch shut. As she turned to go back inside for her purse and keys, a movement beside the house caught her eye. A dark form slipped under the bush. Was that cat still around? Something about the animal's movement had been off—not quite cat-like. But maybe she just hadn't been paying attention.

Still, if the cat had been injured … She crouched down and peered under the branches.

"Here, kitty, kitty," she crooned.

It was dark in the shade of the leaves. Alex couldn't see the cat. She called again, but the animal must have slipped away. Probably for the best—she had enough on her plate. It was most likely a neighbour's house cat, and if it wasn't, she didn't want to know. Dealing with Gran's animals was enough—she didn't want to feel obligated to find a home for a stray as well.

She stood. As she turned her back, she heard the swish of leaves. *Something* was under that bush, whether she could see it or not.

"Morning, Alex!" Mrs Walker waved from the street where she was walking her dog.

"Mrs Walker." Alex stepped out to the footpath. "I have a box of books for the garden group. Would you like me to bring them down later?"

"I can take them now—I'm on my way home."

"Are you sure? They're kind of heavy."

"Show me. We'll see."

Alex led her to the garage where she'd stacked the boxes of books. "Here are all the gardening books." She scratched Mrs Walker's shih-tzu while the older woman perused the volumes.

"This was all she had?" Mrs Walker rifled through the other boxes.

"All her books are here in these boxes. Feel free to take anything else you want. I plan to take them to the used book shop later this week and see what I can get for them, but you're welcome to take anything you'd like."

"Would you take two hundred dollars for the lot?"

"What?"

"I'll buy all Alice's books from you."

What did she want with this lot of rubbish? "Sounds good to me." If she didn't have to haul the books anywhere, that was a win. And she wasn't likely to get two hundred from the second-hand book shop.

"I'll go drop Bonny home and come back with the car and some cash for you."

After loading Mrs Walker's car with books and then dropping the rubbish off, Alex cleared out Gran's clothing without even bothering to look at any of it. She stuffed it all into rubbish bags and drove it to the nearest clothing bin. Let someone else decide what was fit only for rags and what was still useful.

When she returned, she felt lighter. There was still work to do, but most of Gran's personal items had been dealt with. Furniture, kitchen items, garden tools … they were unlikely to reveal illicit affairs or anything else shocking about Gran. The difficulty was going to be the animals. Linda had promised to ask around to see if anyone wanted them. It would be nice if Alex could take them back to Wellington, but there was no way—her flat didn't allow pets, and she didn't have the time to care for a dog.

She let Benji out into the yard to do his business while she sat in the late afternoon sun sipping a glass of wine. A cloud obscured the sun for a moment and she shivered. It felt like autumn in the wake of the storm.

She surveyed the yard. The lawn needed mowing. The place would need to look tidy, whether she planned to sell the house or rent it out. Selling was tempting—a lump sum might give her enough for a down payment on a nice place in Wellington. But Gran's house wasn't going to cover more than a down payment, and maybe having the regular income from a rental would be better.

Benji's barks distracted her from her thoughts. She rolled her eyes. He was at the shrubbery again. No doubt another blackbird.

"Benji, leave the bird alone."

His barks grew more furious and he lunged into the branches. Was there a cat under there? Would the one from earlier still be hanging around? But why would he get upset about a cat—he lived peacefully with two of them.

"Benji! Hush!"

Suddenly, his barks turned to a squeal that had Alex shooting out of her chair. She knew what an animal in pain sounded like.

She made it only a few steps across the lawn when the panicked yelping was cut short. A rustling came from the foliage. She bent to look.

For a moment, she thought she saw the glint of armour plating, the arch of many jointed legs.

"Fuck!" She leapt away. What the hell had she seen? No way could it have been what she thought it was. Her heart beat a rapid drumming in her ears.

"Benji? Come on, boy!"

The bush was silent.

"Benji! Dinnertime!" The dog had never failed to come running when called. Maybe he wasn't her dog, but within minutes of her arrival, he'd decided she was his human. "Come on, Benji!" Her voice quivered.

She glanced around the yard and snatched up a shovel Gran had left sticking upright in the compost pile. Holding it in front of her, she crept back toward where Benji had disappeared. She crouched and peered into the gloom. A dirty tennis ball, a drift of leaves. Nothing else was under there. Not even Benji.

Had he squeezed under the fence into Linda's yard? She listened for a whine, a snuffle, anything …

Silence.

Before she went to Linda's she wanted to make absolutely certain Benji wasn't still under the bush.

"Benji? Come on out, boy!"

When he once again failed to appear, she used the shovel to lift the lower branches. No way was she putting her hands in there. She cursed her decision to read that book—nothing she'd ever read had spooked her into seeing monsters before. *Come on Alex. Get a backbone. Whatever you think you saw is in your imagination.* Maybe Benji had cornered a stoat—those things could be fierce. He might be in there hurt and needing her help.

She dropped the shovel and shoved aside branches, pushing her way between the bush and the fence on hands and knees.

There, among the leaves, was Benji's collar. Her stomach sank. Had he slipped his collar? But where was he? She reached toward the collar. She'd need it when she found him. If something large and leggy hadn't eaten him.

A brown form burst toward her face and she ducked with a scream. With sickle-shaped jaws, too many legs to count, and moving like lightning, the enormous centipede skittered right over her back, each clawed foot scratching as it poked through her T-shirt.

Her scream took on a deep-throated horror she never knew she could make. Her whole body shook and she staggered backward. By the time she turned to face her attacker, the monster was gone.

"OhmygodOhmygodOhmygod! What the fuck was that?"

The word *materpoda* flashed through her brain. A large centipede-like demon, easy to summon, difficult to control.

But she didn't believe in any of that shit. Demons were medieval fictions cooked up to try to explain all the awful, natural stuff life threw at people before they understood science. They weren't real, live, three-metre-long centipedes that ate terriers.

Her whole body shook, and she could barely open the latch to the gate onto the street. She ran to Linda's house and pounded on her door, trying to steady herself. Her voice was breathy when she asked Linda if Benji was in her back yard.

"Well, I don't think so. How would he have gotten there? You're welcome to go round and check. Is everything alright?"

"Yeah. No. He's … he's vanished."

"Oh, you poor dear. He'll be around somewhere. He must be missing his old lady. Don't you worry dear. No doubt he'll show up soon. He won't have gone far. Now you go and check in the back, and I'll be out in a wee bit. I've got dinner on, and I can't leave it at the moment."

Thankful for Linda's absence, Alex ran around to the back.

"Benji? Benji!"

Benji wasn't there. At this point, she didn't expect him to be. That … thing … had eaten him. Her stomach churned and she wanted to vomit. She couldn't face Linda again, so she scurried back out of her yard.

At Gran's house she slammed the door behind her, locking it with jittery fingers. The cats. Where were they?

"Thor? Thunder?" Her voice quavered. The cat tree in the living room was empty. She raced down the hallway to Gran's bedroom, where the cats sometimes slept on her bed.

Her shoulders slumped in relief. There the two felines were, sprawled together in a tangle of limbs on Gran's duvet.

"Just stay here, you two," she told them.

She walked back to the living room and paced the rug, talking to herself.

"Okay, so let's say a giant centipede just ate Benji. And let's say that giant centipede was a materpoda." She paused and leaned against the mantel for support.

"And let's say you summoned this materpoda yourself."

She swallowed and sat down hard on the couch. If she'd summoned that creature, she'd done it in here last night.

She'd seen it.

Here in the living room.

It had been in the house. She shivered.

How had it gotten outside? Could it have gone out when she opened the door to carry boxes out to the car? Surely she would have noticed an animal that big, either inside the house, or when it ran out the door.

She cast her mind back to last night—the book, the candles, the lightning and thunder.

Sucking in a sharp breath, she stood. "The animal flap!" It creaked shortly after the big lightning strike. Thunder had shot into the room, and she assumed he'd been outside, but he'd come in when the storm started. And he'd been dry when she petted him.

The materpoda had gotten out through the animal flap.

Which meant it could get back in through it too.

"Fuck!" Alex dashed to the kitchen and yanked open the middle drawer. Yes! Duct tape! She knelt at the door and ripped off a strip of tape. She slapped it over the animal flap, then pulled off another, and another, and another. She didn't stop until the flap was completely obscured by multiple layers of tape.

Now what?

She rubbed her face. This couldn't be happening, but it was all too real.

The book.

It must have instructions for controlling the demon, or sending it back to … wherever it had been summoned from.

She reached for the door, and then paused. The creature was out there. Did she dare go out?

"Dammit, you're an adult, Alex," she growled at herself. She wasn't afraid of animals. She could brave a giant centipede. Right? Surely her brain was exaggerating its size—it couldn't be *that* big.

Big enough to eat Benji, though. She shuddered. Poor Benji!

"It's just eaten. It won't want to eat me."

She needed that book. Before that ... thing ... got hungry again.

Chapter Seven

Chilopodophobia

Alex pounded on Shelby's door. "Come on, Shelby! Open the damned door!" Where was he? She pounded again.

"What the hell!" Shelby jerked the door open, and then stepped back. "Oh. It's you. What're—"

"I need the book." Alex stepped into the doorway.

"Huh?" He looked at her as though she'd sprouted horns.

"I need the book! Where is it?" Her hands shook, and she clasped them to steady them.

"Didn't you just give me the book?"

Was he deaf? "Yes! And I. Need. It. Now."

"Why do you need—"

"Because I accidentally summoned a demon by reading it aloud to the dog last night, and I need to figure out how to send the damned thing back!"

His calmness made her want to throttle him. "Where's Benji?"

"The demon ate him." She swallowed and blinked back

tears.

He scoffed. "So, you're saying you accidentally summoned a demon and he's eaten your dog?"

"Gran's dog, but yes. More or less."

"Is this some kind of joke?"

Alex spoke through gritted teeth, her heart pounding. "This is not a joke. There is a demon loose in the—"

Shel raised his hand. "Look, I have work to do. Maybe you should go home and sleep this off, whatever it is you've taken."

"I haven't taken anything." She took a calming breath. Was she acting high? Yeah, okay, maybe. What if Shel had come to her door with this story? Another breath. *Get your act together. Don't freak out.* "Would you mind if I borrow the book? Just for a bit."

He clearly wasn't buying her sudden calm. His eyes scrutinised her for a moment. "I suppose. It's in my room."

He turned, and Alex followed into a gloomy living room with the curtains still drawn, then down a carpeted hallway.

"Your parents still away?"

He jumped, eyes round and fearful. "Why are you following me?"

"'Cause I want the book, remember?" Was she being freaky again?

"You could have waited by the door." He was frowning now. No, it was more than a frown. He was looking at her like she might be a serial killer.

Calm down. Don't scare him.

She smiled. "I wanted to ask you, do you think your dad might know something about the book? Something that might help me in my ... ah ... situation."

"Maybe." Shelby scrutinised her again. "But my parents are on holiday in Australia. Stupid, as far as I'm concerned, what with Covid still raging and all, but—" He shut his mouth.

She must still be acting weird. "How about I just wait in the living room." Only serial killers insisted on following a stranger to their bedroom. Besides, Alex imagined it was a stinky man-cave with unwashed socks strewn across the floor and half-eaten pizza in a takeaway box on the bed. She shuddered at the vision as she retraced her steps.

The room was an ordinary lounge—overstuffed grey couch with matching armchairs, glass-topped coffee table, big-screen television, and a log burner. It would have been pleasant if it weren't so dark. She reached for the curtains and paused. Would the materpoda be out there? Holding her breath, she swept the curtains open.

No giant centipede skittering down the footpath. She puffed in relief, but kept vigil at the window, afraid to turn her back in case the demon snuck up on her.

Shelby returned with the book and handed it over. Was it heavier than before? Did it crackle with magical energy? No. *Get a grip.* It was a book—paper and ink. She sank into a chair and opened it. "I was reading this one—the summoning for the materpoda." She scanned the text for more information.

Shelby remained standing. "And you were reading this spell aloud, why?"

She sighed. "Benji was terrified of the storm. I realised my voice calmed him so I picked up some books and started reading aloud."

"And you chose *this* book to read?"

"It was better than *Compost Porn*, trust me."

Shelby snorted. "Compost *what?*"

Alex waved a hand, still scanning the text in front of her. "Gran had strange taste in literature."

"So you were reading this book aloud."

"This *spell*." She tapped the page.

"Right. This spell. To summon a demon." He spoke slowly, as if talking to a child.

"Yeah, a materpoda. It's this big … centipede."

"*Centipede*?" Shelby squeaked.

"Yeah. A couple of metres long, at a guess, though I haven't really seen it stretched out all the way. It was kind of—"

A strange sound made her look up. Shelby's face was grey. His hands shook and he looked like he was going to vomit.

"Shelby?" She jumped to her feet. "Are you okay?"

His eyes were glazed, unseeing. His face grew even paler.

"Okay. Um. Lie down. Can you make it to the couch?" He listed to the right. "Never mind. Lie down on the floor. That's it." She eased him down as he all but collapsed onto the carpet. "Just relax. I'm going to get you some water."

She raced to the kitchen and started tearing open cupboard doors, looking for the glassware. She finally found it and filled a glass at the tap. Rushing back in, she wondered if she should be dialling emergency services. Could he be having a stroke or something? He was so young, it hadn't occurred to her. What was that acronym for stroke symptoms? FACE? What did the letters mean again?

She knelt beside him. He hadn't moved at all while she was gone, and his eyes were still unfocused. "Shelby? Shelby, I've brought you some water. Do you think you can drink a little?" He didn't respond. "Shelby, can you tell me what's wrong? Do I need to dial 111? Come on Shelby, talk to me."

He blinked and his eyes focused on her face. "Shel."

"Pardon?"

"Shel. Call me Shel. Only my parents call me Shelby."

Well, at least he was talking. It might be irrelevant, but it was coherent.

"Shel. Do you think you can sit up and drink some water? Do you need an ambulance?" Her pulse raced. What if he died while she was here?

He shook his head. "No ambulance. I'll sit up in a moment. Put the water on the side table."

She did as he asked and then perched on the couch, watching him as he closed his eyes and took several deep breaths. Finally, he hauled himself upright, leaning his back against the armchair. He reached up for the water and took a sip. Colour slowly returned to his face, though his hands still shook.

"Are you sure you don't need an ambulance?"

"I'm fine. Can you please just go?"

"What's wrong? Does this happen often?" She probably shouldn't pry, but she was still considering calling emergency services. *Something* was wrong when a man just collapsed like that with no warning.

Now colour returned to his face with a vengeance. Was he blushing?

"I ..." He rubbed his face. "I have a phobia of ... something you mentioned."

"What? Centipedes?"

He blanched again, and Alex clapped a hand over her mouth.

"I'm so sorry!"

"Look, can you just go? You've got the book, now get out. You can keep it. I don't think I want it in the house." He waved her away.

"Are you sure you're going to be okay?" She didn't know this guy at all, and he thought she was a serial killer, but she wasn't going to leave him here alone if he was having a medical emergency.

"I'm fine. Please go." Colour was creeping up his neck, and Alex knew it was kinder of her to leave him and save him the ongoing mortification of an audience to his phobia.

Alex stood. "Can you message me in an hour or so, just to let me know you're alright? I'm not trying to be a mother hen or anything, but you just collapsed in front of me, and I know you're here by yourself … I'm not crazy, even if you think I am because I said I summoned a demon, and I'd feel bad if I read of your death in the paper in two weeks."

Shel snorted and smiled weakly. "You mean Friendless Computer Geek Dies at his Desk in Parent's Attic and No One Realises He's Gone Until the Smell Alerts the Neighbours?"

Now it was Alex's turn to blush, because that's exactly what she was thinking. Was she being unfair to him—judging a book by its cover?

"Right. Well, I'll just go and deal with my little … problem." She let herself out and walked quickly back to Gran's, eyes darting everywhere, wondering where the materpoda was now.

When she opened the door, Thunder and Thor meowed their irritation at the taped-over animal flap. Thor made a lunge for the outdoors. Alex blocked him with a foot.

"Oh no you don't. You boys are indoor cats for now." She'd need to set up a litter box for them. Probably best to do it now. She grabbed an old baking tin from the kitchen and filled it with sand from Gran's potting shed. When she placed it in the laundry room for the cats, they sniffed at it with obvious disdain, then returned to Gran's bed.

Her stomach growled. In all the excitement, she'd forgotten to eat dinner. A foray to the fridge yielded a slice of spinach and feta pie Linda had brought her. She slid the pie onto a plate, heated it in the microwave, and poured herself a glass of wine.

She sat at the dining room table, eyeing the book warily while she wolfed down her meal, praying it contained the information she needed to get rid of the materpoda.

Finally she sat down on the couch and paged through the book.

There was nothing in the section on the materpoda that she hadn't read yesterday, but Alex noted again the comment, *control of a Materpoda once summond be more difficult than the Summoning, and attain only by those naturally born unto Magick.*

How did you identify someone naturally born to magic? What did that even mean?

She paged further into the book. Surely there would be a section on getting rid of demons, right?

There it was, right at the very end.

The Summoning of Spirits shall not be undertaken in jest or without dire need. Significant dangers beset the Witch involved in summoning even the most benign of Spirits. The summoner must needs defin a task for a Spirit when it be summon'd or it may chuse to follow its own unpredictable Will. Under the control of an experienced and powerful natural-born Magick wielder, a Spirit will compleat its task and then joyfully return to its hom when the summoning be revers'd.

In the case a Witch neglect to provyde a defin'd task or sufficiently powerful control, any Spirit can become a Danger to the Magick wielder and others. In the case that a Spirit cannot be returned by banishment, the only recourse be Death.

Spirits be frightfully difficult in the killing, only with Magick. Banishment be recommended.

Alex turned the page. A woodcut of a gruesome-looking creature with horns and long claws graced the final page of the book.

"That's it?" She paged back again, thumbing through the

entire book at speed. "You're not going to even explain what a banishment is?" Witches were apparently supposed to know that already. Or maybe there was a companion book? Even if there was, Alex didn't have it.

She threw the book down and rubbed her face. "What the hell am I supposed to do now?"

A loud hiss emanated from Gran's bedroom, and Alex rushed down the hallway to find both cats sitting on the windowsill, backs arched, with their fur standing out like hedgehog quills. Their eyes were fixed on something outside.

Alex crept to the window to see what had upset the cats. *Please let it be a dog and not a giant centipede.*

Her silent plea went unanswered. As she reached the window and glanced down, she sucked in a breath.

The creature was a rich russet colour with a shiny body at least three metres long and thirty centimetres wide. It scuttled through the grass on dozens of half-metre-long legs. Whip-like antennae tapped the ground ahead of its wicked-looking black jaws. Its eyes were small black golf balls on either side of its head. It wove back and forth across the yard, antennae tapping rapidly. Its movement reminded her of Benji's snuffling exploration every time they went for a walk.

She pulled her phone out of her pocket. Maybe someone could identify it if she posted a picture online. Sort of like those sightings of black panthers that always turned out to be nothing more than large house cats, maybe this materpoda was just ... a really big house centipede. Or maybe it was one of those Australian giant centipedes. Did people keep those things as pets? Maybe one had escaped.

Her hands shook as she raised the phone and snapped a picture. In the fading light outside, her flash automatically went off. By the time its bright reflection in the window cleared from her vision, the creature had vanished.

Alex swiped to the photo. A brilliant starburst of light on a black background. No demon. Damn.

Chapter Eight

Missing Dog

She didn't sleep well. The cats were disgruntled, howling to be let out half the night, and when she did doze off, her dreams were filled with leggy monsters chasing Benji on his leash as she fled with him. She woke fuzzy-headed and irritable.

Her stomach felt like it was full of bricks, so she ignored food and made herself a coffee. She resisted the urge to drink it on the back deck—she wasn't ready to face that thing again yet.

That thing. Maybe there was something online about it. She googled *materpoda*.

Google responded: *Do you mean meterpodu?*

The links that came up were irrelevant and a little bizarre—a gay meet-up page on Facebook, the index from what looked like a Latin textbook, and a couple of Twitter posts in a foreign language she didn't recognise, but which did not translate to anything resembling, *I saw this great big centipede today …*

She googled *demons*. This got lots of hits of ugly creatures from mythology, but none that looked like a centipede.

She googled *witchcraft* and *summoning*. Gazillions of hits, none of them mentioning materpodas.

She googled *giant centipede* and read some nice little articles about the ones in Australia, which didn't come anywhere close to the size of the one currently residing in Gran's back yard.

She leaned back in her chair with a huff. What do you do when Google fails to provide an answer?

Maybe Dex's letters had more information in them. It was a long shot, but the book was of little help, and Google was a bust—there weren't all that many options.

She picked up the stack of unread letters and opened the next one.

12 September 1976

Dear Alice,

I hope you read this before you hear about it through the ladies' gossip chain. Belle is pregnant again. I know it will upset you, but it would look strange if I didn't go through the motions wouldn't it? She wanted another child so badly, and I do care for her, even if it isn't the same as it is with you.

Meet me tomorrow behind the rugby clubrooms. Nine o'clock.

Love,

Dex

Well. Dex was having his cake and eating it, too. A flare of indignation rose in Alex's chest. Then she shook herself. Gran was cheating on her husband. She was no better than Dex.

She opened the next letter.

20 September 1976

My Dearest Alice,

Please don't be angry with me. Don't cut me out. I waited for hours behind the rugby clubrooms for you. Why did you run out of the church social when you saw me? And I know you were not ill for the committee meeting yesterday.

I will wait for you again tonight. I know you have your knitting group meeting at the hall. I'll be in the gardens behind the hall when you finish.

Love,

Dex

"Ha! Serves you right." Of course, the mountain of letters still to come was proof Gran had given him another chance.

Alex read on.

A dozen letters later, Gran and Dex had made up, Belle had lost the baby, and Dex hadn't mentioned the book once.

Alex tossed another letter onto the *read* pile. Her stomach growled. Maybe she should eat something.

As she headed to the kitchen, a knock sounded at the door. She'd barely opened it before Linda started talking.

"Morning, Alex! Beautiful day, isn't it? I hope I didn't wake you. It is a little early, but Alice was always an early riser, and I remember you were never far behind her, were you? Not like teens these days, sleeping in until noon or later. Why, Emma Lyttle, from my book club, her boy Lucas apparently doesn't go to sleep until three in the morning, and then she says she's lucky if he's awake for dinner!"

"Shocking," Alex said, not pointing out that a mere seven years ago, Linda was rolling her eyes at Gran, saying 'kids these days' about Alex herself. "Did you need me for anything?"

"Oh! Sorry, I got sidetracked. I came over to bring you this." She handed over an old biscuit tin Alex remembered from her time with Gran.

"Are these your rhubarb bars?" Alex asked, peeking

inside.

Linda nodded. "I remembered they were your favourite. Thought you might need some comfort food."

More food? Did Alex look like she couldn't take care of herself? She caught herself before she said anything snarky. Linda pushed all of Alex's buttons, but she had a good heart. "Thanks. Yeah, comfort food is a good thing."

"I also wanted to ask if you'd found little Benji."

Alex shook her head. "No sign of him at all." She bit her tongue to stop herself mentioning he'd been eaten by a monstrous centipede that was currently hanging out in Gran's back yard.

"Oh dear. Well, Ken Silver, from just down the street—do you remember Ken? Used to do model train set-ups in his living room. He has that cute little toy poodle, and—"

"Yeah, I remember him," Alex lied. She had no interest in hearing Ken's life story.

"Right, well, Ken stopped by this morning to tell me to be on the lookout, because his little poodle is missing."

Alex's throat went dry. "Missing?"

Linda nodded, eyes wide. "Just like Benji. And I doubt it's a coincidence. I reckon there's a thief around, snatching up pet dogs and selling them off. No doubt you'll find both dogs on Trade Me before long."

Alex didn't think so. She gave a weak smile, trying to mask her racing heart. "Maybe they've run off together—doggy love or something."

Linda laughed. "Well we can hope so. Though let's hope they don't come back with a litter of puppies."

Unlikely, given that Benji was a neutered male. And because he was currently working his way through the digestive system of a demon. "Well, thanks for letting me know, Linda. I wish I could invite you in for a cup of tea and to enjoy these rhubarb bars with me, but I'm meeting with Gran's lawyer shortly and need to get ready," she lied.

"Oh, well. Good luck. I'll see you later."

Alex shut the door and swore under her breath. Of course the demon wasn't just hanging out in Gran's yard. She ran her fingers through her hair. What was she going to do? She couldn't let the thing eat its way through the entire neighbourhood's pet population.

Surely Dex's family had more information—old papers, letters, more books maybe? Somewhere there had to be information about how to get rid of this creature.

Giving up on the idea of eating—her stomach was roiling again—she snatched up the book and Dex's letters, shoved them into a tote bag, and hurried over to Shelby's house.

Five minutes later she knocked on Shelby's door. Should she have waited, or messaged first? It was only eight o'clock in the morning. Would Shel be up yet?

She knocked again.

Shel had definitely not been up yet. He blinked against the light as he pulled the door open, his hair standing on end. He wore a T-shirt that proclaimed, *I'm not procrastinating, I'm doing side quests* over a pair of baggy grey track shorts, and his feet were bare.

"You again? No." He swung the door shut.

Alex jammed her foot in the doorway and pushed the door back open. "Look, I need your help."

He raised his hands, as if to fend her off. "I can't help you. Not if it has to do with that—" his face paled.

"Would it make it easier if I referred to it as a materpoda?" She clenched the edge of the door. He had to help.

Who else could she ask?

"A mater-what? Have you given your imaginary creature a name now?"

"Please. It's called a materpoda; I didn't make it up. And it's eaten another dog. I've got to get rid of it somehow, and I've come up with nothing. Your family had this book" — she waved it in the air— "for decades. Surely you have other things in the family—books, papers, whatever—that might help." Was she freaking out too much? Scaring him? Acting like a lunatic? How could she not, when she expected to see a giant centipede around every corner?

He frowned at her. "Have you googled it?"

She rolled her eyes. "Of *course* I googled it—do you think I'm stupid or something?"

"No. I think you're—never mind. If nothing came up on Google, it's either a figment of your imagination, or you weren't searching for the right thing. I'm betting on the imagination."

"Look, I *heard* the thing eating Benji! It ran across my back! The cats were freaking out about it last night too; it's not just me. And I *know* how to do a Google search. Just because I'm not some computer geek doesn't mean I'm incompetent."

Shelby looked smug. "Most people have no idea how to do an effective Google search."

"Well, fine," snapped Alex. "Show me then, mister computer whiz."

He stepped back, inviting her in. "Come on. We'll do a proper search, but don't expect to find anything."

As she followed him inside, he ran a hand through his hair. "Lemme just get dressed." He vanished down the hallway. Alex flopped onto the couch in the living room after pulling back the curtains to let light in. How could anyone live in a cave like this?

Shelby appeared in the doorway a few minutes later. "Coffee?"

Alex suppressed a snort—*getting dressed* apparently meant putting on a different worn T-shirt and some slightly less baggy shorts. "Yes please." At least he was being civil. Or maybe he hadn't had his morning coffee yet and needed it in order to deal with her.

"Black, right?"

Alex nodded, and Shelby vanished into the kitchen. The sound of a grinder and the smell of fresh coffee beans lifted her opinion of him. At least he didn't drink instant.

But the wait for the coffee felt interminable. She needed to get her information and deal with the materpoda before it ate any more pets. Playing the crazy serial killer wasn't going to win Shelby's help, though. When he finally returned with coffees in hand, she summoned all the politeness and calm she could.

Taking the offered mug, she said, "Sorry I barged in on you while you were still asleep."

He shrugged. "Nah. I've been awake for hours. Woke at five with the solution to a coding problem in my head. Figured I'd better get it written before I forgot it. But now I'm desperate for coffee."

Be polite and not crazy. He had skills that were possibly useful to her if he agreed to help. *Make small talk.*

"So, what is it you do, exactly?"

Shelby smiled. "I work for a VR game company."

"Scarlet Pimpernel. Yeah. They do some interesting stuff."

Shel's eyebrows rose and his smile grew. "You've played their games?"

"No. I'm not really into computer games, but I've

checked out their website—I like that their games are based on fixing humanitarian crises."

"Yeah. They're a great company to work for."

"So you write code for the games?"

His eyes sparkled. "Yeah, we're working on a new VR game right now that will create a virtual volcanic eruption in Auckland. Players will be able to go around the real city and rescue people, put out fires, that sort of thing."

In spite of her impatience, Alex was intrigued. "Cool. Sort of like Pokemon Go, but with a humanitarian mission?"

"Uh huh. If it goes well, we'll do other disasters in other cities around the world. It's pretty intensive for each city, because each one is bespoke, you know."

"Sounds like it." Alex didn't have much to add. That level of computing was way beyond her knowledge—she didn't even know what questions to ask about his work. Besides, it was time to get on with her problem.

Shelby gestured for her to follow and led her down a dim hallway. "So what exactly is it you're looking for?"

"Anything that might help me get rid of this … demon I've summoned."

"Riiiight."

Chapter Nine

Dexter Saunders

Alex followed Shelby back to his bedroom office. It wasn't quite the cave she had imagined—though it was dark with drawn curtains, it was reasonably tidy, and there were no smelly socks or greasy pizza boxes in sight. A large desk dominated the wall opposite the bed, two enormous monitors perched on top, alongside a tall black desktop computer.

"Wow. You've got quite the set-up here."

Shelby whipped open the curtains and pushed aside a stained coffee cup. "It's not bad. The water cooler conversations are pretty one-sided though." He touched the keyboard, and the monitors sprang to life. "I take it you've done the obvious searches?"

"Like giant centipede—sorry!" she added as Shelby blanched. "Yes. I've done all those."

"Did you check Google Scholar?"

Alex wished she could wipe the know-it-all look off his face by saying *of course I checked Scholar*, but it hadn't occurred to her. She reluctantly shook her head.

Shelby sat down in the space-age-looking gaming chair, and Alex drew up next to him, eyes on his screen.

He typed in a series of searches, scanning the hits so quickly it made Alex's head swim. He clicked on a book about witchcraft in Europe and scrolled through the pages.

"Lots of details about supposed cannibalism and orgies. Too bad you're not interested in that." His face went red. "I mean ... you know ... from a research perspective."

Alex couldn't suppress her snort of laughter.

He slowed his scrolling. "Wait. Here's something referencing a document about exorcising household demons." He clicked through a few links. "Damn. The original doesn't seem to be online, and it's in Latin anyway."

Alex sighed. "Surely if there was a book about summoning demons, there would be one about getting rid of them." She paged through the book as Shelby continued scrolling. Maybe there was a clue she'd missed. Maybe the publisher had produced other witchcraft books. "This was printed at the Peacock and Bible. Maybe if we search that printer?"

The search yielded nothing of use. "Well, it's not like they would have had a website or anything," Shelby said.

"Did your grandfather leave behind any papers, books, things like that?"

"You want to go through my grandfather's things? I don't think you'll find references to imaginary demons there."

Dammit, the materpoda *wasn't* imaginary. It took effort to unclench her fists and respond without snapping. "He gave my gran a book on summoning demons—who knows what he might have had?"

Shelby frowned. "I suppose you have a point. But I have no idea what is still left of Grandpa's things, or where it might be."

"Presumably your parents know. When will they be back?"

"Not for weeks." Shelby opened a different window and typed a message to P Saunders.

You available to talk?

Sure thing. Everything alright?

Yep. Just have a question.

He opened a video chat and an image of a middle-aged man with salt and pepper hair and a trim beard popped up on the screen.

"Hey Dad. How's it going? How's Darwin?"

The man smiled. "Great! Had a fabulous cruise yesterday." His eyebrows rose. "Who's the friend?"

"Uh ... she's not a friend. She's a ..."

"I'm Alex, Alice Blackburn's granddaughter. She lived just down the street from you and passed away last week."

"Alex found some letters from your dad to her gran. Apparently, they, uh ..."

Peter snorted. "Had an affair."

"You knew?"

"Yeah. I'm pretty sure Mum did, too."

"And she stayed with him?" Shelby's eyebrows rose.

"I don't think Mum cared much, so long as he supported her and the kids and kept it discreet. The expectations of marriage were different back then. So, is that why you rang?"

Shelby glanced at Alex, and then turned back to the screen. "We were curious, I guess. Wanted to know more."

"I'm not sure how much of your grandpa's things we still have, and I can't say I remember anything related to your grandmother, Alex. But you're welcome to have a look through them. They'd be in a cardboard box at the back of the closet in the spare bedroom."

"Thanks."

"No worries. Sorry to hear about your grandmother, Alex. Nice meeting you."

Alex and Shelby both said goodbye, and then Shelby dug out the box Peter had mentioned.

"Let's look for books first," Alex suggested.

They lifted out photographs, Dex's pilot licence, a creased and stained cap advertising *Saunders Spraying*, a Korea Medal on a faded blue and yellow ribbon, a stack of letters, and several yellowed newspaper clippings. There was also a starched christening gown bearing a pinned-on label that read *Made by Grandma Parker, 1929*.

Alex lifted up the christening gown and peered into the box. "Aha!" Her pulse quickened in anticipation.

At the very bottom of the box lay a book. She snatched it up and turned it over.

Her shoulders sagged. "A Bible."

"Open it," Shelby suggested. "It might have writing in it, or papers tucked inside."

The cracked leather binding threatened to break as she opened the cover. "You sure we should be doing this? This is your family Bible."

Shelby shrugged. "It's not like we use it or anything—I've never even seen it, so I'm guessing it's been in this box since Grandpa died."

Inside the front cover was the family record. Some of the names were written in faded, flowery script that Alex couldn't read. She scanned them, finding the record of Dex Saunders' birth on 23 August 1929 to Clive and Mary Saunders (nee Parker).

"I think Dad's great-grandmother was named Catherine," Shel commented.

"Could she be Catherine Parker?" Alex pointed at the

record of a girl born on 2 December 1861 to Robert and Isabella Deacon.

"The same Grandma Parker who made the christening gown? She would have been sixty-eight when she made the gown." He shrugged. "Could be, I suppose."

"She was the one who recovered the book from her mother's house."

"So Isabella Deacon was the witch."

"The one in the unmarked grave."

They sat in silence for a few moments. Isabella's birth wasn't recorded—she would have been part of someone else's family at the time.

Alex turned the page. "A death registry too." She scanned the page and snorted. "They didn't even record her death."

"Of course not."

She thumbed through the Bible, looking for anything that might have been stuck between the pages. Nothing. "I don't know what I expected. If they didn't even record Isabella Deacon's death, they certainly wouldn't have recorded anything else about her."

"No, and I can't imagine anyone would store magical spells inside a Bible. Should we check these letters?" Shelby sorted through them. "Most of them seem to be written by my grandfather to his parents during the Korean War."

"Those won't be of use. Are there others?"

"Um … only these two. From Charles Cartwright?" He handed one to her and opened the other.

Alex pulled out the letter and skimmed its contents.

7 April 1954

Dex,

Congratulations on your upcoming nuptials. Hope the girl is as pretty as the army nurses! I'm still happily single—seems a decorated pilot makes me a desirable catch, so I'm taking advantage of the situation for as long as it lasts …

The letter went on to describe Charles' daily life after the war. Nothing of interest to Alex. She stuffed it back in its envelope. "Worthless. Yours?"

"Same." He began to pack everything back into the box. "You know that book could have been a hoax—a joke between our grandparents."

Alex growled in frustration. "I summoned a demon with it—it's no hoax. Where else would we find Isabella's things, or information on local witchcraft—do you think there was a witches' coven here? I know nothing about witchcraft in New Zealand."

"You're assuming witchcraft is actually real."

Alex huffed. "Look, I don't blame you for being sceptical. If I hadn't felt the thing run across my skin, I might have thought it was fake too. Can you humour me? Let's assume witchcraft is actually a thing that people did, at least in the past. Where would we find information on it in New Zealand?"

Shelby rolled his eyes. "Well if I was looking for historical records, I'd start in the local library. We could check their catalogue online."

"Good idea."

Back in Shel's bedroom office, Alex leaned over his shoulder as he typed in various searches of the library's catalogue. *Witchcraft* yielded books about medieval Europe, *Witchcraft New Zealand* yielded novels about witches written by New Zealand authors, *Demons* brought up nothing.

"Let's just look for local history. If we can find any reference to local witches, maybe we can find other families who might have books handed down from that time."

Shelby paused, rolling his eyes at the idea of references

to local witches. Then he typed in a search. "Wow! There's a lot of local history books. Lemme see if I can narrow it down."

They eventually found two books that included historical references to Rifton.

Alex shouldered her bag. "You coming?" Why did she want his company?

Shelby shook his head. "No way. This is your problem, not mine."

"This book came from your family!" She jabbed the summoning book at him.

"I'm not the one who thinks they accidentally summoned a demon. Besides, I have work to do. Just because I work from home doesn't mean I don't have to get my job done."

Alex held up her hands. He was right. This was her problem. "Fine. Thanks for your help. Mind if I hang on to the book until I get this sorted?"

Shelby pushed the book away. "I don't ever want to see that book again. It's yours."

Fifteen minutes later, Alex sat in the library, two slim volumes on the table in front of her. She no longer had a local library card, so she had no choice but to read the books here.

The first she opened was a history of the region written by an amateur historian for the commemoration of the centennial of the Rifton Hall. It was truly dreadful. It reminded her of an information report she'd written in year six—a random assortment of facts, poorly organised and written in the rambling fashion of someone recounting stories to their friends.

At least it was organised by town, so she only had to

wade through part of it.

She read about the construction of the first hall in 1864, and how James Farthing, the carpenter, had to resort to using wooden pegs because he ran out of nails.

She read about the fire at the school in 1902, lit by a pair of troublemaking brothers who didn't want to go to school the next day.

She read about Geoffrey Lochead, one of the first Europeans to run sheep here, who did his first shearing (of 200 sheep) on the parlour rug, turned upside down in the paddock. Alex laughed at that one—she could almost hear the conversation at home afterwards when Mrs Lochead asked where the parlour rug had gotten to.

And she read about the first local Agricultural and Pastoral show, in which some joker had included a disgruntled cat in the poultry display.

But there was no mention of witches or witchcraft, or any strange creatures hanging around people's back gardens.

She shoved the book aside and opened the second. It was focused on the churches of the area. To Alex's dismay, it was even more boring than the first book—lists of church committee members; dates of construction, expansion and renovation; descriptions of leaded glass imported from Europe. It nearly put her to sleep.

Three sentences at the end of the section on Rifton's Anglican church contained the only useful information:

It is interesting to note the two unmarked graves situated just outside the cemetery proper. At least one of the graves is rumoured to be that of a woman believed to be a witch descended from a long line of sorcerers in England. Perhaps she hoped to escape persecution in New Zealand, but the fact she was buried without record indicates her troubles may have followed her across the sea.

So, maybe there was once a witch in Rifton. Could there

be witches here today?
    How would she find them?
    And would they help her?

Interlude Two

1918: Mary Mary Quite Contrary

Mary tied the strings of her crisp apron snugly at her back. She shut her eyes and prayed for strength to make it through one more day. She'd hoped it would be easier to bear Clive's absence, now the war was over and he would be coming home soon. But she was worn down by the stress of the past two years, running the pub by herself. It wasn't the work that ground her to dust—she enjoyed being in charge of the business. There was an art to brewing beer, and her customers all said that hers was the finest ale in New Zealand. She loved the warm smell of the yeast, the bitter tang of hops. She worked long hours, rising early to tend to her garden and her hop plants, which Clive had obtained from a grower in Nelson shortly before the war. After washing the dust off, she would head to the pub for several hours in the brewery before welcoming her first customer of the day.

She loved her customers. Most were farm labour-
ers—the local station owners and their permanent
staff were joined seasonally by shearers, swagmen,
and travellers on the train. The locals looked after
her on the rare occasion an itinerant tried to take advantage of the lone female publican.

No, it wasn't the work that ground her down. It
was the other women in town, with their sneering
looks and their prohibition petition. Clive couldn't
return soon enough for her liking. Not that the
women in town would change, but she'd handle it
better with Clive at her back.

She simply had to hold out until he returned. She
straightened her shoulders and unlocked the door,
turning the sign to *open* before heading back to the
kitchen to check on the pies destined for tonight's
dinner crowd.

An hour later, shouting on the street outside
caught her attention. No, not shouting. Chanting.
The Presbyterian women's group was at it again.

She frowned and threw down the knife she'd
been using, lest she be tempted to sink it into Eunice
Glandovy's face. Because Eunice would be there—the
loudest of them all, and the leader of her gaggle of
meddling, self-important hens.

Hurling the door open, Mary waved her arms.
"Get away from my doorway!"

"Not until we shut down your den of iniquity!"
Eunice shouted.

"I run an honest business and you know it." That

Eunice's husband washed up in the pub most days wasn't her doing. Mary couldn't blame the man for doing what he could to avoid Eunice's company.

"An honest business?" Eunice laughed. "Is it an honest business for a married woman whose husband is off fighting for King and country to lure all the young men in the district to her door each evening to imbibe the devil's drink?"

If only she was allowed to remain open after six o'clock, maybe there would be some truth to the statement, but prohibitionists like Eunice had seen to it that the nation's war effort included curtailing pubs' operating hours. "I am keeping Clive's business alive so he has something to return to when he comes home."

"You're luring our men into sin and debauchery!"

Mary shook her head. "Your husband needs no luring." She suspected he was lurking nearby, waiting for his wife to go home so he could secure his daily pint before closing time.

Eunice's hens squawked and hissed as their leader sucked in a scandalised breath. Then the shouting began in earnest. "Sign the pledge!" they called. "Save Rifton from the riff-raff!" Their shouts filled the air as Eunice stalked toward Mary, finger wagging.

"We're watching you, Mary Saunders. We know what goes on in that devil's den you call a business. You'd better hope Mr Saunders doesn't hear about it."

What the hell was she talking about? It was a

damn good thing Mary had left the knife in the kitchen. She vibrated with rage. "Clive is well aware I am successfully running his business."

Eunice snorted. "Is that what you call it?"

"Back off, Eunice." Bill Saunders' deep voice cut through the shrill cries of the women. Mary tried not to let her relief show. Her brother-in-law swept up the steps with several of his workers in tow. "Mary's got better things to do than tell you what a witch you are." The men strode past her, Bill giving her a wink, and the others tipping their hats to her.

"By all means, stay out here and shirk your household duties. I've got dinner and drinks to prepare, especially since Mr Glandovy's obviously not getting supper at home today, so he'll need to eat *somewhere*." Mary turned and stepped back into the pub. Pressing her back against the door, she squeezed her eyes shut and tried to tamp down her anger.

"Go on. Let it out. She's enough to make a saint swear." Laughter laced Bill's voice.

Mary let out a breath on a laugh and opened her eyes. "She's going to be the death of me. Now, what can I get you? I'm afraid I'm fresh out of devil's brew, but I've just tapped a barrel of stout I think is the best I've made yet."

"Pride, too." Bill's eyes twinkled with mischief. "The devil's own daughter."

"The witch's granddaughter no less," added old George McMillan. "Brewing up the finest potions this side of Wellington. I'll have me a pint of that new stout, if you please."

Mary smiled at the men as she rounded the bar to draw their drinks. Bill rested a hand briefly on her arm as she passed. "You okay?"

She nodded. "I am now. Thanks."

"Want me to send one of the boys down tomorrow? I can spare a lad, now the lambing's done." Bill was as protective of her as any brother could be. Any guilt she'd felt over being glad he'd been sent home from the war with his left hand missing vanished the first time he'd silently stood beside her in the face of the Presbyterian ladies.

"No. I'll be fine. Thank you for offering, though."

He nodded. Like his brother, he was protective, but understood her iron will. She would manage Eunice, the business, and her household by herself.

Eunice and her followers had deterred the train patrons, but Mary's regulars calmly stepped around them to take their usual places. All except Eunice's husband, who slipped in the door five minutes before six, after the women had abandoned their vigil, to guzzle a pint and apologise for his wife.

Back at home, Mary ate dinner—the last of the mince and cheese pies, washing it down with the new stout. It *was* the best yet. Maybe Clive would be home in time to taste it.

She was washing up her few dishes by the light of the kerosene lamp when a rock crashed through the kitchen window, showering the floor with glass.

"Devil's brewer!" The shout was followed by the shattering of a window in the parlour, and then a third window in the bedroom.

A white-hot flash of rage roared in Mary's veins. She snatched Clive's rifle from the chest in the hall, then hurled open the door, shooting into the night.

"Get the hell away from my house!" She let off another round. Pounding feet sounded on the shingle of the lane. Mary gritted her teeth, restraining herself from firing toward the sound.

When she was sure the rock throwers were gone, she turned back inside. There was glass everywhere, and a chilly, damp wind swirled in through the gaping window frames. She needed to find something to close up the broken windows before the rain arrived.

But anger drove her now. Instead of searching for a hammer and boards for the windows, she plucked a small, aged book from a box beside her bed. She brushed her fingers lightly over the embossed letters on the cover—*Formulae for the Summoning of Minor Angels and Daemons.* Did she dare? Mother hadn't hesitated to make use of the book. She'd always laughed at the women who scorned her because she was the witch's daughter. "They have no idea." She'd never told Mary exactly what she did with her witchcraft, but Mary had grown suspicious when, after Grandma's death, strange misfortunes befell every one of the town councillors. Ted Watson had lost all his teeth over the course of three days. William Grey had sprouted fur on his hands—his wife had to shave it off daily, and he was rarely seen without gloves on.

Only her father seemed to be immune from the town councillors' troubles. But after his death, she'd found the bills from the specialist in Christchurch. Electrical stimulation therapy for impotence, they'd read.

She knew her mother had blamed the town council for Grandmother's death. Now she understood the anger that had driven her.

She opened the book.

"*Felis daemonicus* should do nicely," she muttered as she paged to the familiar spell. She hadn't actually summoned a demon before, but she'd read the book over and over, wondering if it was actually possible to summon a being from another world. Had her mother ever done so?

Well, she would find out tonight. Her mother had been discreet, but Mary had learned a thing or two about witchcraft by lurking silently around the house while her mother thought she was outside playing or dutifully doing her chores.

She laid out her pentagram, reciting the words she'd heard Mother say, and lighting the candles. Within the circle, she began the incantation. The breeze picked up outside and the candles flickered, threatening to blow out. She ignored the need to deal with the windows and kept reciting the summoning.

On the final word, there was a loud crack and a flash of light that made Mary wince and blink. When her eyes refocused, a sleek storm-grey cat sat in the circle with her. It blinked malevolent yellow eyes at her.

Well, what do you want? The cat's voice was a rumble like distant thunder in her mind. It sounded ... vindictive. Excellent.

"Eunice Glandovy's prize chickens. Go kill them all."

If cats could smile, this one did. His laugh rumbled in her chest. Thunder. She would call him Thunder.

Chapter Ten

A Household Demon

After lunch, Alex read through more of Gran's letters from Dex, desperate for any mention of the book and the spells in it.

Of course, the letters weren't the only way Gran and Dex communicated. They lived in the same town and sat on the same church committee. They might very well have discussed the book in person.

7 February 1984

My Dearest Alice,

You are a free woman! Or nearly so. Congratulations on your empty nest. Have you given any thought to dissolving your marriage now that the children are grown? Surely at this point, they would not be unduly harmed by a split.

Let's talk about our future, my dear. When is Daniel's next trip out of town? I'll make a neighbourly visit to bring some vegetables from Belle's garden.

Love,

Dex

The jerk! Asking Gran to divorce her husband while he was still married? None of the subsequent letters referenced Dex's neighbourly visit, but Alex knew Gran hadn't divorced.

16 October 1986

My Dearest Alice,

I wish I could hold you and kiss away your grief. It is unfair to have a child taken away as Mark has been. I hope you got the flowers Belle and I sent.

Love,

Dex

Mark would have been Alex's uncle. Her mum used to tell stories about how Mark tormented her with worms slipped down the back of her shirt when they were kids. He'd died in some sort of accident—Alex couldn't remember what it was. Or maybe Mum had never told her.

There was a gap of several years before the next letter.

10 August 1990

My Dearest Alice,

Thank you for the flowers, including the beautiful note you included with them. Belle was never my true love—that place is yours—but I did care for her, and I love our children and soon-to-be grandchild.

Alex threw the letter down. There was no useful information here. That book of spells had been forgotten on Gran's bookcase in 1976 and nobody had even thought about it until she'd picked it up two days ago.

Thor jumped onto the couch next to her and rubbed his head against her shoulder. Thunder padded to the door and meowed.

"I know you both want out. But until I know that thing isn't out there, you're just going to have to stay in."

Was it still out there? Regardless of whether she found information to help her or not, she was going to need to find the thing in order to banish or kill it. Her hands grew sweaty as she contemplated poking her head under the shrubbery. Maybe if she had a weapon …

"Come on Alex. You're going to have to face this thing sometime. Better to do it in the afternoon sun."

She slipped out the door, nudging the cats back with her toes as they tried to slink past her. Her first stop was the garage, where she scanned the tools. The long-handled spade would deliver a good blow, but she didn't think it was heavy enough to knock out a three-metre-long centipede. Could centipedes *be* knocked out? Would a blow to the head even kill one? Were they like cockroaches—able to live for weeks without a head? She shuddered at the thought.

She considered the mattock—it certainly had a nice heavy head, but the handle was short. She'd have to get far too close to the creature to hit it.

Her eyes lit on the old-fashioned chipping hoe. That might be the best tool. It wasn't quite as heavy as the mattock, but it had a nice long handle. Could she use it to chop the creature into pieces? Her stomach churned. How could she even think about killing an animal that size with a garden tool?

One way or another, it had to die. Imagine going back to her boss at Biosecurity NZ and saying, "By the way, while I was on leave I accidentally introduced a large predator to the country." So much for New Zealand's "Predator Free by 2050" goal. And the paperwork? Yeah, that would never do.

Chipping hoe it was. She swung it over her shoulder and headed to the yard.

Gran's section wasn't large, but the plantings were mature and dense. Alex parted the branches of an azalea, holding her face well away from the plant, unwilling to get too close. Nothing but darkness.

103

Shit. She was going to have to stick her head in there to see anything. Swallowing her fear, she leaned in. Leaves brushed her cheeks, and the fruity smell of decay filled her nostrils. Dead leaves lay underneath. A few straggly weeds struggled in the shade. No giant centipede.

The branches sprang back into place as she moved on. She bent down and peered underneath the arching leaves of a flax bush. Something rustled and she tensed. Holding her breath, she eased the hoe along the ground underneath the flax. A dark shape burst from the bush and she yelped, dropping the hoe and staggering to her feet, heart pounding.

"Damn." Her heartbeat slowly returned to normal as a thrush hopped through the branches of Gran's apple tree, flicking its tail in obvious irritation.

She picked up her hoe and resumed the search. As she leaned into the next bush—a dense pittosporum with sticky seed capsules that tugged at her hair—a fat spider dropped onto her hand. She leapt out of the bush with a yelp.

"Get a grip," she scolded herself. "You're not even afraid of spiders."

She used the handle of the hoe to poke into a cluster of tall ornamental grasses in the back corner. No way was she going to stick her hands into that thick foliage. The tiny lizard that skittered out made her jump.

"Get a hold of yourself," she growled.

She finished her circuit of the yard, heart pounding, waiting for the demon's appearance. But if there was a giant centipede hiding there, it was underground, not among the leaf litter. The thought made her jittery. Did materpodas dig? What if they could tunnel underground and pop up wherever they wanted?

No. No. No. Regular centipedes didn't dig, why would a giant one do it?

Did giant demonic centipedes behave like the ordinary ones? What if they had other skills, different behaviours? Maybe they climbed trees, sprouted wings, shot acid at your eyes. It could be anywhere, doing anything, for all she knew. Her skin prickled, and she whirled, brandishing the hoe, expecting to see the materpoda rearing up at her back.

The yard was empty.

She returned to the house, taking the hoe with her. It made her feel safer to have a weapon close at hand.

Alex still had half a lasagne left from the large pan one of the women from Gran's church had brought over after the funeral. She pulled it out of the fridge and was cutting herself a piece to heat up for dinner when her phone pinged with an incoming message.

When she opened it, she found three messages from Shel that had all come in over the past fifteen minutes.

Are you available?

As soon as you see this message, please respond.

I need you to come over here NOW!

Alex swore and tapped a quick message in response.
On my way. I'll bring dinner.

Maybe if she was nice to him, he'd stop thinking she was a complete nut-case. Not that it really mattered what he thought, but she might need him later.

She snapped the lid back onto the lasagne pan, tucked it under her arm, snatched up her tote bag with the book in it, and raced out the door.

She didn't even have to knock when she reached Shelby's place. As she stepped up to the door it opened.

"In! Quick!"

She darted in and Shelby slammed the door behind her and locked it. He was pale and breathing hard.

"What's wrong?"

"The … the … that demon. It's on the back deck."

She put her hands on her hips. "Oh. So you believe me now?"

His finger shook as he pointed. "It's out there!"

Why hadn't she brought the hoe? She strode to the back of the house, setting the lasagne and her bag on the dining room table as she passed. In the kitchen, she peered out to the deck. "I don't see—oh shit." Where there had appeared to be only wooden decking, a form rippled into view. Long and leggy, there was no question it was the materpoda. It skittered forward a metre and then froze. The instant it did so, it vanished.

She felt Shelby come up behind her. "It's invisible," she whispered. "Except—"

"When it moves. Yeah. I noticed that." Shel's voice came out as a squeak.

She glanced at him. "You were on the deck?"

He nodded, visibly trembling. "You need to get rid of that thing now."

"I don't know *how*."

"Just kill it!"

"With what? My bare hands?"

"It's a bug—squish it. Stomp on it or something." He sucked in a breath. "I've got it!" He dashed into the attached garage, while Alex kept her eyes on the spot where the materpoda had vanished. She wanted to be able to track it when it moved again.

Shel was back in a moment, waving a brightly coloured can of fly spray. "This stuff kills everything."

Alex held out her hand for the can. "Let's try it. You stay

here at the window while I go to the door. I assume the thing will run when I step onto the deck. Your job is to watch where it goes because I won't be able to see it while I'm opening the door. If I lose it, you'll need to tell me where to spray."

Shel looked like he might vomit. But he must have known the only other job was the one she was taking on— actually spraying the damned thing at close range. He nodded. "Where is it right now?"

"Last it was visible, it was right underneath the chair on the left. I haven't seen it move since, so I assume it's still there."

She shook the can. Good. It was pretty full. She didn't know how much fly spray it would take to kill a materpoda, but she wouldn't be surprised if she needed the whole can. She squared her shoulders. She could do this. Easy as—just spray and walk away, right? "You ready?"

Shel nodded.

Moving as slowly and quietly as possible, Alex eased open the back door. She peeked around it as she stepped out—nothing visible under the chair. "Is it still there?" she called to Shel through the kitchen window.

"I haven't seen it move."

Right. Alex held her breath as she crept toward the chair. One step, two steps, she rolled her feet to the decking as silently as possible. She could see nothing, but she'd watched the creature disappear in front of her eyes, and then reappear. About a metre from the chair she crouched and shot a spray underneath.

The materpoda burst into view, tumbling the chair in its dash away from the spray. Alex instinctively reared away, adrenaline coursing through her veins. It was all she could do to stand her ground and follow its movement.

It stopped behind a large basket full of firewood and vanished again.

Could the materpoda hear her pounding heart? With her eyes glued to the basket, hands shaking, Alex once again began creeping toward the demon. Had any of the fly spray hit it? Would it take effect immediately, or take time to kill the creature? She wasn't going to take any chances. She'd unload the whole can on it if she could.

She reached the basket, shot her arm over the top and sprayed blindly in the space behind it. The materpoda shot out of the space, hugging the wall of the house as it darted away.

Horror flooded her chest. "No!" She'd forgotten to shut the door. The demon was headed straight for it. A moment later, a scream came from inside the house.

Alex raced in to find Shelby huddled on the kitchen bench white-faced and whimpering as the materpoda circled the kitchen like a pinball, hugging the walls and knocking over a rubbish bin in its way. Alex caught it on its way out in a stream of fly spray, but the creature didn't slow down.

It rocketed into the dining room, careening around the walls before stopping abruptly and vanishing behind the floor-length curtains across the sliding glass door.

Alex wasted no time in stealth. She pounded across the room and tore back the curtains, a stream of fly spray already aimed where she last saw the demon. But she wasn't fast enough. The materpoda shot off into the living room, and her spray only dampened the curtains. It ricocheted around the room before scurrying underneath the couch.

"Aha! Gotcha now." Alex jammed the spray can underneath the couch and fogged the whole space with poison.

The demon seemed to pour out from under the couch directly toward her. She cried out and fell backward as the creature raced up her body, over her face, and dashed down the hallway.

Shelby peeked out of the kitchen wielding a long kitchen knife that shook violently in his hand. "Did you get it?"

Alex scrambled to her feet and picked up the spray can she'd dropped. "No. It ran off down the hall."

With their dubious weapons, the pair stalked down the hallway, Alex in the lead and Shelby cringing behind her. She popped her head into the bathroom first. Centipedes loved bathtubs—maybe the materpoda would be there.

But the bathtub was empty, even when she sprayed it. She carefully shut the door behind them before they moved down the hallway.

Next was the master bedroom. Alex scanned the room. The only real hiding spot would be under the bed. Of course, the creature could hide in plain sight, so there was no saying where it would be, but it definitely seemed to prefer to be under things. Was it tiring to turn invisible? Easier to simply hide under something? Not keen to have the materpoda burst out into her face again, she stretched her arm as far as it would go, ducked her head, and sprayed under the bed.

Nothing came shooting out from under it. Shel waved his knife around the corners of the room. Still, nothing moved.

Alex shut the door as they quietly moved to the next room.

The bed in the spare bedroom was a trundle—no space underneath. They quickly swept the corners of the room and found it empty.

That left only Shelby's room. They crept in, and Alex went straight for the space underneath Shelby's desk. The fly spray didn't send a demon flying out, so she stood and turned toward the bed. Shelby was waving his knife at the floor near the closet. Something caught Alex's eye above him.

Damn. They climb. "Shel!"

He looked up at her shout, just as the materpoda dropped from the ceiling. Shel let out a bloodcurdling scream as the beast landed on his back and shot away out the bedroom door.

Alex lunged after the demon as Shel slumped to the floor. She pounded down the hallway, turning the corner just in time to see the demon's rear end vanish out the back door. She slammed it shut and pressed her back to it, shaking so hard, she could barely stand. The spray can dropped from her fingers and she sank to the floor, her mind blank except for the panicked swear words streaming through it.

Chapter Eleven

Just Like Kittens

Alex took a deep breath, then another. "Shelby." Shit. She'd left him prone and colourless on his bedroom floor. Heaving herself up on shaking limbs, she staggered to his room.

"Shel?"

He stirred as she crouched down beside him.

"Shel, are you okay?"

He groaned and rolled onto his back. "I think I'm gonna be sick."

"Please not on the carpet. Are you hurt?"

He shook his head, groaned again, and then lurched to his feet. He pushed past Alex and stumbled into the bathroom. A moment later, sounds of vomiting emanated from the loo.

Lovely. Alex had to admit, chasing a giant fast-as-lightning centipede around the house had been terrifying, but fainting and vomiting? It was a bit pathetic.

Well. Nothing she could do for him at the moment. She wandered back to the kitchen to get away from the disturbing sounds of retching. What now?

The lasagne still sat on the table. She'd been hungry before her showdown with the demon. Although she didn't feel hungry anymore, she could eat. And while she ate, she'd figure out what to do next. The normalcy of rummaging around for cutlery and plates and microwaving dinner eased the jittering in her hands. They were almost steady as she reached into a high cabinet for a water glass.

She poured two tall glasses of water—Shelby would need one.

When he finally trudged into the kitchen, she was sitting at the breakfast bar picking at a steaming plateful of lasagne. She wordlessly handed him a glass of water. He took it and slumped onto the stool beside her. His complexion was waxy, but he was at least upright and sipping water.

"I brought dinner." She pointed to the pan of lasagne sitting on the bench. "Help yourself."

"Maybe later. I couldn't eat now if you paid me."

Alex nodded. "At least finish your water. It'll help."

After a moment of silence, Shelby whispered, "I'm sorry I didn't believe you. Did you get it?"

Alex sighed. "Well, I emptied nearly the entire can of spray at it, and I'm pretty sure plenty of it hit home. But it dashed out the back door—I'd say the spray was as effective as water."

"You mean it's still out there, in my back yard?" His voice rose an octave.

"Well, at least it's not inside the house now."

"I can't have it in my yard!" Full panic was setting in now. The water in his glass sloshed as his hand shook.

Alex shut her eyes for a moment, willing herself not to snap at him. He had a phobia. He couldn't control that, and he hadn't even believed her before. In spite of it, he'd been willing to help her. Give him a break. But his panic was only feeding her own nerves. In truth, it was hard *not* to freak out about an enormous pet-eating centipede.

"Once I've eaten, I'll go out the back and see if I can find it. Maybe the spray just takes time to work. It could be lying out there dead." She glanced out the window. The sun was going down. She'd need to get out there soon. The last thing she wanted was to be searching for the thing in the dark.

She finished her dinner, Shel a jittery silence next to her. When she was done, she loaded her dishes into the dishwasher and rolled the stress from her shoulders. She could do this. Hadn't she wanted to study animals when she did her biology degree? Well, this was her chance to learn about the biology of a materpoda. What would the title of the paper be? *Effects of the Application of Insecticide on Demonic Chilopoda.*

Some drudge at Biosecurity would no doubt be required to read it and provide a summary to her superiors.

Especially if the fly spray hadn't worked.

"I'm going to have a look for it. Maybe you should try to eat something."

He nodded, but didn't move as she grabbed a shovel from the garage and then slipped out the back door, being careful to shut it this time.

Just as she had at Gran's place, she poked and peered under the bushes, moving systematically around the yard. There was no sign of the demon, and thankfully there weren't even any birds or spiders to startle her. She relaxed a little—the thing wasn't going to jump out at her. But was it dead? She needed to lay eyes on it to be sure. Where could it be?

When she turned back toward the house, her stomach clenched. The deck was about thirty centimetres off the ground, and the space underneath was gloomy and dark, perfect for hiding a large, demonic centipede. She wasn't going to be able to see anything under there without light, though.

The torch function of her phone—that would do. She swept the beam through the narrow space under the deck. Her first sweep revealed nothing, but when she swung the beam back more slowly, it landed on a tableau that sent shivers down her spine.

The materpoda lay curled around a mound of white spheres the size of grapefruit—there must have been twenty or more. It lifted each one and gently swiped its mouthparts over it—cleaning each before nestling it back with the others. Soft musical ticking noises emanated from it—from *her*—like a lullaby. Her antennae caressed the orbs with feathery touches.

Eggs. A shiver of fear coursed through Alex's body. But as she watched the materpoda clucking over her eggs, something shifted inside her chest. She remembered the nest of newborn kittens she'd found under the deck at home when she was eight years old. The kittens had been wet and slimy—eyes tightly sealed, and as appealing as drowned rats. Yet the mother cat purred and licked them all over as though they were the most beautiful objects in the world. Those kittens lit her interest in animals and the natural world and led directly to her degree in biology.

The materpoda was a monster.

The materpoda was a mother.

The shift in perspective unsettled her.

She eased herself silently to her feet and tiptoed across the deck to avoid disturbing the family below, just as she'd done at age eight. She stepped through the door and gently closed it behind her.

Shel was eating lasagne when she told him what she'd seen. "Eggs?" His fork froze halfway to his mouth. "You mean the thing is *reproducing*?"

Alex squeezed her eyes shut, as though she could snuff out what she'd seen. Shel's terror brought her own surging to the fore again. "Yeah."

He set down his fork with a clatter. "We've got to kill them all."

Her eyes flew open. That's exactly what her dad had said about the kittens, and the statement sparked the same fury in her now as it had then. "They're babies! Not even born yet."

"Which is exactly why we need to nail them now, before they hatch and go … who knows where? What's going to happen if those things keep multiplying?"

Another pest in New Zealand. And one hell of a pest. He was right. They needed to do something, and fast.

Yet … "I can't kill babies." She knew it was crazy, but watching that mother demon caring for her eggs just … "It would be like killing kittens."

"Come on. You work for Biosecurity. You know the risks of something like this getting out."

"How do you know I work for Biosecurity?" She'd never talked about herself to Shelby. She definitely hadn't told him where she worked.

He rolled his eyes. "I googled you of course. Got your degree at Victoria University. You like long walks on the beach and" —he wrinkled his nose— "strolling through graveyards. Honestly? Who puts *strolling through graveyards* on their Tinder profile?"

"At least my profile photo isn't photoshopped," she snapped back.

Shelby's face flushed. "Whatever. The point is, you work for Biosecurity, and you know we need to exterminate this thing before it multiplies."

She did. Her mind flew back to those kittens. When she announced their discovery, Dad had argued that, as one of New Zealand's worst predator problems, the feral cats should be destroyed. He was right. The only way to protect New Zealand's unique biodiversity was to be ruthless about exotic species. How many pest problems could have been avoided entirely if someone had acted quickly to eradicate an animal the moment it entered the country?

Still, she hadn't let Dad kill the kittens. She'd gotten creative. Maybe she could be creative now and save the materpoda and its babies, and still protect the country from a marauding demonic centipede.

"We should smash the eggs. We can't let a hoard of giant … giant …" Shelby's face lost all colour as he tried to say the next word.

"And what do you think their mother is going to do if we smash her babies?" The vision of a giant, pissed-off centipede made her shudder.

"So we kill the big one first. We can't let them hatch!"

Alex wasn't squeamish about bugs. And her approach to them was pragmatic—aphids on the potted herbs on her windowsill got squished without a second thought, but spiders indoors were scooped up and deposited outside. Spiders were useful, after all, and aphids were pests. Anyway, spiders and aphids were just bugs—they didn't have feelings, their lives were short.

The materpoda was more. The book called materpodas demons, whatever that meant. Clearly that demon cared for her babies. She wasn't 'just a bug'.

"She's out there caring for her young, and you want to—"

Shelby leaned in, eyes wide. "It's eating household pets." He stood and carried his plate, lasagne only half eaten, to the sink.

Alex winced. There was that. They'd have to think creatively. "What if we fed her?" she mused. "Do you think she would stop hunting pets?"

He slammed his plate onto the kitchen bench. "We are not feeding a fucking demon! Not while it's got a bloody *nest* under my deck! We need to kill the thing. Now."

And there was the real problem with killing the materpoda. "How? The fly spray obviously had no effect on her whatsoever."

"We could shoot it."

He must be nuts. "You ever shot a gun? I don't even think it's legal to fire a gun under your deck—that close to the house?"

"The axe! We've got one for splitting firewood."

Alex scrubbed her hands over her face. "I just … I'm not real happy about the idea of killing her. She's a *mum*."

"It's a monster."

"Fine. You do it then."

Shelby blanched. "No way. This is *your* problem—you summoned the fucking thing."

"With your great-great-whatever-grandmother's book."

He held up his hands. "I had nothing to do with that book. You're the one who decided to read it aloud."

"There has to be another way to deal with her. She came from *somewhere*, she can go back there."

Shelby sighed. "We've tried that, and there's no information about how to do it anywhere."

"There has to be information somewhere. We just need to search harder."

"All the while that *thing* is living under my deck and chowing through the neighbourhood cats and dogs."

Alex growled in frustration. "There *has* to be a w—" Her

117

heart lurched as she remembered the same argument with Dad. Would the solution she devised for the cats work with the materpoda? "What if we caught her and kept her in captivity until we figured out how to send her back?"

Shelby's eyes went wide. "No. Fucking. Way. I am *not* keeping that thing as a pet."

Exactly like Dad. Alex almost laughed. "Fine. I will." She stood. "It will take me a day or two to source a cage, and then I'll get her out from under your porch and you won't have to deal with her again."

When Dad had agreed to let Alex catch, raise, spay and then give away the kittens and their mother, he hadn't expected her to follow through on it. Even at the time, she knew he expected her to fail, and then he'd swoop in and destroy the animals.

It had made her even more determined. She'd learned patience. She'd learned how to approach wild and wary animals. She'd learned how to coax and entice animals, rather than chase and bully them. She'd forced herself to ignore her fear of being scratched and bitten. And she'd silently patched up her bleeding hands on the multiple occasions she *had* been scratched and bitten.

Surely she could set aside her fear of the materpoda to do the same.

All she needed was a little time. And a big cage.

Chapter Twelve

The Demon Run

After an evening of surfing the internet looking for the best deals on dog runs, Alex fell into a fitful sleep. In the morning, she shrugged off her bleariness with a cup of coffee and headed to a stock yard manufacturer and retailer in an industrial suburb of Christchurch.

According to their website, they were open to the public, but it was clear they did most of their business with farm supply companies. The place was basically a giant warehouse and workshop with a tiny office in one corner. Alex stepped into the office to the smell of hot metal and stale coffee. The cluttered desk was unstaffed, next to a water cooler with a pair of worn work gloves draped over the top. There was no indication the office was meant to receive visitors, and she felt like a trespasser.

The crackling of a welder echoed from the open door into the workshop. Alex stepped through the door. "Hello?" The sound of welding continued. She raised her voice and took a few steps into the shop. "Hello!"

"Can I help you?"

Alex yelped and spun toward the voice, heart hammering. "Um. Yeah. I … uh. I'm interested in a dog run."

The man wore blue coveralls and work gloves. He looked like he was trying to suppress a smile. "Sure thing. Come into the office. Have you had a look at our standard dog runs?"

"Yeah. I was thinking the two-by-four-metre one, but I need one with a top."

"Our runs are one point eight metres tall. You won't need a top. No dog can jump that high." He sat down at the computer and started typing.

"Well, that's just it. This isn't going to house a dog."

"What'cha putting in it?" The question was light and curious. Thankfully, Alex had considered her response beforehand, or she would have sputtered and fumbled.

"A parrot."

"Huh. Cool." He clicked a few things on the screen. "We could do the two by four and add a roof. That'd be two extra panels … we're looking at two thousand plus GST."

Ouch. But she knew this was going to be expensive—she'd manage. "That sounds fine. Do you deliver?" Her rental car didn't have a trailer hitch, and there was no way those big panels would fit inside the car.

"We do, but we're backed up on deliveries—can't get you in until next Thursday at the earliest."

That wouldn't do. Maybe she could rent a moving van. "Can I pick it up here instead?"

"We can have the run ready for you within a couple of hours. You'll need a friend to help load, unload, and assemble it—the panels aren't light."

She paid, cringing again at the cost, and promised to return in the afternoon.

On her way back to Gran's, she stopped at the butcher's

shop. She scanned the case. What would a demon partial to toy poodles like to eat? Whatever she liked, she would need a lot of it. Whole chickens seemed to be about the right size, but would the materpoda eat chicken? Beef or pork seemed like the better bet, given what she had already consumed. But the eye-watering prices of beef and pork steered her back to the poultry. How about chicken drumsticks at $6.50 per kilo? She asked for twelve kilos of them.

The butcher raised her eyebrows. "Lemme see if I've got more in the back." She returned with a plastic bag full and began weighing them out. "Having a party?"

"Something like that." She sure hoped the materpoda ate chicken, because there was no way she could eat twelve kilos of drumsticks.

Back at Gran's, Alex messaged Shel. Surely he'd agree to help if it got the materpoda out from under his deck, right?

> Can I get your help this afternoon? I've got to pick up the cage for the materpoda, and it's a two-person job.

I suppose. How big is it?

> Assembled, it's 2m x 4m, but it comes in big panels.

WTF? That's huge!

> So's the materpoda.

Fair enough. What time?

> Around 1pm. I've got to rent a truck from in town to carry it.

Just get a trailer from the petrol station.

> No tow bar.

Mum's car has one. I'll pick you up at

one.

Didn't he say this was her problem? And now he was not only agreeing to help, but offering his mum's car? Alex smiled. The guy was growing on her.

She reserved a trailer for the afternoon, and then rummaged around in Gran's garage for the things she thought she'd need for a materpoda enclosure. Did they drink water from a dish? She had no idea, but she wasn't about to cage an animal without water. She found a shallow plastic tub filled with an assortment of old, broken and bent items. She tipped the entire contents into the rubbish bin, rinsed out the tub and set it aside for a water dish. Then she sorted through a collection of odd bits of wood, pulling out pieces large enough to be fashioned into some sort of shelter. It didn't need to be much, but clearly the demon liked hiding under things. And the eggs would need protection from the elements.

She scrounged a box of nails and a hammer, and spent an hour cobbling together what had to be the ugliest bit of carpentry ever. At least it had been free, and she was pretty sure the materpoda wouldn't care how it looked.

Water and shelter taken care of, she dusted off her hands and headed inside for lunch.

Shel pulled up at one o'clock in a powder blue station wagon.

She slipped into the passenger seat. "Thanks for this. I wasn't looking forward to the hassle of renting a truck."

They picked up the trailer Alex had reserved, and she gave him directions to Stock Solutions, where she'd bought the run.

He followed the directions in silence, eyes focused on the road, a frown on his face. He had offered the car, offered to drive. Why was he so grumpy now?

"Look, I'm sorry to drag you back into this. Sorry to drag you into it at all. I … thanks for helping today. I could have asked Linda but—"

Shel snorted and his frown eased. "Even if you *had* been able to explain to her why you were erecting a big dog run in your grandmother's back yard, it would have taken twelve years for her to stop talking and actually help."

Alex smiled. "Gran used to check before she stepped out the front door. If Linda was in her yard, she'd sneak around the back so Linda wouldn't see her. She was probably sorry she taught me that trick later, when Linda was such a good source of my whereabouts."

"Wait. Did you live with your gran?"

"After Mum and Dad died. Yeah." The memory of Mum and Dad's death was sharp again, in the wake of Gran's passing.

"Shit. I'm sorry. I mean, not that you lived with your gran—I'm sure she was nice and all—but that your parents died."

Alex blinked back tears. She was almost thankful for this nightmare with the materpoda, because it prevented her thinking about the loss of Gran, the loss of all her family. "Thanks. Yeah, Gran was great, but I was a complete bitch to her. I regret that now. She tried so hard to take care of me, and I pushed her away." She gave a wry laugh. "That's why Linda's snooping was so useful to her. I was always sneaking out, skipping school, causing trouble. But between Linda next door and Mrs Walker living down on the corner, I rarely got away with it."

"Who's Mrs Walker?"

That's right, he'd gone to high school in Christchurch and wouldn't have had Mrs Walker. "My high school English teacher. She and Gran were both in the local garden group. Any trouble I made at school, Mrs Walker told Gran all about it."

"Damn. Makes me glad I went to school in town."

Alex glanced over at him. "Were you a troublemaker?"

He laughed. "I wanted to be. Wanted to be badass, you know? But I was usually too busy coding to be out scrawling graffiti on walls. Besides, my friends all lived in town and I was stuck out here. We hung out on Slack after school, not in the alley behind the gym where the real troublemakers did."

"And you never did anything nefarious online?"

He blushed. "Well …"

"Come on. Out with it!" Alex grinned at him.

"Me and my mate Harrison wrote this computer game that was … let's just say it was a game only teenage boys could have come up with."

"What was the game?" Alex's thoughts turned sour. "It wasn't some sick rape game, was it?"

"No, no! We never would have done that! It was a game where you asked girls out. Of course all the girls were drawn like pin-up models. They always said yes to a first date, but then you had to do things in order to keep them as your girl-friend."

"What sorts of things?" Did she even want to know?

"You had to bring them flowers, give them chocolates, give them foot massages—stuff like that. And we had cool tasks like rescuing them from dragons, plucking them out of towers they were trapped in—you know, all the knight-in-shining-armour tropes."

"So, what was the goal?"

"You have to ask?"

Alex snorted a laugh. "Really?"

"We were horny teens! You got points for every thoughtful thing you did for your girlfriend, and if you got enough points, you got to have sex with her."

Alex threw her head back with laughter. "Wait. You didn't animate that part did you?"

"Nah. You just followed her into a bedroom and the door shut behind you. Little hearts floated up from the door." He chuckled.

Alex was still giggling about Shel's dating game when they pulled up at Stock Solutions. They quickly loaded the cage onto the trailer and headed back to Gran's.

The cage walls were heavy and awkward to manoeuvre. The guys at Stock Solutions had made it seem so easy.

"All you've got to do is line them up, slip the clips on and insert the bolts," they'd said.

Yeah, right.

"Okay, got it." Shel's voice was strained with the effort of holding two large panels steady while Alex tried to slip the joining clips onto the uprights.

"Wait … okay … can you keep them more still?" The wobbling pipes slipped from the clip, which clattered to the ground. "Fuck." Alex picked up the clip.

"Can you hurry? This isn't easy."

"I'm going as fast as I can. If you'd hold them still—"

"If I could hold them still, I would. They're not light, you know."

Alex clamped the clip over the poles again and screwed the bolt finger tight. "One on." The remaining three clips went more easily than the first, and Shel sighed as he let go.

"Well, that's one corner. Just three more to go."

"And the roof," Alex reminded him.

Shel groaned.

They set another panel in place. Shel steadied it so Alex could affix the clips. "So, I told you what sort of trouble I got into in high school; what did you do when you snuck out of the house?"

Alex laughed. "Well, once I poured milk into Kelly Johnson's school shoes."

"What?" The panel shook a little as he laughed. "Why did you do that? And where were her shoes?"

"She was a bitch. Told everyone at school my parents weren't actually dead—they just didn't want me. She kicked her shoes off on the porch every day when she got home, as you do. They were the good leather ones, you know—I was surprised at how much milk they held. They must have been waterproof." She tightened down one of the clips.

"So you snuck out and tortured your enemies at night?"

"Only that once." Alex's smile faded. "Mostly I went to the cemetery."

"Really? Kids hung out there?"

Alex began fixing another clip. "No. Just me. I'd sit with my back against a gravestone, thinking."

All the laughter was gone from Shel's voice when he asked, "About your parents?"

"Yes and no. Mostly I was having a pity party for myself. I grew up in Auckland, so coming here at age thirteen was rough. This place was a shithole, and Gran was overprotective—at least I thought so at thirteen."

"Every thirteen-year-old thinks adults are overprotective."

"Yeah. I get that now." Alex blew out a breath. "I was just angry at the world for all the shit it threw at me."

Shel met her eyes with compassion. "No surprise. Sounds like you had a lot to deal with."

126

She broke his gaze when she felt her eyes filling with tears. He must have seen it, because he asked, "Did you ever get caught? For the milk in the shoe prank?"

Alex laughed, tightening another bolt. "Nope. You should have heard her at school the next day, complaining about her ruined shoes. She assumed her little brother had done it and was outraged because their parents refused to punish him, because there was no milk missing from the fridge."

They made quick work of the last wall panel, and then installed the door.

"Just the roof to go. Easy peasy, right?" Alex eyed the remaining panels lying on the grass and frowned.

"If you work at Stock Solutions, maybe," Shel grumbled.

They managed the roof, with a few choice swear words thrown in when Shelby's finger got caught between the wall and roof panel. But by that point, Alex was able to finish the job while Shelby wrapped his smashed finger in a tea towel filled with ice.

When they finally had the cage fully assembled, they stepped back and surveyed their work.

Shel frowned. "So, how are you going to get the thing into the cage?"

Chapter Thirteen

To Catch a Demon

"Well …" She wasn't exactly going to pick the materpoda up and carry her down the street in her arms like a stray cat. And she wouldn't even know where to attach a leash. Could she bundle her into a dog carrier? Even the largest carrier seemed like it would be too small. "Um …" Her face heated. "Maybe I can herd her?"

Shel tossed the wrench back into Gran's toolbox and turned to face her. "You mean you bought this huge cage, roped me into spending hours putting it together, and you don't even know how you're going to get the thing into it?"

"I'll figure something out."

"Yeah. Like what? This isn't a cat or a dog we're talking about. It's a giant fucking—" His face paled.

"Centipede?" She might not have all the answers, but at least she could talk about the thing without fainting. "Look, I'll figure something out."

"I want that thing gone. I didn't sleep a wink last night knowing it was under the deck. What if it got into the house?

What if it bit me when I stepped out of the door? For all we know, the thing's poisonous."

Damn. She hadn't thought of that.

She ran a hand through her hair. "I'll wear gloves. I might not even have to handle her at all." She considered the twelve kilos of chicken drumsticks in the fridge. "I might be able to lure her out with food."

"What? Drag a dog on a leash past it and then lead it at a run down the street?"

"Something like that, but not with a dog."

"Oh, that'll be interesting—what will the neighbours say when they see you dash by with that thing nipping at your heels?"

Alex sighed. "Would you rather I just leave her where she is?"

"No. I'd rather you kill it."

"Sorry. Can't do that. And I'm not going to argue about it again." She rolled the tension from her shoulders. "Thanks for helping to put the cage up. I'm going to have a bite to eat, grab a few things and then I'll be down to your place to catch the materpoda. I'll have her out of there before dark."

She hoped.

Forty-five minutes later, Alex pushed open the gate to Shel's back yard, propping it open behind her. In one hand she carried a large torch from Gran's junk drawer. In the other was a bag full of chicken drumsticks. She rounded the house and peered through the kitchen window to where Shel was washing dishes. He glanced up, and she waved, hoping the smile she gave him looked more confident than it felt.

She crouched and peered under the deck. The materpoda glittered in the light of her torch. The coils of her body wound around the eggs and she tapped them lightly with her antennae. She was emitting those musical clicks again that sounded like a lullaby. How could a creature so terrifying be so maternal?

Well, here went nothing. She opened the bag of chicken and pulled out a drumstick. She tucked the first one under the deck—just far enough that she was certain the materpoda couldn't miss it. Then she dropped another a few metres away, toward the open gate. She dropped the third in the gateway itself, and then stood beside it, waiting.

She had a good view of the first drumstick. How long would it take for the materpoda to come over and eat it? Did materpodas even *like* chicken? She leaned against the fence, eyes glued to the drumstick.

The sun lowered in the western sky. It dipped behind the neighbouring houses, and still the materpoda hadn't ventured toward the chicken.

She remembered the first time she tried enticing the mother cat out. She'd bought a can of cat food with her pocket money and set it several metres from the deck. Then she'd dropped spoonfuls of the food in a trail to the deck, flicking the last spoonful underneath toward the cat and kittens. Then she'd sat down to wait beside the can.

It had taken hours. The mama cat had snarfed up the first dollop quickly, and her nose twitched as she sniffed the air for more. Each dollop, further from the safety of the deck, had taken longer and longer for her to work up the courage to eat. When she'd finally reached the can, Alex had been so excited she'd reached right out to the cat, scaring it back under the deck. It was days before she could coax it out again.

Coaxing the materpoda out was the same. It would require patience.

130

As the light fell, she lost sight of the drumstick under the deck, but she kept her eyes trained on the spot.

Something rustled in the leaves under the deck. She tensed, straining to see anything in the gloom. She could shine her torch over there, but she didn't want to startle the materpoda if she was creeping out to eat her offering.

A streetlight winked on, but all it did was cast the back yard into deeper shadow. The house windows remained dark. Was Shel inside watching too?

There was the rustling again. Was it coming from the grass now? Alex's heart thumped in her chest. As much as she wanted to see the materpoda come scuttling out of the darkness toward her, the prospect still made her jittery. She took a silent step backward, away from the final chicken leg. Slowly, she reached into the bag to pull out another drumstick. When the materpoda came out, she wanted to be ready to lure her further.

The minutes ticked by. The darkness remained silent. Alex cursed the streetlight, shining on her and ruining her night vision, but doing nothing to illuminate the scene she wanted to see. A sharp line of shadow sliced across the path, and the only visible part of her trail of meat was the final drumstick, glistening dully in the light a few centimetres from the darkness.

There it was again—a shuffling. Definitely in the grass, and moving her way. She adjusted her grip on the drumstick in her hand, its skin slipping greasily between her fingers.

The sound came in fits and starts, as though the creature were snuffling around. She imagined it scurrying ahead, sniffing—did materpoda sniff or did they sense smells with their antennae, like insects?—then stopping when it smelled something interesting.

Questing. The thought made her shiver, and the hair on

the back of her neck prickled. This wasn't a cat or dog—it was no ordinary creature. She didn't even know what the thing could do, other than make itself invisible and eat household pets.

Now wasn't the time for frightening conjecture. The shuffling sound grew closer. Alex stepped back another pace, her heartbeat pounding in her ears. She lowered the drumstick to the ground and quietly drew out another, never taking her eyes off the spot the sound seemed to be emanating from.

The shuffling paused on the edge of the darkness. Sensing the food just over the edge of the shadow perhaps. Maybe the demon was shy of the light. Again, she cursed the streetlight.

Her eyes strained to pick up the glint of light on the demon's carapace, but all was black within the shadow. *Come on. Take the bait. Come out into the light.*

More shuffling. Alex's breath was shallow and fast as her apprehension grew. Here it came. It wasn't stopping now. It arrowed toward the drumstick.

A form emerged from the darkness—melon-sized and covered in bristles. The tension whooshed out of Alex, and her shoulders dropped. "Shit." All that anticipation for a bloody hedgehog. The hedgie waddled to the drumstick, gave it a sniff and a nibble, then shuffled on through the gate and into the front yard, disappearing under a hydrangea next to the house.

With the spell of anticipation broken, Alex's impatience surged. She checked the time—she'd been waiting over two hours. Time to check on the materpoda—maybe she didn't like chicken at all. Maybe she was still curled up with her eggs—did materpoda even hunt while they were incubating their eggs? Maybe they were like penguins—spending months at a time not eating while they tended their eggs.

She flicked on her torch and stepped into the back yard, sweeping the beam over the grass where she'd placed the chicken lures.

The drumsticks were gone.

She frowned. The hedgehog couldn't have eaten them—each one was half its size. She paced toward the deck, scanning the edge where she'd left the first drumstick.

It was nowhere to be seen.

She crouched at the edge of the deck and peered under. The eggs glowed in the reflected light from her torch. The materpoda wasn't there.

Her palms began to sweat and her skin prickled. How could it have disappeared while she was watching? She stood and swept the beam of light around the back yard. Was it creeping around under the bushes? She didn't want to poke around in the dark to find out.

With her light trained on the grass, she retraced her steps. Maybe she could see which way the materpoda had gone. It had obviously eaten the first few drumsticks, but had avoided the light.

Unfortunately, an animal with a hundred dainty legs didn't leave footprints. She reached the spot where she'd dropped the last drumstick that had remained in shadow and scanned for any sign of where the creature had gone from there. Not a blade of grass seemed to be out of place—there was no sign that anything had come this way.

She let out a frustrated huff. How was she going to lure this thing all the way down the street to Gran's house if it refused to venture out under the streetlights? It would take some more thought.

At least she now knew it would eat chicken. Maybe she hadn't caught the beast, but she'd learned valuable information. She went to collect the final two drumsticks under the glow of the lights.

They were gone.

A shiver ran down Alex's spine.

How had the materpoda snatched up two drumsticks in plain sight without her noticing?

And where exactly was it now?

She nearly bolted to Shel's door and pounded on it to be let in.

But she was here to catch the demon. Maybe she hadn't seen it take the drumsticks, but it was taking them—taking her bait.

She took a deep breath to calm herself. Trying hard not to think about the giant centipede creeping around unseen somewhere nearby, she stepped into Shel's front yard. She dropped a chicken leg in the grass. *Here materpoda. Come on. Follow me home.*

On the footpath, she placed another drumstick in the darkest corner she could find. Then she paced slowly back to Gran's, placing a trail of chicken behind her all the way. Furtive glances behind her revealed nothing. No demon snuffling up her offerings. Not even a curious hedgehog.

When she got to Gran's, she left the gate open behind her and dropped a trail of bait leading into the back yard and the open door of the cage. She crumpled the now empty chicken bag and shoved it into her pocket, and then sat down on the edge of the back deck to wait.

After a moment she scurried to the compost bin, picked up the shovel Gran always kept there, and carried it back to her post on the deck. Its heft calmed her nerves slightly. As a bonus, she could use it to shove the cage door shut when the materpoda arrived.

With the shovel across her knees, she waited. Her eyes

grew accustomed to the gloom, and she was confident she'd see the materpoda when it arrived.

The hours crawled by. Alex shivered as the night grew cooler. She wished she'd thought to wear a warmer jersey.

Her eyelids grew heavy, and now she wished she had a thermos of coffee. She checked the time—one o'clock. No wonder she was tired. Was the materpoda even following her trail? She might stay awake all night here, and the demon wouldn't come. What if it ate its fill before it got here? Maybe she should have left smaller pieces of chicken along the way. What if it decided it didn't like chicken, after tasting a little of it? What if it got sidetracked by a tasty neighbourhood cat?

She considered going inside and giving up.

And then what would she do?

She *had* to catch this creature. It was either that, or kill it, and she couldn't do that—at least not until she'd given this plan her best shot.

She stretched and yawned, trying to keep herself alert. She could do this.

Her eyes flew open. Where was she? Her face pressed against the ridged boards of the deck. The shovel lay heavily across her legs.

A rustle in the darkness, and she remembered. The materpoda! She was supposed to be waiting for it, and she'd fallen asleep instead. Damn it!

She just managed to stop herself from bolting upright. Instead she listened intently for a moment. There was that rustling again. The materpoda? She inched a hand to the shovel resting against her legs, holding it steady as she eased to sitting. Her body protested its hard bed—there was a kink in her neck, but she didn't dare move more than she had to, even to roll her shoulders and ease the ache.

The materpoda was there, in the back yard, its exoskeleton gleaming in the moonlight. Alex tightened her grip on the shovel and tried to keep her breathing as shallow and silent as possible.

The demon scurried back and forth across the grass in what looked like a frenzy, tapping its antennae lightly in front of it. Was it looking for more chicken? Alex tensed, ready to slam the cage door shut the instant the materpoda was inside. In its snuffling and scurrying it bypassed the door, angling directly for the chicken at the back of the cage. *Shit*. She didn't count on it not being able to find the door. It met the side of the cage and jerked back. Easing close again, it tapped gently on the galvanised mesh. The mesh jingled musically under the animal's touch, and the materpoda jumped back, as if startled. It approached again with the same tapping of antennae. When the chain link mesh jingled back this time, it didn't jump away, but instead increased the force of its tapping, making the mesh sing.

With a lurch, it launched itself up the side of the cage, chain link jangling under the patter of a hundred feet. Alex sucked in a breath, startled by the sudden motion and noise. On top of the cage now, the materpoda began rhythmically tapping its feet, setting the whole cage jingling in a complex, repeating pattern.

Alex's mouth fell open. Just like when she'd heard the materpoda's clicks to its eggs, she felt there was more to the sound than simple noise. There was cadence, rhythm, meaning behind those tapping feet. And the materpoda was using the cage to amplify the sound. Was she trying to communicate with other materpodas? Alex shivered at the thought of more of the demons here.

The materpoda's performance continued for several minutes, during which Alex remained mesmerised. What was it trying to communicate? And to whom? The biologist in her sparked with excitement. This! This is what she'd dreamed of when she first decided to study biology—discovery, adventure, solving the mysteries of living things.

With a tinge of amusement, she realised the materpoda's rhythm reminded her of the song 'Call Me Maybe', which had been one of her favourites in high school. Without thinking, she started to tap her foot to the beat.

In the blink of an eye, the demon stopped its pattering rhythm and darted forward. It seemed to flow along the top of the cage and over the edge, in through the open door and back along the ceiling, hanging upside down. It flowed down the back wall, snatched up the drumstick Alex had left there, and streaked out along the ground.

By the time Alex thought to shut the door, the demon was gone.

Chapter Fourteen

Materpoda Mayhem

"You didn't catch it?" Shel's dismay was perfectly audible down the phone line when she rang him the next morning.

"No, but you'll never believe what she did!" Shel's disappointment didn't dampen Alex's excitement about what she'd witnessed last night. Knowing that no one else had probably ever seen the same made her giddy.

Breathless, she recounted the night's events to Shel, describing in great detail the materpoda's use of the cage.

"She was like a kid with a megaphone. She was using the cage to shout a message. Do you think materpodas can talk to one another? What if they have a language?"

"It was *in the cage* and you didn't catch it?" Shel was clearly not as excited about the social life of materpodas as Alex was.

"I'll catch her tonight. I know she likes chicken now."

"And if it's as fast as you say it is, how will you close the door before it gets out?"

"I'll put more chicken in there or something, so she stays

longer." She was irritated that Shel wasn't excited about her discovery.

Well, what did she expect? The guy was terrified of centipedes and clearly wasn't interested in wildlife or anything outdoors.

"Look, I'm sorry I didn't catch her last night, but I'm sure I can get her tonight. I'll sleep this afternoon so I don't fall asleep at night, and I'll put more food in the cage, so she can't just grab it and run."

Shel sighed. "Fine."

Alex had just hung up the phone when there was a knock at the door. She opened it to find Linda on the front step, a concerned frown on her face.

"Alex! How are you this morning?" She forged ahead without waiting for Alex's reply. "I thought you should know that Julie Cameron's bichon frise has gone missing, and something got into my chook house last night and killed four of my lovely girls, including poor Loretta." Her lips quivered for a moment before she regained control. "And yesterday, David found a dead cat on the footpath." She shuddered. "He said it looked like it had been flayed."

"Probably struck by a car," Alex reasoned. "They can sometimes run a fair distance before collapsing and dying."

Linda leaned forward. "Not the way David described this poor animal—torn apart, he said!"

Alex's stomach soured. Had she whipped the materpoda into a feeding frenzy last night?

"I thought you ought to know, so you can keep your grandmother's cats indoors—some hoodlum has it in for our pets. It must be those gangs—the ones that come out from Christchurch on their motorbikes. Up to no good those men are."

Alex was certain that Christchurch gangs had nothing to

do with the disappearance of the neighbourhood pets. But the importance of protecting animals was real. She gestured to the taped-over animal flap in Gran's door. "I've already confined them indoors."

"Oh, good! I imagine you would, what with Benji having disappeared." Linda continued her monologue, commenting on the sad state of a society in which bored young men killed law-abiding citizens' beloved pets. Alex tuned her out, exhausted from the previous night, and sick to the stomach at what the materpoda had done.

Eventually Linda must have noticed her glazed eyes. "Are you alright, dear?"

Alex shook herself out of her trance. "I didn't sleep well last night. You know, dealing with Gran's passing and all," she lied. Yes, she was struggling to come to terms with Gran's death, but that had nothing to do with her poor sleep.

"Oh, love." Linda patted Alex's arm. "It must be terrible for you. And here I am nattering away. Go take a nap. Everything will look more optimistic after some sleep."

It wasn't bad advice, and Alex took it as soon as she'd closed the door behind Linda.

Crouching down at the edge of the deck, Alex shone her light into the darkness. *Shit.* The materpoda wasn't there. A shiver of unease coursed through her. If she wasn't curled around her eggs, where was she? Maybe somewhere else in the yard? She systematically scoured the plantings, peeking underneath branches and pushing back foliage to inspect hidden corners. The creature was nowhere to be found.

Now what? She couldn't lure an animal that wasn't present. Maybe she could lay a trail of drumsticks for her from her nest to the cage anyway. Surely she would return to the nest, and then hopefully follow the trail as she had done last night.

She'd rigged up a rope on the cage door, so she could pull it shut from Gran's deck. Her blanket, snacks and coffee were already waiting for her beside a deck chair—all set for another vigil.

She simply needed to be sure the materpoda would follow the trail of chicken again, and then linger long enough in the cage so she could slam the door shut.

But if the animal wasn't here …

Oh! She wasn't here. What if she took the eggs and put *them* in the cage? When the materpoda came back and found the nest empty, might she follow the trail of food to her eggs?

She crouched down at the edge of the deck again and peered at the nest. Still no materpoda, but the eggs gleamed in the light of her torch. She pulled a plastic bag from her pocket—good thing she'd shoved it in there last night. It was a little slimy from the chicken, but it would hold the materpoda eggs nicely.

Her hands were jittery as she contemplated her next move. The deck was low, and she'd have to shimmy underneath it on her stomach to reach the eggs. She swept the light around the area, just to be certain the materpoda wasn't nearby. What would it do if it found her stealing its eggs? It clearly had some maternal instincts—would it protect the eggs by attacking?

With no materpoda in sight, now was the time to snag the eggs. A shiver of excitement ran through her, or was that fear? Commando-crawl to the eggs and snatch them? What could go wrong? The torch beam bobbed in her hand, and she wished she had a head-torch instead. The damp ground was drifted with leaves that rustled as she inchwormed

141

through them. Why did Shel's parents have to build such a big deck? The four-metre crawl to the eggs felt like a kilometre in the claustrophobic space.

Half a metre from the nest, she set down the torch and reached for the first egg.

The materpoda winked into view an instant before pain sliced into Alex's hand. She screamed, yanked her hand back and rolled away from the nest. The materpoda followed, unimpeded by the low deck beams. A sweet almond-like scent filled Alex's nostrils as dozens of claws scrabbled for purchase on her arms, face and body. She scrambled blindly backwards, toward the light of the yard. Another jab of pain lanced through her panic as the materpoda latched onto her forearm and held tight. The pair tumbled out from under the deck and rolled onto the grass. All of Alex's excitement at the adventure fled with the terror of having a giant centipede wrapped around her body, jaws embedded in her arm and countless clawed limbs clinging to her in a hideous embrace. She kicked and thrashed. She pushed at the demon's head, desperate to release its jaws. A series of angry clicks emanated from it, but it held fast.

"Get. Off. Me!" Alex growled through gritted teeth. She punched at what looked like eyes. The materpoda flinched and let go, but immediately took another bite. Alex cried out at the pain. "Fuck!"

She punched the eyes again, this time not stopping with one hit, but keeping up a barrage. The materpoda let out another series of clicks, which Alex figured was the equivalent of swearing. It let go of her arm, but instead of jumping off her, it shifted toward her head, opening its jaws wide as if it was aiming to catch her face in its vice-like mandibles.

Alex screamed, shut her eyes and flung her arms up to protect her head.

A loud crack resonated, and she felt a shudder go through the materpoda's body. Then another crack, and the beast leapt off her. Something gripped her shoulder, and she yelped before recognising it as a human hand.

"Can you stand? We need to get inside before it attacks again." Shel.

Her whole arm throbbed, and she felt as though all her muscles had turned to jelly. "I ... I don't know."

His eyes darted away from her to something out of her line of sight. "Alex, you need to get up. Now."

As if in slow motion, the materpoda's form spun through the air toward Shel. They could *jump*? Standing with a cricket bat raised like a professional cricketer, Shel faced the oncoming demon, his face set in a grimace that was half terror, half determination. He swung, and the bat connected with the materpoda's head with a loud crack. The materpoda cartwheeled back into the yard, tumbling in a tangle of legs into the middle of the vegetable garden.

Suddenly the world sped up again.

"We have to go, Alex!" Dropping the bat, Shel hauled her to her feet. He grabbed her around the waist, pulling her good arm over his shoulder, and dragged her into the house, slamming the door behind them.

Her whole body shook. Her arm throbbed. Shel all but carried her into the living room and deposited her on the couch. He picked up her bitten arm and swore. "I'll be right back."

She couldn't shake the feeling of all those feet all over her body, the spiky jaws sinking into her arm. She tried to raise the arm to look at it, but she couldn't. She shut her eyes. "Fuck, fuck, fuck."

"This might sting." When had Shel returned? Something was wrapped around her arm, pressing tightly against it. Had he dressed the wounds already? Why couldn't she remember it?

The pressure on her arm let up. She opened her eyes to see what he was doing. His face was white and his hands trembled as he poured antiseptic onto a paper towel and pressed it to the wounds on her arm and hand. She flinched.

"Sorry." He didn't stop, despite his apology. "All the punctures have bled a lot. I don't think they'll get infected. But …"

"I can't move my arm." Alex felt panic setting in. "It's swelling, isn't it?"

Shelby nodded. "And it's gone a weird shade of purple. How do you feel?"

"I don't know. My arm is screaming. I feel like I can't take a breath, but that could be fear, not venom."

"You're shaking like a leaf." Shelby finished with the antiseptic and pulled out a roll of gauze. "I'm going to wrap these up, but you need to tell me if the bandage starts to feel tight—I don't know how much that arm is going to swell."

Alex nodded, shut her eyes and focused on breathing. Her skin felt clammy, her lips were cold, and every breath took more effort than the last. Her senses seemed fuzzy— sounds were muffled and sensations distant.

An arm around her shoulder pulled her into a sitting position. She tried to open her eyes, but couldn't. "Open your mouth." A firm hand on her jaw forced her to comply. "I'm giving you an antihistamine. You'll need to swallow it with water." Something dry and bitter landed on her tongue, and then the smooth edge of a glass touched her lip. When water poured into her mouth, she reflexively swallowed, and then coughed as a drop of water went down the wrong way. She felt herself lowered back down, and a blanket pulled over her.

"Do you want me to call an ambulance?"

Her eyes wouldn't open, but she shook her head. "What would we tell them?" The water and warmth of the blanket had helped a little.

"You look like you're struggling to breathe. Maybe we should call the ambulance."

Again she shook her head. "Just shock. Raise my feet." Her legs seemed to float into the air. Were they even attached to her body? She wished she could open her eyes.

Chapter Fifteen

More than Gardening

"Alex? Alex! Talk to me, Alex. If you don't wake up, I'm going to call the ambulance." The voice filtering through her brain held a note of panic that dragged her through what felt like molasses to consciousness.

Someone was shaking her by the shoulders. Shelby. And he was crushing her arm. Why was he doing that? And why couldn't she open her eyes?

"Stop it." Her mouth felt sticky, her words slurred.

"Thank God. I thought you were dead."

Why would he think … oh, yeah. The materpoda attack came back to her. "I feel like shit."

Shelby laughed. "Can you sit up?"

Sit up? She wasn't even certain she could open her eyes. "Do I have to?"

"I think you should try to eat something. I'll make breakfast."

Breakfast? But it wasn't even night time yet. She wrenched her eyes open. The lids felt like lead and she only managed to crack them slightly. Shelby hovered over her, worry lines wrinkling his face.

"What time is it?"

"About eight in the morning."

Alex groaned and bit back a curse.

"No. Don't close your eyes again." He slipped an arm under her shoulders and hauled her upright on the couch. She flopped against the back, her stomach churning and her vision swimming. He held her upright with a hand on each shoulder, obviously aware of how dizzy she was.

She glanced past him to the floor, where a couple of rumpled blankets and a pillow lay. "You slept on the floor?"

He nodded. "I wanted to keep an eye on you. Didn't sleep a whole lot, to be honest."

Alex tried to rub her face, but only one hand obeyed her brain's instruction. Her attention turned to her injured arm, wrapped in gauze stained red with blood. The fingers sticking out the end of the bandages looked like fat sausages. "Shit."

"How does it feel?"

"Like it's been mauled by a demon."

Shel snorted a laugh and the worry on his face eased a little. "I thought you were going to die." He squeezed her shoulders.

Poor guy. He must have been frantic. She vaguely remembered telling him not to call the ambulance. She reached up with her good arm and clasped his hand. "Thanks. For coming out and beating the thing off me. And for taking care of me after. I think you saved my life."

She ran her hand through her hair and dislodged a leaf. "God. I must look like hell."

He smiled. "Yeah. You do." He tugged at a lock of her hair and pulled off a long strand of something crusted in dirt. "Lots of spiderwebs under the deck."

"I suppose I need to get back to Gran's and clean up." *If I can stand.*

"Not until you've had breakfast." He'd watched over her all night and was offering to make her breakfast? She fought the urge to cry—no one had taken care of her for so long. "Are you up to eggs?"

Alex wasn't convinced her stomach could keep anything down. "Maybe just some toast."

"Sure thing." He disappeared into the kitchen.

She should get up, do something—at least use the toilet—but the room seemed to be spinning slightly, and she was afraid to even try to stand. She stared at her swollen arm—maybe if she watched it she could convince it to move. But try as she might, it lay still on her lap. She tried to lift her fingers, one by one, flex her wrist, straighten her elbow—but her arm remained immobile. She tried to lift her arm at the shoulder. The limb twitched slightly, but didn't rise. It was as if it didn't even belong to her.

With her good hand, she lifted her swollen one. Pain lanced up her arm and she dropped it back to her knee. "Shit." She leaned her head back and shut her eyes, trying not to think about what sort of venom was coursing through her body, trying not to wonder when, or if, she'd regain use of her arm. Trying not to stress about the fact she hadn't caught the demon, and she had no idea where it was now, and it was her freaking dominant hand that was immobilised by venom and swelling.

"You having trouble breathing again?" She hadn't even heard Shel return.

She opened her eyes and sighed. "No. Just freaking out."

He nodded and set a plate of toast and a glass of juice on the coffee table in front of her.

"Thanks." She leaned forward to reach the food, and her injured arm slid off her knee and thumped to the seat of the couch. The sensation of watching her own limb move on its own turned her stomach. "Oh shit." She felt the blood drain from her face and she leaned back against the couch again.

"You can't move it at all?" The worry lines were back on Shel's face.

She shook her head. "And I can't feel the skin at all. Plenty of pain inside, but it's almost like it's not my limb." She struggled not to cry. This couldn't possibly be happening. This whole thing was a nightmare, and Gran wasn't even around to help her through it.

"Here. Sit up again." Shel was at her side. He lifted her arm and gently folded it across her stomach. "Hold it with your other hand." Then he looped a triangle bandage around it and over her shoulders. He tied the corners behind her neck and carefully tucked her fingers inside the loop.

She bent her neck, trying to free the hair that had gotten stuck under the sling. Shel gently pulled the strands loose for her. Then he tugged her ponytail out—the elastic was barely holding any hair anymore. Most had been pulled out in the struggle with the materpoda. He ran his fingers through her hair, gently untangling the worst of the knots, and then refastened it in the elastic.

It was the last straw—the gentle ministrations reminded her of how her mother used to calm her whenever she'd been sick or hurt. They reminded her of all she had taken for granted, all she'd lost. Her blinking wasn't enough to hold back the tears. She hiccupped a sob.

Shelby jumped up and stepped back. "I'm sorry. Did I do something wrong?"

Tears obscured Alex's vision, and his response to them embarrassed her. She shook her head. "I just ... it's ... it's been a really hard week, what with Gran and now this. I'm sorry. I'm imposing on you. You've done so much for me already. I'm sure you have other stuff to do, and—" she tried to rise, and the room spun.

Shelby lunged, grabbed her by the shoulders and pushed her back onto the couch. "You're not imposing." His mouth quirked into a small smile. "I feel like I'm living in my high school fantasy game."

Alex's next sob came out half laugh as she remembered his story from earlier. "I'm hardly a pin-up girl, and it wasn't a dragon."

He shrugged. "It was still terrifying." He patted her shoulder. "Eat. You'll feel better with something in your stomach."

Just before he disappeared back into the kitchen, he turned. "And for the record, I'd prefer you over a pin-up girl any day."

She was glad he couldn't see her blush. What the heck was that? She's sitting on his couch covered in dirt and spiderwebs, with a mangled arm and he's … flirting?

She took a bite of toast, chewing thoughtfully and trying to piece together her memories of the past sixteen hours. The materpoda had been invisible—of course it had been. It must have been sitting still, just like it had done on the deck the day before. Why hadn't she considered that possibility before she reached out to grab the eggs? Thank God Shel had been there. He must think she was an idiot, crawling under there.

He was terrified of centipedes. And still, he'd come out with a—she cast her mind back to the chaotic scene— "cricket bat," she said aloud as he re-entered the room carrying his own breakfast. "You attacked the materpoda with a cricket bat."

"I did." He sat down next to her and set his coffee on the table. On his lap, his plate held an egg sandwich piled with mouth-watering toppings—avocado, sprouts, cheese—and Alex began to wish she'd agreed to eggs.

She tore her eyes from his breakfast to look at him. "I underestimated you."

He laughed and took a bite of his sandwich.

"No, really. I feel like I need to apologise. You seemed like this …"

"Squeamish computer geek?"

"Well, yeah. But—"

"No need to apologise—I *am* a squeamish computer geek. I'm not exactly comfortable with animals of any sort, and certainly not … you-know-whats."

"But you still came out and beat it with a cricket bat."

"I'm squeamish, I'm not completely heartless—it was mauling you!"

"Yeah. I underestimated you. Sorry. And thanks." They ate in silence for a few minutes. The toast and orange juice was helping, just as Shelby had predicted. She was feeling less dizzy, less emotionally fragile. "So, if you'd put materpodas in your game, what would be the bonus for saving a damsel in distress from one?"

Shelby chuckled. "Well let's see. The dragon was worth a hundred points. The rabid dog and the purse snatcher were fifty points. I'd probably put the materpoda around seventy-five."

Alex raised her eyebrows at him. "And what would an extra seventy-five points get you?"

Shelby blushed. "Well it would get you another date of course. But if you were smart, you'd spend the points on a good sword for when you made it to the dragon."

Alex sighed. "If only we could use your points to buy a

materpoda trap. Or better yet, a materpoda transport device to send her back to wherever she came from."

"Yeah," he agreed. "But then we'd be screwed when we got to the dragon."

Alex laughed. "Alright. Save your seventy-five points from the materpoda for your sword. And I'll give you an extra twenty if you'll make me a cup of coffee." And maybe she'd throw in a date, too. Shelby was growing on her.

Shelby laughed and stood. "As you wish, m'lady."

Alex never finished her coffee—she fell asleep between sips, vaguely aware of Shel catching the mug before it slipped from her fingers. When she woke, shortly before one o'clock, her arm was still swollen, but she could twitch her fingers and move her elbow and shoulder a little. It was enough to allow her to manage to use the toilet—with difficulty. Wiggling her jeans down wasn't too hard, but pulling them back up took ten minutes.

Shelby, still hovering over her like a mother hen, made her an egg sandwich for lunch, just like the one he'd eaten for breakfast. She hoped he'd gotten some work done while she was asleep—did he keep normal work hours? She would have headed home, but he insisted she eat more before she left. He really was sweet. She could get used to being taken care of like this.

"So, how are we going to kill that monster?"

Alex's head snapped up from her sandwich. "We're not killing it. We've discussed that."

"After what it did to you last night? Alex, the thing is deadly."

"And I can catch it so it doesn't hurt anyone else."

"Then what? I assume you still haven't managed to figure out how to undo the summoning."

Alex sighed. Of course not. She'd spent the past forty-

eight hours thinking only about how she was going to cap-
ture the materpoda. She was no closer to a solution for sending it back to its home than she was before.

"I'll work on that this afternoon."

"And when you still can't figure it out?"

Alex's anger flared. "It won't be your problem. I'll catch
the materpoda tonight, and then you don't ever have to think
about it again. I'll get out of your hair, and you can forget all
of this."

He snorted. "Not likely."

"Whatever. It's not your problem." She finished the last
bite of sandwich and took her plate to the sink, her irritation
subsiding. Of course he'd assume she'd want to kill the animal after it had attacked her. He might even kill it himself—
after his performance with the cricket bat, she wouldn't put
it past him. Warmth suffused her chest. She could take care
of herself—she'd proven that—but it was nice to have Shel
helping her.

"Thanks for lunch. And breakfast." She sighed. "And
everything else. I'll be back at dusk."

Alex's attempt to get some sleep that afternoon was interrupted by another knock on the door.

"Mrs Walker. Hi." What did she want?

"Hi Alex. I was wondering if we could chat for a bit."
Her eyes dropped from Alex's face. "What happened to your
arm?"

"Um. A little accident. What is it you wanted to talk
about?"

"Oh, just something about your grandmother."

Alex invited her in and made tea while Mrs Walker settled in an armchair.

"So, what about Gran?" Alex handed her former teacher a cup of mint tea.

"Well, first, I was wondering if you've gone through all of Alice's books yet."

Alex nodded and waved at the empty shelves. "They're all gone."

"And you're sure you haven't missed any?"

What was she getting at? "I've been through every shelf and cupboard. Why do you ask?"

Mrs Walker fidgeted, running her fingers over the mug in her hand. "As I mentioned to you before, Alice had some unusual books. There was one in particular that the garden group is keen to … retain among our members."

"A gardening book?"

"Not exactly."

Oh. Understanding dawned. What did a gardening group want with a book about summoning demons? Unless they weren't really a gardening group …

Alex leaned forward. "You're asking about the demon summoning book? What do you know about it?"

Mrs Walker's eyes opened wide. Then she smiled. "I thought you were holding back something. Where's the book?"

"I have it, but I'm afraid I'd like to hold onto it, at least for now." How much should she tell Mrs Walker? Was the garden group a front for a witches' coven? Might they be able to help her? Or was she reading too much into this conversation? Maybe it was simply a curiosity to the garden group. Or maybe it had been owned by one of their members ages ago and was passed from person to person within the group over the years.

"I see. How much do you know about the book?" Mrs Walker asked.

"I know it was given to Gran by Dex Saunders, and that it originally came from his great-great-great-grandmother, Isabella Deacon."

Mrs Walker nodded. Clearly this wasn't news to her. "And have you read it?"

"I have. Have you?"

"Yes." Mrs Walker spun her cup in her hands, as if considering her next words. "The garden group has occasionally ... made use of the book."

Excitement shot through Alex's body. "You've summoned demons? Maybe you can help me."

Mrs Walker held up a hand. "I don't recommend trying any of the summonings. Unless you've been practising magic since you left home. I know Alice didn't teach you anything."

There it was—the sinking feeling of bombing an English assignment. Alex's shoulders slumped. "Well, here's the thing. I accidentally summoned a demon a few days ago."

"Accidentally?"

Alex nodded. "I just need to know how to send the demon back. If you can tell me how it's done, that'd be perfect."

Mrs Walker shook her head. "But I can't."

"Mrs Walker, the demon I summoned is eating neighbourhood cats and dogs. It did this to my arm." She waved her good hand at the sling. "I *have* to send it back. Please tell me how."

"I would tell you if I could, but I don't know how to banish a demon. None of the women in the garden group do."

Alex's brief flare of hope died, settling like a lump of coal in her stomach. "So, you've summoned demons, but not sent them back?" The thought of other materpodas lurking in Rifton made her shiver. "Did you kill them?"

"Oh no. Demons are virtually indestructible. You can

only kill them with powerful magic. May I ask what you summoned?"

"A materpoda."

Mrs Walker paled a little. "I see. Yes, I can see why you're eager to send it away." She glanced around the room. "And where is it?"

"Well, it's laid eggs under the Saunders' back deck."

"Oh. Oh dear. Yes. This is serious."

Interlude Three

2004: Gran's Cat

Alice clutched the cooling mug in her hands, unable to swallow even Jane Walker's mint and lemon verbena tea.

The other women of the Rifton Garden Group frowned at her, worry written in the wrinkles on their foreheads.

"She told me not to come after her. She doesn't want anything to do with me." Alice sniffed. "But how will I keep her safe? Her parents entrusted her to me, and now I've lost her."

"What you need is someone to keep an eye on her, if she won't come back." Jane nodded, as though the solution was obvious.

Ellen rolled her eyes. "Who is she going to get to do that? She doesn't even know where Alex is staying."

"She could hire a private investigator," Pauline

suggested, picking up a cookie and biting into it. Tea and cookies were the group's first response to most problems. And for most, it did the trick. Not so much for Alex's disappearance though.

"Or ..." Margaret set down her mug. "She could summon a familiar."

The women all froze, but it wasn't the stillness of shock, rather the stillness of thought.

After a moment, Sharon nodded. "The right one would be able to seek her out. Shadow her."

"And bring back regular reports of how she was doing," Jane added.

"A familiar?" Alice dabbled in the same magic the other members of the garden group did, but she'd never considered anything beyond the simple potions, lotions and tonics the women referred to as 'hedge witch' magic.

Margaret nodded. "Like my Leo."

Alice turned sharply to Margaret. "Leo is a familiar?" Margaret's lanky house cat was a regular fixture at garden group meetings, but Alice hadn't known he was anything other than an ordinary cat.

Margaret's smile was sly. "I summoned him back when Mother was ill with dementia—he'd keep watch so I could get some sleep. He'd wake me up if she decided to wander." She shrugged. "He was so useful to have around, I never even considered sending him away. Don't know what I'd do without him now."

"But I don't know how to summon a familiar."

Margaret smiled. "It was your book I used. The

one Dex gave you years ago."

"The one—oh!" Alice rose from her seat. "Now where did I put it? It's been ages since I looked at it." She scanned the bookshelf in the living room where they were gathered, but didn't see it. "No. I would have kept it in my bedroom, away from Alex's notice." She drifted down the hallway. It wasn't on the shelves in her room. What had she done with it? She wracked her memory.

That's right! When Margaret had returned it, she'd been in the middle of repainting the bedroom. She'd tossed it into a box. Opening the closet door, she surveyed the teetering stacks of boxes inside.

"It would have been 1998," she muttered. She pulled out the third box in the middle stack. They weren't labelled, but it didn't matter; she knew exactly what was where.

Opening the box, she rifled down about halfway. "Aha!" *Formulae for the Summoning of Minor Angels and Daemons.* She caressed the cracked leather, thinking about Dex, who'd given her the book all those years ago. It had been strange, as gifts from secret lovers went, but she'd treasured every little token back then. Rousing herself from her thoughts, she headed back to the living room. "Found it."

A ripple of excitement coursed through the women. Margaret reached for the book, and Ellen shifted close to her on the couch to peer over her shoulder. Everyone's eyes were on Margaret as she paged through the book, looking for the spell she wanted.

"Ah, here it is—*Felis daemonicus*."

"*Daemonicus?*" Alice frowned. "That doesn't sound very nice. Are you certain it's safe?"

"Well, Leo is perhaps more bloodthirsty than your average house cat, but he mostly takes his aggression out on rats." She considered for a moment. "There was that one time he took after Alfred Smythe's bloody Rottweiler. That was rather unfortunate." She smiled. "But I was the only witness, and no one would have believed a cat could do that much damage to a dog so big anyway."

"Besides, that dog was a menace," Pauline added. "Chased the neighbours' kids home from school every day."

"Didn't he also bite Lachie Robertson?" Sharon asked.

"On the butt. Which is why you shouldn't carry dog treats in your back pocket." Margaret giggled. Then she waved her hand. "The point is, that dog was more of a demon than my Leo has ever been."

"But how will a ... cat ... tell me how Alex is doing?"

"Ah! Because it won't be a cat. It will be a familiar—technically a demon, but one who does your will."

"But Leo doesn't talk."

"He does to me—mind-to-mind. In fact, he's a much better conversationalist than Edward ever was."

"Margaret!" Sharon cried. "Edward was your husband. Besides, you shouldn't speak ill of the dead or they'll come back and haunt you."

Pauline snorted. "Everyone knows Edward was a bore."

"Ladies! Focus." Ellen brought them back to the task at hand. "We need some candles."

"And space." Sharon jumped up and dragged her chair to the wall. The other women bustled around, setting up a pentagram. The actions were familiar and integral to Alice's long friendship with these women. Some of the tension in her muscles eased.

Ten minutes later, Alice chanted the summoning for *Felis daemonicus*, with her friends gathered around her.

The flash of light came with a thunderous crack, and Alice smiled as a trim black cat with luminous eyes appeared in the middle of the circle. It glared at her. *Well?* Its voice was a musical growl in her head. Impatient. *What is it? I'm sure you'll have some bloody errand or something for me. You didn't summon me here because you had an extra plate of liver pâté to give away, did you?*

"I'd like you to find my granddaughter Alex. See how she's doing and then let me know where she is and if she's okay."

Oh you would? And I'd like a couple of juicy pigeons to fall dead at my feet and lose all their feathers so I don't have to get that horrible fluff in my mouth when I eat them. Fat lot of good wishing that will do me.

He was a rude creature, that's for sure. But Alice was used to rude. In fact, she thought Alex and this familiar might get along well if they ever met.

"How about a nice can of tuna when you get back?"

The cat huffed aloud, then spoke again in her mind. *I suppose it'll have to do, won't it?* He sauntered toward the door and meowed loudly. *I can't go find your granddaughter if you don't open the fucking door.*

Alice quickly let him out, and then turned to the other women. "Are all familiars that snarky?"

Margaret laughed. "Well, they *are* cats. But he'll come round. Just feed him well, and before you know it he'll be as friendly as Leo."

Chapter Sixteen

More than a Cat

Well, so much for the local witches' coven. Who purposely summons demons without knowing how to get rid of them? Mrs Walker had assured Alex that she'd talk to the other women in the garden group to see if anyone knew how to banish a demon, but Alex wasn't hopeful. She wouldn't even say what demons the group had summoned in the past. What else was lurking out there? Talk about biosecurity risks!

If there were already demons out there, did it matter if she sent the materpoda back?

She caught sight of Benji's collar, hanging on the coat hook by the back door. She looked down at her swollen arm.

Yeah. It mattered. Maybe the demons the garden group had summoned were small and innocuous. The materpoda was not.

Her phone pinged with an incoming text. Her boss, scheduling a meeting for next week.

Next week? Shit. She was due to return to Wellington in four days. There was still a ton of Gran's stuff to dispose of, two cats to rehome, and a demon to banish before then.

She was never going to get it all finished in time, especially if she didn't get her butt in gear.

With laptop, summoning book and a glass of wine, she plopped down on the couch. She wasn't going to be able to focus on anything until the materpoda was gone, so working out how to get rid of it was priority number one.

Thor and Thunder sauntered into the room as she settled herself.

"Hey there you two," she greeted them. Both leapt to the couch with little feline grunts. Thor was first to rub up against her thigh, begging for a scratch. Thunder, not far behind, swatted Thor out of the way as Alex rubbed his ears. "There's enough for both of you, you bully." She wished she could use both hands, but her injured one gave no more than a twitch when she tried to raise it. Thunder sniffed at her injured arm with intense interest. Thor joined him, letting out a low growl as he investigated.

"Yeah, I feel the same about it," Alex said.

Thor began licking her fingers—the only part of her arm visible around the bandages. It felt creepy, precisely because she *couldn't* feel it. She tried to pull her arm away from him, but it wouldn't obey. Gently she pushed at Thor with her good hand. "Stop now."

He growled and kept licking. When she persisted pushing him away, he hissed and swatted at her.

"Okay. Have it your way." Alex wasn't interested in being mauled by a cat too. She turned her attention to Thunder, scratching him under the chin while he purred. As long as she didn't watch Thor licking her, it didn't bother her, given that she couldn't feel it.

Petting Thunder was relaxing. Tension eased as she focused on the purring animal under her fingers. Minutes later, she was shocked out of her blissful trance. She could *feel* Thor's tongue. She turned back to him and let out a cry at the sight of her fingers—the swelling was nearly gone, and the sick purple was fading to a more healthy looking flesh colour. *What. The. Fuck.* She wiggled her fingers, and they actually moved.

Having licked all of her fingers, Thor tugged at the sling and bandages as if to say, 'Take these off so I can fix the rest.'

Alex was not letting a cat lick a bunch of puncture wounds. That was a recipe for infection. She pushed the cat away.

But Thor wouldn't take no for an answer. He gnawed at the edge of the bandages and raked his claws through the sling.

"Stop!" Again Alex pushed the cat away from her.

Thor hissed and turned wild eyes on her, ears laid back.

"What?" she asked him. "You're not licking it. No way."

Thor returned to her fingers and bit down hard. With sensation restored in her fingers, she felt every sharp little tooth.

"What the hell?" She tried to push him off, but Thor dug his claws into her arm and clung. First a freaking demon, and now Gran's cat had gone nuts. She flicked her fingers, the only part of her arm she could move, in a futile attempt to dislodge the cat. He let go of her fingers, and blood welled from the wounds. Fantastic. Now she had a cat bite to deal with too.

To her astonishment, Thor licked the bite he'd just delivered to her finger. The wounds instantly stopped bleeding. The skin re-formed, and within moments, there was no sign of the bite at all.

"What are you?" She stared at the cat, as though he

would suddenly transform into … she didn't know what. What kind of creature healed wounds by licking them?

Thor growled and tugged at the bandage again. This time, Alex shrugged out of the sling and began unwinding the bandages.

She didn't remember much about the damage to her arm—a lot of blood, at least one terrifying hole in the meat of her forearm. The idea of getting a good look at the damage, compounded by swelling, made her stomach churn. She wasn't generally squeamish but when it was her own body it was different.

Thor didn't waste a moment. As soon as a bit of skin was revealed, he started licking.

Alex unwound the final layer of gauze and grimaced at what she saw. Four festering holes, puffy around the edges, set in an arm that looked more like a baked ham than an appendage. The iodine Shel had used on the wounds lent a rusty cast to the skin around them as though it was oven-browned, lymph oozed from the holes like shiny honey glaze, and the arm was twice the circumference it should have been. "Fuck." She leaned her head back against the cushions and shut her eyes as her stomach flipped and flopped.

She should probably see a doctor. Surely she should be on antibiotics, and probably antihistamines too.

But, damn it, she had stuff to do. And not enough time to do it. Going to the urgent care clinic would take half her day. Maybe she could put it off until tomorrow. After all, she did feel better now than she had first thing in the morning. By tomorrow, she might not even need to see a doctor.

And what would she tell the doctor? That she'd been bitten by a giant demonic centipede while she was trying to collect its eggs? Yeah, no. Wasn't happening.

Right now, she needed to focus on figuring out how to send the demon back to where it came from. She'd start by re-reading the summoning book. Maybe she'd missed something before.

Opening her eyes, she avoided glancing down at her arm again. Thor was blocking most of her view of it anyway, still licking away. Fine. Whatever made him happy. She leaned down and picked up the summoning book, laying it on the seat beside her and flipping it open. She began at the first page, reading the entire book from cover to cover in the hope of finding some nugget of useful information.

A third of the way through, on a page devoted to a demon called the Leockock—a bipedal creature with a hooked beak, spotted fur and wings ending in fierce looking claws—she found her first snippet of useful information.

To summon a Leockock be a difernt mater from other demons. The summoning needs be performd in revers, as their heads be backwards.

Huh? Alex peered at the woodcut drawing again. What she'd thought was a demon looking over its shoulder at the viewer was actually a creature looking straight ahead. Okay. Backwards head. How that translated to a different form of summoning, she couldn't say.

Out flie Leockock, strength be thine. Winged Catamount seek Master fine. Submission thy command, thy only wish. Content thyself with bread and fish.

Was that the summoning, or the reverse of the summoning? The text gave no indication. And was 'performing a summoning in reverse' the same as reversing a summoning, the same as a banishment? Presumably if it was, you could work out the banishment from the summoning.

Alex stared at the words, trying to make meaning from them.

What if the banishment involved reading the summoning backwards? She scanned the Leockock summoning from the end of the last sentence.

Fish and bread with thyself content. Wish only thy command, thy submission. Fine master seek catamount winged. Thine be strength, Leockock flie out.

A thrill ran through her. It made sense! Well, sort of. As much as any of the summonings made sense. She quickly flicked back to the materpoda page.

Backwards, the summoning read: *Thrall and command, voyc my wish. Call my witness and now me find. Fawn and fox loveth materpod. Dawn and dusk 'twixt firelight be gone.*

Could it be that simple?

Did she simply have to read the summoning out backwards?

Could she do it right now, or did she have to be near the materpoda when she did it? Logic said she needed to be near the materpoda—otherwise a witch could send someone else's demon back by mistake.

A knock at the door made her jump. Thor, who she'd forgotten about entirely, spooked and leapt off her. She looked down at her slightly damp arm, and all thought of the person at the door vanished.

Her arm was no longer swollen. The deep, angry puncture wounds the materpoda had left were faint pink puckers of skin. She raised her arm—it moved easily, with just a small twinge of discomfort. Lifting her eyes to Thor, primly washing his face in the middle of the room, she asked again, "What are you?"

Thor raised his head, looked her in the eye, and meowed.

Is this why Mrs Walker had told her, before leaving, that she should consider keeping Gran's cats? Were *they* the demons the garden group had summoned?

The knocking sounded again, louder this time, and Alex

jumped from the couch. It had to be Linda—the woman would have noticed she hadn't come home last night. She wouldn't be able to resist poking her nose into Alex's business and wheedling information out of her that she could canvass around to all her friends.

She'd just tell the woman she spent the night with a friend in Christchurch because she needed a break from the memories in Gran's house. Hopefully Linda hadn't noticed her rental car had spent the night in the driveway. Thunder raised a sleepy head from where he lay curled beside her, sighed, and then sank back into a doze. Thor trotted beside her to the door, tail held high.

"Don't think you're getting out, mate," she told the cat. She picked him up, holding him firmly against her chest as she plastered a fake smile on her face and opened the door.

"Oh! What are you doing here?"

Shel's shoulders slumped and he scuffed a toe against the doormat. "Um. Just checking you're okay."

She didn't really need checking on. And he could have simply texted. But, oddly, it didn't bother her that he'd stopped by. "I'm sorry. I was expecting Linda. You know how she is." She felt a little bad about practically storming out of his place earlier, after he'd taken care of her for the whole night and half the day. She stepped back. "Come in."

Thor squirmed in her arms and broke free of her grasp. Expecting him to bolt for freedom, Alex lunged at the door and slammed it shut.

But Thor was twining himself around Shel's legs, purring loudly, rubbing his head against his shoes and shins in apparent ecstasy.

Shel stood frozen for a moment, watching the cat. Then he carefully lifted one foot high, extracting it from Thor's reach, and took a step further into the room. "Um."

Alex laughed. "He obviously likes you."

"Yeah. I'm not really an animal person." He lifted his eyes from the cat, and when they landed on Alex's injured arm, they went wide. "Your arm!"

"You will *not* believe what happened." She wanted to tell him—he was the only one she could tell, and now that he was here, she was glad for his company. "Stay for a cup of tea?"

"Yeah. Sure."

Alex waved him into the living room. "Have a seat." She filled the kettle and pulled down two mugs, humming to herself and revelling in the use of her injured arm. It was the miraculous healing of her arm giving her this bubbly feeling in her chest, not the presence of Shel. She certainly wasn't happy about Shel butting in and trying to look after her.

While the water came to a boil, Alex pulled out a box of crackers and a slightly dried-out brie she'd opened three days ago and hadn't finished yet. She would feed Shel, show him she could take care of him as well as herself, though cheese and crackers didn't stack up to the amazing lunch he'd made for her.

"What are you humming?"

Was she still humming? Yes, and she caught herself dancing around the kitchen a little as she moved from cupboard to fridge. She laughed. "You know that song, 'Call Me Maybe'?"

"The one by Carly Rae Jepsen?"

"Yeah. That's the one. The materpoda's tapping and rattling of the cage the other night reminded me of that song. Now I can't get it out of my head."

Shel snorted. "Maybe the materpoda wasn't trying to communicate. Maybe it was doing karaoke."

"Nah. It was more like a one-man band." She poured the

water into their mugs and carried everything into the living room on a tray.

Both cats sat next to Shel. Thor rubbed against his elbow, purring. As Alex set down the tray, Thor leapt to Shel's shoulder, causing him to flinch.

"Thor! Stop that!" Alex lifted the cat and sat him on her own lap as she settled on the other end of the couch from Shel. "He's been ... weird ... since I got back today."

"How so?" Shel reached out to pick up his tea.

"Well the strangest thing is that he healed my arm."

"What?" His tea stopped halfway to his mouth.

Alex explained how he insisted on licking it. "And everywhere he licked, the swelling went down, the wounds closed up."

Shel stared at Thor with wide eyes. "That's seriously creepy."

"I know, right?"

"Weren't you freaking out?"

"I was, but then I got sidetracked." Alex turned to the other reason for her giddy mood. "I've figured out what a banishment is!"

"Really?"

"Yeah." She picked up the summoning book and read the passage about the Leockock. "Now, the Leockock summoning is: *Out flie Leockock, strength be*—"

"Stop!" Shel slapped a hand over the book so Alex couldn't read more. "Don't read it aloud!"

"Oh. Right." She scooted closer to Shel and pointed to the summoning she was about to read. "Read it forwards and then read it backwards. It makes sense both ways. And the materpoda summoning does too. All I have to do to send it away is read the spell backwards."

He took the book from her and silently read. Then he

paged to the materpoda summoning. "I guess they make sense backwards. A little anyway."

"So tonight, all I have to do is lure the materpoda back to the cage, say the spell backwards and *poof!* Problem gone."

"You sure there's not more to it than that?"

"Absolutely. You'll see."

Chapter Seventeen

Send Her Home

As dusk fell, Alex set her lure again. She piled half a dozen drumsticks in the back of the cage and left a trail of chicken from Gran's house to Shelby's house.

In Shelby's back yard, she waved to him through the window, and then crouched down to shine her light under the deck.

Her nerves calmed a little when she saw the materpoda tending to her eggs. First hurdle cleared. She tucked her last drumstick under the edge of the deck, flashed a thumbs-up to Shel, and then hurried back to Gran's to wait.

Once again, she'd prepared a station on the back deck for waiting. Coffee, snacks and a blanket would keep her awake and comfortable all night. Her rope system meant all she had to do was yank on the rope as soon as the materpoda was inside the cage.

She settled into the deck chair and arranged everything so it was within easy reach. Now it was simply a matter of waiting.

And waiting.

And waiting.

The night was dark and quiet, with a gentle breeze that barely stirred the leaves on the back yard shrubbery. She read the news on her phone, played a couple of mobile games, and checked her social media feeds. She drank a cup of coffee and munched a few cookies.

She checked the time—11:36 pm. Damn. It was going to be another long night.

The moon crept into the sky overhead. The back yard was washed in blue light.

A cat ghosted along the top of the fence on silent feet. Hopefully it would be far away when the materpoda showed up.

She closed her eyes, listening to the small, indistinct sounds around her. Her muscles relaxed and her mind drifted. Sounds faded. She forced her eyelids up. *No. You will not fall asleep.* Picking up her phone, she scrolled again through her social media feeds in an effort to stave off sleep and boredom.

She read the latest issue of *New Zealand Geographic*, which included an interesting article on bioluminescence.

She finished off the coffee and cookies.

She downloaded a new game for her phone, played it once and decided it was boring. She deleted it.

The moon tracked to the other side of the house and dipped behind it. Inky blackness pooled in the yard.

Alex shivered and pulled the blanket around her shoulders. Her mind wandered back over the events of the past two days. The mystery of the materpoda was only a part of the jumble of unsettling events. There was Thor, who looked like a cat but had … healing powers? It just wasn't possible. So what *was* Thor? And how had her grandmother—wait a minute. She mentally paged through the summoning book again. Somewhere in there she remembered a demon that looked a lot like a cat. The woodblock print showed a fierce-looking feline in the classic Halloween cat pose—back arched, tail fluffed and stiff—with a woman who looked like she was scolding it. Could Thor be a demon?

Impossible ... wasn't it? But if he was, did that mean Thunder was, too? Or was Thunder an ordinary cat?

Were Gran's cats the demons the garden group had summoned? Mrs Walker had studiously refused to tell her anything about the garden group's use of the book. If they had summoned cat-like demons, why had they done it? Had it been accidental, like her summoning of the materpoda? Why would anyone purposely summon a demon? You'd have to be mad to do so.

You'd also have to be mad to sit in the dark waiting for a three-metre-long centipede.

Was she crazy? Maybe this whole thing with the materpoda was in her head. Maybe Gran's death had pushed her over the edge. This could be one huge, bizarre hallucination.

It must be madness that made her wish Shelby were here with her. He'd be nothing but a liability when the materpoda showed up.

Except he'd beaten the demon off with a cricket bat when it was attacking her. The memory of him caring for her afterwards warmed her whole body. She smiled into the dark.

Then she shook her head. Hero worship. That's all it was. He wasn't interested in her, and even if they didn't live far away from each other, he wasn't the kind of guy she was interested in either. She was drawn to outdoorsy types. Fellow biologists. A guy who spent all his time indoors? Who didn't like animals? Not for her.

Somewhere in the neighbourhood, two cats began howling at each other. The altercation didn't last long, and then silence descended again.

A car door slammed a few houses away. A minute later, a vehicle motored past.

She looked at the time again—4:45 am.

She wished she hadn't drunk so much coffee—she desperately needed to pee.

A train hummed in the distance, growing louder as it sped across the Canterbury Plains, and then fading again on its way toward the West Coast.

Trucks hissed past on the main highway a kilometre away.

The inky sky above lightened to grey that slowly gave way to deep magenta.

The blackness of night drained from the yard, revealing the pale flesh of chicken drumsticks still lying where Alex had left them the night before. A fly buzzed past to land on the drumstick closest to her.

Her phone dinged. Shel.

Did you get it?

Alex sighed and hauled herself out of the deck chair, stiff muscles complaining about the long night.

She never came.

WTF? I can't deal with another day of it. The thing was dancing on the roof last night! I'm trapped in the house and don't dare go into the back yard!

What was Alex supposed to do about that? It wasn't her fault the demon didn't follow her bait trail. She gathered the detritus of her vigil and stepped inside.

I'll try again tonight.

**If you know how to send it back, why
not do it now, from my back deck?**

Why hadn't she thought of that? Of course she could do it that way. The weight settling in her chest lifted, and her exhaustion from a sleepless night dissipated.

Good idea. I'll be over soon.

The morning was chilly, but promised warmth. As she walked to Shel's house, she picked up the trail of chicken she'd left the night before. A jogger passed as she retrieved one piece and dropped it into a plastic bag.

"Morning," she said with a bright smile, trying to pretend collecting raw meat off the pavement was a perfectly normal thing to do.

The jogger raised an eyebrow—amusement and confusion warring on his face. "Morning."

She hurried on before more of the neighbours saw her.

Just before she arrived at Shel's house, the trail of chicken ended. So the materpoda had started to follow the trail. Had it found something tastier to go after? She hoped Linda didn't stop by with news of more vanished pets this morning.

She let herself into Shel's back yard and shone a light under the deck. The materpoda was tending to her eggs again, picking up each one and swiping it with her mouthparts as she clicked to them. Alex frowned. Something was different about the eggs today. They were darker, a black shadow clearly visible inside each egg. What did that mean? Were the eggs rotting in spite of the materpoda's care? Or were they developing—getting closer to hatching? A tingle of fear shot up Alex's spine, thinking about twenty hungry baby materpodas running around.

She straightened up. It would all be fine. She would send them all back right now, and that would be that.

Carefully, she stepped onto the porch. She didn't want to disturb the materpoda, but thought she should get as close as possible to it before doing the spell. Who knew what the range was on a banishment spell, but she figured the closer the better.

When she thought she was directly over the materpoda's nest, she opened the book, turned to the materpoda page and began to read the summoning backwards.

"Thrall and command, voyc my wish. Call my witness and now me find. Fawn and fox loveth materpod. Dawn and dusk 'twixt firelight be gone."

Nothing happened. Of course, she wasn't sure what *should* happen except that the materpoda should vanish. She stepped off the deck and peered underneath.

The materpoda continued to clean her eggs, completely unaffected by the spell.

"Damn." Maybe she hadn't used the right authoritative voice? It was essentially a command—maybe it needed to be recited in a commanding way. She stepped back onto the porch and raised her voice, reading the spell once again.

After the final *be gone*, which she read with particular emphasis, she paused, holding her breath. In the silence she could hear the musical clicking of the materpoda singing to her eggs.

"Fuck." She read the spell again.

And again.

And again.

The materpoda remained firmly under the deck.

Alex squeezed her eyes shut in frustration. Dammit, she was sure this would work.

A rapping at the kitchen window made her open her eyes. Shel raised his eyebrows in a question. She frowned and shook her head, then turned her attention back to the materpoda beneath her feet.

There it was. That same rhythm the materpoda was making the other night by rattling the cage. She was singing it to her eggs. Alex began tapping it with her fingers on her thighs—what was the significance of the rhythm to the materpoda?

As her tapping continued, the materpoda's clicking grew louder. A rustling sounded under her feet, and suddenly, a pair of antennae poked between the boards of the deck. Alex yelped and stumbled away from them, ceasing her tapping. The antennae retreated, and a moment later the materpoda began its clicking again.

Huh. Interesting. Alex began tapping again while she slowly stepped off the deck. She stopped about five metres away and turned to watch. The materpoda was just visible—she'd left her nest and now lurked at the edge of the decking. She skittered back and forth, as if she wanted to follow Alex's tapping, but dared not come out from the safety of darkness. Her movement grew more and more frantic. Alex's tapping was causing her stress. No. The tapping was attractive to her—not wanting to leave the shadow of the deck was causing her stress.

Alex stilled her hands and the materpoda froze along with them. Then it let out a burst of clicks. Alex responded with a series of taps, mimicking the materpoda's rhythm. The demon inched a third of its body out from under the deck. Could she lure it out, all the way to Gran's house, with tapping instead of food?

She kept tapping. The materpoda responded by launching back into the 'song' it sang to its eggs. Alex slowly backed toward the gate to the yard. The materpoda inched further out until most of its body was out from under the deck. Its antennae quested toward Alex.

Come on. All you have to do is follow me. She wasn't convinced that leading a giant centipede down the footpath at nine in the morning was a good idea, but she wasn't going to waste the opportunity if it was willing to follow her.

It certainly *wanted* to follow her. Its antennae tapped rapidly as it skirted the edge of the deck. The yard was still mostly in shadow, but when it reached a sunbeam, it hissed and drew back. How much of the route to Gran's house was in the sun at this hour? Alex tapped louder, humming along with the beat now—she swore it sounded just like that Carly Rae Jepsen song.

Her attention was fixed on the materpoda, so when a large kitchen knife suddenly spun through the air past her head, she barely had time to react before it struck the demon, point first, between the eyes.

The knife clanged and bounced off the demon's head. In a flash, the materpoda darted back under the deck.

Alex whirled around to a white-faced Shel, standing behind her clutching three more knives. "What the hell are you doing?"

"I'm trying to get rid of that monster, like we should have done the minute we saw it."

"All you did was scare her away." She waved toward the deck. "I had her moving—she was following me."

"So you could do what with it? You still don't know how to send the thing back where it came from, and what's going to happen when those eggs hatch? Will you be able to deal with twenty fucking demons crawling around? Crawling around in *my back yard*, I might add. This has gone on too long. It has to end now."

"I'm *trying*." Alex gritted her teeth. "Just let me catch her, and it'll all be my problem, not yours."

Shel laughed. "You said that yesterday, yet that thing is

still under my deck."

Alex rubbed her face. "For God's sake, Shel. Don't be such a wimp. It's only been a couple of days."

"I am not a wimp."

"Well, you're sure—"

"Hello?" A voice rang out from the gate. "Um. Hi." A gangly teenage girl stepped nervously forward. "Sorry to bother you, but I wonder if you've seen my dog." Alex's stomach churned as the girl continued. "She's a little Jack Russell terrier. Mum let her out last night to do wees in the yard and she never came back in."

"Sorry, we haven't seen her," Alex said.

"Well, if you do, can you ring?" She held out a slip of paper with a number on it. "It's not like her to run off."

Alex swallowed the bile rising in her throat and took the paper.

They stood in silence as the girl turned and left.

"I swear I will catch the materpoda tonight as soon as it's dark." Alex didn't wait for Shel's argument, but marched out the gate behind the girl.

Chapter Eighteen

Caught

Shel wouldn't be brave enough to try to kill the materpoda without Alex around. At least that's what she hoped. And after watching that kitchen knife bounce off the materpoda's carapace, she wasn't sure he'd succeed, even if he tried. Mrs Walker must have been right when she said they were virtually insdestructible.

Back at Gran's, she opened up the summoning book again.

Proper summonings and banishments recuire the carful selection of wax candles. Tallow be not pure enough of flame as that produced by the industrie of bees. E'en the wicke be critical to entice demons forth. Some be better summoned forth out of doors, others be more delicat of constitution and will not arise but in a snug abode. E'en with the best care a demon may chuse not to show itself, remaining with its brethren in the pits of Hell from whence they arise.

How had she missed that part when she read the book before? Of course she needed candles—wasn't that a critical part of any spell ever depicted in movies and books? Candles and a pentagram, whatever that was.

And she'd lit candles the night of the storm, because of the power outage. Of course! She was pretty sure Gran's candles weren't beeswax, though. They were cheap paraffin candles. She supposed paraffin candles hadn't been a thing when the summoning book was written. Gran's candles had proven adequate for summoning, so she assumed they were fine for a banishment.

Did she need to worry about the pentagram thing? She tried to remember where in the room she'd placed the candles the night of the storm. How many had she even lit? Four. Didn't a pentagram have five sides? If a pentagram was important, wouldn't she have needed five candles?

Pentagrams must be a movie thing, not a real thing.

Should she go back to Shel's and try again, using the candles?

No. She didn't want to have another argument with him. Besides, she was exhausted from being up all night. She'd wait until evening and lure the materpoda to Gran's house first.

A disturbing thought intruded. She'd summoned the materpoda inside the house. What if she needed to do the banishment in the same place? Would she have to bring the demon into the house? She shuddered.

She'd try it outdoors first. No sense in risking bringing it inside and then not being able to return it to its world or to the cage.

Her decisions made, she stumbled to her old bedroom to sleep the remainder of the morning.

In the afternoon, a second-hand dealer arrived to appraise Gran's furniture—Jason from Backstreet Antiques.

"Well, she didn't exactly go for quality, did she? Look, this chest of drawers isn't solid walnut it's just a cheap veneer job. And there's a lot of wear on the arms of the couch. That'll need reupholstery."

Alex knew it was his way of convincing her to accept whatever pathetic amount he'd eventually offer her for the stuff, but he had a point. None of Gran's furniture had been particularly high quality when she'd bought it, and all of it was old. Still, it irritated her to hear him dismiss Gran's belongings like they were nothing but rubbish. She was happy to usher him out of the house half an hour later with a promise to consider his offer once he sent it via email.

Truth was, she'd probably accept whatever he offered—she didn't have the time or inclination to spend weeks disposing of Gran's things—but she still felt the urge to purge his sliminess from the house when he was gone. She threw open all the windows until the sickly smell of his cologne dispersed.

She struggled to eat dinner—her stomach was in knots. This *had* to work—both capturing the materpoda and performing the banishment. It was Thursday. She had to be back at work on Monday. If the banishment worked tonight, that would give her three days to finish dealing with Gran's things.

The real estate agent was going to come through and discuss her options tomorrow—she was tempted by the idea of keeping Gran's house as a rental property, but she wasn't sure what might need to be done to it in order to bring it up to standard. The agency she'd called was happy to either sell it for her or to manage the rental if she chose to go down that route. She knew she wouldn't be able to finalise anything before she went back to Wellington, but once the agency had the key, she should be able to handle most things without flying back down.

Oh shit. The realtor would need to see the back yard.

What if she managed to catch the materpoda but not get rid of it tonight? She couldn't have a realtor poking around the place if there was a three-metre-long demon in a cage out the back.

Well, she'd deal with that in the morning if she had to. One crisis at a time.

As the sun set behind the mountains, she headed down the street to Shel's house, leaving a few chicken drumsticks along the way. She was going to pull out all the stops tonight. The path to the cage in Gran's back yard was going to be irresistible.

Without even a glance at the kitchen window—she was still annoyed at Shel about the knife incident—she checked for the materpoda, shining a light underneath the deck. The nest appeared untended. Not wanting to be fooled a second time by an invisible demon, she tossed a small pebble at the nest. The materpoda burst into motion, and into view, and Alex leapt away, not wanting to be the object of her anger again.

As soon as she'd retreated a few metres, she began tapping against her legs in the rhythm now seemingly stuck in her head.

The materpoda's antennae emerged from under the deck, tapping in a blur of motion. The demon darted out, straight toward Alex, and she skittered backwards toward the gate, heart pounding. Was this a good idea? The materpoda was *fast*.

The demon reached the first of the drumsticks and paused. Alex stopped tapping while the creature crunched through bone and sinew. Disgusting.

When it finished eating, it began to turn back toward the deck. *Oh no you don't!* Alex resumed tapping, and the materpoda instantly homed back in on her. She dashed backwards out the gate, beyond the next drumstick. Again the materpoda darted forward, but was distracted by the food. Perfect.

When she reached the street, the materpoda suddenly vanished. Alex didn't even remember blinking—one instant she was staring at the demon, and the next instant it was gone. She swore, then clamped her mouth shut—she didn't want to scare it. Not that she thought the materpoda had anything to be frightened of. Alex was the one who should be frightened. She knew exactly who was the predator and who was the prey in this situation. Especially when she couldn't see the materpoda. Her palms grew sweaty as she envisioned the leggy demon leaping out at her.

A scrape of claw on concrete drew her attention. There in the shadows was the materpoda. How had she moved three metres in an instant? Alex rubbed the sweat off her hands before resuming her tapping.

The materpoda preferred the shadows. Every time they passed a streetlamp, it skittered around the pool of light the lamp cast.

Alex didn't dare turn her back on the creature, so she trotted awkwardly backward to Gran's house in fits and starts, tapping out the materpoda's favourite tune with nervous energy all the way.

When she eased into the shadows next to Gran's house, she turned and ran to the back yard, taking up her position, rope in hand, ready to slam the cage door shut as soon as the materpoda entered.

Staring at the inky darkness waiting for the demon to round the corner of the house, her knees began to shake. What if it didn't come? What if it decided she was tastier than the chicken inside the cage? What if—

Meow!

A black cat trotted out of the shadows, tail held high.

Thor? How did he get out?

She remembered throwing open the windows to get rid of the scent of the icky antiques dealer. Shit. "Thor!" she whispered. "C'mere boy."

The cat ignored her, his attention captured by something else. He arched his back, hair puffing out in all directions, and hissed.

In a rush, the materpoda rounded the corner of the house. Thor turned and bolted directly into the cage, demon snapping at his tail.

"No!" Alex screamed as both demon and cat barrelled toward the back wall of the cage. The chain link rattled and Alex flinched, trying to distinguish between fur and exoskeleton. Thor was a goner.

The materpoda slammed into the back wall and skittered upward, drawing Alex's eye that way. Where was—

What? Thor was somehow on top of the cage. On the outside. He glared at her and howled, as if to say, 'Shut the bloody door!'

Alex yanked on the rope and the door clanged shut. Darting forward, she slammed the latch into place.

The materpoda ricocheted around the cage, frantically seeking an exit, and clicking furiously. It lunged at Thor, where he sat on the roof. Thor hissed and swatted at the sickle-like jaws that poked through the cage mesh. The materpoda lunged again, and Thor leapt calmly off the cage onto the ground, turning and howling at the demon for good measure before trotting away.

It wasn't until Thor had vanished back into the shadows that Alex realised she'd sunk to her knees beside the cage, her legs shaking so much they wouldn't hold her upright. Then the materpoda lunged at her.

She swore and stumbled away—the demon's body might

not fit through the mesh, but those sickle-shaped jaws could easily poke through.

Out of the materpoda's range, and with the adrenaline receding, Alex's brain began working again. She frowned. The materpoda was frantic. It was racing around the cage, bashing into walls, overturning its water dish. It was going to hurt itself if it didn't calm down.

She began tapping her thighs again. It had no effect. Maybe the materpoda couldn't hear it over the racket she was making.

The eggs. Of course the materpoda was frantic. She was trapped away from her eggs. She was unlikely to calm down until she had her eggs with her again.

Alex grabbed one of Gran's cloth grocery bags and jogged back to Shel's house. She shimmied under the deck, bag in one hand, torch in the other, to collect the eggs.

When she lifted the first one, she nearly dropped it. It was warm—hot-water-bottle warm—and pulsed in her hand. How close were these things to hatching? She shivered and quickly shoved it into the bag. She counted as she grabbed each one and placed it into the bag—twenty-one eggs.

That was a lot of potential demon babies.

Laden with a bag full of warm, squirming eggs, she dragged herself out from under the deck and hurried back to Gran's house.

On the way, she passed a man walking his dog, and thanked her lucky stars he hadn't decided to go out earlier.

She dashed into the back yard, where the materpoda was clicking loudly. Calling to her eggs? Or cursing Alex? Maybe it was good Alex couldn't understand her.

As she neared the cage, the materpoda lunged at her. The entire cage shivered under the demon's onslaught. How was she going to get the grapefruit-sized eggs into the cage without letting the materpoda out? They wouldn't fit through the gaps in the chain link. Could she stretch a gap or cut a larger one? No, a larger hole in the cage was a bad idea—the babies would easily escape through it. In fact, given the adult was able to slip out the animal flap, she was a little worried the babies would be able to fit through the gaps even without a larger hole.

The materpoda lunged again, hurling itself against the door and making it rattle on its hinges. Damn. If she opened the door, the materpoda would be through it in a second. No way could she hold it shut against that sort of pounding.

"Okay. Think," she muttered. She needed something to hold the door, so that when she opened it, it could only move a tiny bit. Just enough to squeeze the eggs in. "Rope!"

She set the bag of eggs on the ground and then jogged to Gran's garage. She had thrown away most of the junk in the garage, but kept a hank of rope because she used it for holding the boot of the car closed when she took stuff to the tip.

She cut off two chunks of rope. Was this stuff even strong enough? She cut two more lengths. If she tied the door at four places, it should be enough, right? She hoped so.

Returning to the cage, she almost lost her nerve. Tying the rope on was going to be challenging, with the materpoda lunging at her and sticking those wicked mandibles through the fencing. Pushing the eggs through was going to require getting close to the materpoda, too.

Her arm twitched with the memory of those vicious fangs sinking into her flesh. Did she really need to return the materpoda's eggs to her?

We've got to kill them all. Shel's voice sounded in her head. He wouldn't hesitate, with eggs in hand and materpoda locked up. He'd smash the eggs rather than put himself in danger or risk unleashing the materpoda again.

It was a sensible option.

It would make the task of returning the materpoda to wherever she'd come from easier.

It would be safer.

But she couldn't do it.

The materpoda *cared* about these eggs.

"Okay love, relax and let me get your babies back to you." Alex's gentle voice did nothing to placate the demon.

The materpoda's frenzied attacks increased in intensity as Alex crouched to slip the first piece of rope through the mesh. She didn't know which was shaking more, the cage under the demon's blows, or her hands. One of the demon's venom fangs slid against her fingers as she poked the rope through. She jerked her hands back with a yelp. Dammit! She almost had the rope in.

Come on Alex, you're Steve Irwin, Bear Grylls. You studied biology because you wanted to work with animals. You can do this.

And if she was bitten, maybe she could get Thor to lick her arm again. She shook her head and laughed—when had her life gotten so crazy?

She darted forward, determined to get the rope secured, and wishing she hadn't thrown away all of Gran's gardening gloves. A little protection would be nice.

Another glancing blow of the materpoda's fangs left a long scratch across the back of Alex's hand. It burned like a hundred bee stings, but Alex didn't pull back this time. She managed to thread the rope around the door and the cage wall. With jittery fingers, she tied it in a loose loop so it would allow the door to open, but not too far. Then she stumbled back, her hand stinging and dripping blood. She pressed the hem of her T-shirt against her hand to stanch the blood. It stung a lot, but wasn't much more than a scratch. Hopefully the venom wouldn't affect her.

Just three more ropes to go.

The materpoda took the rope Alex had just tied into its jaws and began to chew.

"No!" Alex surged forward and grabbed the rope, yanking it out of the demon's mouth.

The materpoda clicked angrily at her. Alex opened her mouth to yell back, and then snapped it shut again.

This wasn't the way to calm an animal. *Come on. Remember the kittens. You know how to soothe an animal. And you know that getting upset and yelling is exactly the wrong thing to do.*

She took a deep breath. "Come on love, step back and let me work so we can get your babies back to you," she crooned.

The materpoda clicked again and hurled herself against the cage.

"Well, that was effective," she muttered. "Now what?" She tapped her hand nervously against her thigh.

The materpoda stilled, antennae vibrating.

Tapping! Of course. That's how the materpoda communicated—with clicks. She tapped again, using the same rhythm she had used to lure the materpoda into the cage.

The demon remained still. Listening? Alex stepped forward. The materpoda didn't lunge at her. She finished a repetition of the rhythm, and stopped—she needed both hands to tie the rope around the door.

She worked quickly, slipping the rope through and tying the knot to secure it. Unfortunately, it wasn't quick enough. The materpoda grew restless the moment Alex stopped tapping, and by the time she had gotten the rope looped through the mesh, the demon was trying to bite her again.

Alex let go of the rope and began tapping again. How

was she going to tie a knot one-handed?

She tried tapping her toes, but it didn't make much sound on the grass. The materpoda became restless again.

She could make clicking sounds with her tongue. Would that work? She gave it a go—nothing to lose after all, except maybe her fingers.

Clicking to the rhythm of the tune stuck in her head, she stepped forward again to thread the rope through the cage door. The materpoda didn't back away, but it didn't attack. It kept up a patter with its antennae, tapping against Alex's shaking fingers as she worked.

The second rope secured, she began on the third, still clicking away with her tongue. The materpoda matched her movements, shifting and continuing its antennal exploration of her hands.

By the time she was threading the final rope through the mesh, Alex was no longer shaking. The fingers on her right hand—the one that had been scratched—were beginning to swell a little, but they still moved. She worked quickly, securing the rope and then reaching for the bag of eggs.

Her nerves returned as she prepared to unlatch the door. Would the ropes hold? Would the door open enough to get the eggs through, but not enough to let the materpoda out?

Clicking as though her life depended on it, Alex eased open the latch. The materpoda followed her every move. She opened the door just far enough to admit an egg. The materpoda's antennae quested out the opening and Alex froze for a moment, terrified it would bolt out, somehow squeezing through the impossibly small crack.

When the demon remained inside, she reached into the bag and pulled out an egg.

The moment the egg was out, the materpoda lunged. It pressed itself against the door, pushing at the crack and stretching the ropes taut. Alex clicked her tongue louder, hoping to soothe the demon and stop its assault on the door.

One of the rope loops snapped. Shit! She needed to get the eggs into the cage now! Abandoning her clicking, which was no longer keeping the materpoda calm, she hauled the eggs out of the bag as quickly as possible, rolling them into the cage one by one. As each one entered, the materpoda tapped her antennae on it briefly before resuming her assault on the door. Did she know how many eggs she should have? Good thing Alex had collected them all.

A second rope loop snapped. Alex shook out the last of the eggs and rolled it into the cage. When the materpoda turned to check it, she slammed the door shut and secured the latch.

Chapter Nineteen

On the Dark Web

Alex stumbled into the house and flopped onto the couch.

Her scratched hand throbbed, and the fingers were still swelling. She was wrung out after her ordeal catching the materpoda. She considered texting Shel to tell him she'd caught it.

But the night wasn't over. There was still a demon to banish. She wouldn't contact Shel until she could tell him the beast was gone for good.

She lay on the couch with her eyes closed, trying to dredge up the energy to go back outside and perform the banishment. She'd need candles and the book. She still didn't know how close she had to be to the materpoda in order to send it back, but she'd try setting up on the deck first. Where would the candles go? Could she recreate the arrangement she'd had during the storm?

An insistent *meow* startled her awake. Damn. She'd dozed off. The meow sounded again from outside. Thor. He must be stuck outside, because she'd taped the cat flap closed. She tumbled off the couch and groped through the dark room to the door.

"Yes, I'll open the cat door again, now that it's safe." She flicked a light on and caught sight of her scratched hand. Yuck. It was purple and swollen. She could still move the fingers, but the skin was tight and hot. That materpoda venom was nasty stuff. She peeled the tape off the cat flap, balled it up and threw it in the rubbish. Thor sauntered in, and Alex crouched down to present her scratched hand to him.

"Want to fix this for me?" she asked.

Thor gave her a baleful look. The message was clear—*I am not your servant.*

"Please?"

He gave her hand sniff and a perfunctory lick, then padded off to his food dish. Alex huffed and stood, flexing her hand. It was improving, even with one lick. She shook her head—everything about the past few days was weird.

The clock on the stove told her it was past midnight. She'd dozed longer than she thought. No worries. There was plenty of time. It was probably better she'd had some sleep before attempting the banishment anyway. The materpoda would still be gone by morning.

She gathered four candles and took them to the back deck. When she glanced into the cage, her heart stopped— the materpoda was gone.

Then it moved, nudging the last of the eggs under the shelter Alex had made. Whew! She didn't want to think about what she'd do if the materpoda escaped.

She arranged the candles and struck a match. It promptly blew out in the breeze.

Twelve matches and a few choice swear words later, all four candle flames danced and guttered. Hopefully they'd stay lit long enough to do the job.

She opened the book and held it near one of the flickering candles. Turning to the page for the materpoda, she read.

"Thrall and command, voyc my wish. Call my witness and now me find. Fawn and fox loveth materpod. Dawn and dusk 'twixt firelight be gone."

The materpoda clicked at her eggs. A gust of wind blew two of the candles out. Ugh! Once again, the spell had failed.

She relit the two candles and re-read the summoning, infusing her voice with what she hoped was authority.

Still nothing.

Okay. Maybe she needed to be closer to the materpoda to make it work. She moved off the deck, arranging the candles so the materpoda's cage sat between them. The wind was stronger now, and the yard wasn't as sheltered as the deck. She lit match after match, struggling to keep the flames alive long enough to ignite the candles. At this rate, she was going to run out of matches.

The candle flames danced and threatened to go out. The moment she had the fourth one lit, she began to read, racing through the words before another gust of wind extinguished them.

She finished moments before a violent gust snuffed out all four candles at once.

Alex held her breath in the darkness.

Click, click, click, click. The materpoda was singing to her eggs.

Fuck.

A smattering of rain splashed down, driven by swirling wind.

Alex wasn't going to get the candles lit again.

She sighed in frustration. It wouldn't work anyway. She could try over and over all night, and it wasn't going to work. She was doing something wrong, and she needed to come up with a new idea.

Wind shook the trees in the yard, and the rain started in earnest. Alex scooped up the candles and hurried back inside.

Alex tossed and turned the rest of the night, trying to sleep, but with her mind spinning. How was she going to get rid of the materpoda? What was she doing wrong? If the spell worked, would the eggs go back too, or did she have to deal with them separately? What was she going to do about the realtor coming tomorrow? Did she need to ask for another week off work? Would the second-hand dealer take all of Gran's furniture, or would she have to find someone else to take what he didn't want? And what was she going to do with Thor and Thunder? What the hell had she been doing with her time—this stupid demon had made her forget everything she should have been dealing with the past eleven days.

She wished she'd gotten a flexible airplane ticket.

By morning, she'd decided to cancel the realtor's visit.

When she checked her email, she found the second-hand dealer had offered her a pathetic $150 for just two pieces of Gran's furniture. She declined his offer.

Shortly after nine o'clock, as she was nursing a second cup of coffee and frowning over the local animal shelter options, she got a phone call from Gran's lawyer.

"Seems she had a one-hundred-thousand-dollar life insurance policy, and you're the listed beneficiary.

"Oh!" Alex hadn't even considered there might be life insurance.

"And I have good news from the bank—your grand-mother was debt-free. Not even a mortgage on the house. So once we've gathered all her assets together, you'll have another substantial sum coming."

Alex reeled a little. A hundred thousand dollars, plus Gran's house and whatever else they found she had? Alex's bank account hovered around three thousand dollars, most of it earmarked for next month's student loan payments. She could barely imagine a hundred thousand dollars.

The lawyer provided her with the necessary details to claim the insurance money, and Alex completed the paperwork online, not quite believing this turn of events.

When Thor and Thunder jumped onto the table to walk over her computer keyboard and beg attention, she looked at them anew. "How would you two like to move to Wellington?" She could find a new flat that allowed pets. She could see it now—a place with a yard. She'd build the cats a little outdoor run, and—

She shook herself out of her daydream. There was a demon in Gran's back yard, and that was her top priority.

Her phone buzzed with an incoming text. Shel.

Well?

> **Materpoda and eggs all in the cage.**

Not gone?

Of course he wouldn't be satisfied until they were banished entirely from the world.

> **Banishment failed last night. Something to do with my candles, maybe? Or might have to be done indoors.**

I have some ideas.

Three dots appeared, indicating he was typing more. Alex rolled her eyes and typed over him.

> **If they involve killing, I don't want to hear them.**

An instant later, his next message popped up.

Too complicated to explain over text.

Then a second message.

No killing.

And a third.

I'm coming over. Be there in 5 min.

Well. A flash of irritation burned in her chest. This wasn't his problem anymore.

Don't bother. I've got this.

He didn't respond, and a few minutes later, both cats leapt up from where they lay on the back of the couch and trotted toward the door. A knock sounded, and Alex shook her head. "How did you know he was out there?"

She opened the door. Shel had a laptop tucked under one arm. His smile faltered under Alex's frown.

"You know you don't need to worry about this anymore," she said without inviting him in. "It's not your problem."

Shelby shrugged. "I haven't done much, just a bit of poking around." Then he smiled shyly. "Besides, it was a bit too quiet at home, after all the excitement of the past couple of days."

She rolled her eyes as her irritation melted. "Wait till I tell you about last night—you might wish for some quiet." She stepped back and waved him inside.

The instant Shelby crossed the threshold, the cats accosted him, rubbing around his ankles, purring loudly, tails in the air.

For a moment he went stiff. Then he bent to gingerly touch each cat with the tips of his fingers. Thor reared up to rub his head more firmly against Shel's hand.

"He's showing you how to do it right," Alex said. Then

she laughed. "You're certainly a cat magnet. You sure your pockets aren't full of catnip?"

Shel straightened, his eyes still on the cats. "I've never had a cat. I didn't know they were so friendly—aren't they supposed to be sort of snobby and aloof?"

"They are to everyone else. Believe me—I don't get that kind of reception when I come in the door, and I feed them. Seriously, you sure you're not carrying catnip?" She bent and picked up Thunder in an attempt to clear his path. "Have a seat. I'll put on the kettle." She shooed Thor away from Shel's feet and kept a firm hold on Thunder until Shel had made his way to the couch. Both cats gravitated to him as soon as he sat down, and by the time Alex walked in with two steaming mugs of tea, they were draped over him like lap rugs. The sight made her smile.

"So tell me about last night," Shel said from beneath his furry mantle.

Alex recounted the adventures of the previous night, including Thor's miraculous escape from the cage.

Thor's ears swivelled toward her as she spoke, and she scratched his head. "I'm beginning to think he isn't actually a cat at all."

Shel's eyebrows rose. "What would he be, if not a cat?"

"Another demon is my guess. Two weeks ago, I'd have laughed at anyone who suggested he wasn't feline, but after seeing the materpoda … well, maybe I'm a little more open minded. Besides, there's a demon in the book that looks like a cat, and Mrs Walker said that Gran's garden group had used the book in the past."

"What?" Shel leaned forward.

Alex told him about Mrs Walker's visit. "She refused to tell me *what* they'd summoned or why, but …" She let the sentence trail off. "Thor sure isn't an ordinary cat."

"Yeah. Everything's been … out of the ordinary."

Alex snorted a laugh. "That's an understatement. I keep thinking I must be insane, hallucinating or something."

"Well, if you are, I am too. And so are a bunch of other folks." He lifted the cats off his lap and replaced them with his computer, opening it up and signing in. "I was doing some searching online and found an interesting witchcraft forum."

"Where'd you find that? I've searched every keyword I can think of and haven't found a thing."

Shel fidgeted. "No, you wouldn't have found this. It's on the Dark Web."

"What's the Dark Web?"

"It's websites that are encrypted—designed not to be discoverable by normal search engines. It's used a lot by—"

"Criminals?"

"Yeah. You've got to kind of be careful what you search for. There's some scary stuff there—stuff you don't even want to know about."

"And you've spent a lot of time hanging out on the Dark Web?" He said he wasn't hanging around alleyways smoking cigarettes as a teen, but he might have been doing the equivalent online. And here she thought he was a decent guy.

"No! Not at all. I very briefly held a job with the Police ICT unit, thinking I'd use my programming skills to catch criminals." He made a face. "The first week, I was searching out information on a child pornography ring. I had to dive into the Dark Web, because that's where those guys operate, and I realised I can't handle that sort of thing. It broke me. I gave two weeks' notice on my second day on the job. So much for doing something worthwhile with my life." His shoulders slumped.

"Hey, don't feel bad. I wouldn't be able to do that stuff

either."

"You'd do fine. You're not a wimp like me. You caught that demon after seeing what it could do to you."

Alex laughed. "Don't beat yourself up. You create games that encourage empathy, reward good citizenship, and value lives. That's awesome."

"Yeah, maybe."

He looked so dejected, she wanted to hug him. Time to change the subject. "So, what did you find out on this witch-craft forum?"

His eyes brightened and he clicked to a diagram that had clearly been lifted from an old book. "This is the pentagram used for the summoning of a demon. From what I read, the candles go at the points of the star, and the atmospheric conditions and location of the pentagram are critical to suc-cess." He clicked to a discussion forum and scrolled down the page. "There's this woman who—according to her—has a revolving menagerie of demons she summons to do shit for her, like give her ex-husband flat tyres and nosebleeds."

"Gee. She sounds like a lovely woman."

"Yeah. Don't piss her off, eh? Anyway, listen to this com-ment she made about someone's botched summoning:

"You must learn to invoke and banish. Learn to cast your circle clockwise and counterclockwise in order to open portals and make the most use of the demons at your disposal. You must learn to feel the rhythm of the light, working in harmony with all five points of your pentagram."

"Can I see that?" Alex slid the laptop onto her own knees and scrolled down.

WitchBitch: What sort of candles are you using? I find the only ones that work for me are the eight-inch Colonial Crafts brand hand-dipped organic beeswax ones. Blue.

PissinmyCauldron: And for Pete's sake, practise the banishment before you do the invocation! I can't tell you how many apprentices have been devoured by the demons they summon because they can't send them back. Safety first! Banishment is hard. Invocation is way easier. If you're struggling with the invocation, you probably shouldn't even be practising witchcraft.

GhostWhisperer: Well, if we're talking about safety, DON'T STEP THROUGH THE PORTAL! Stay well away from the centre of your pentagram as you cast the spell. My great-aunt was actually sucked into a portal because she stood too close.

StarBaby: Yeah, portals suck.

Alex sighed and passed the computer back. "The problem with all that pentagram stuff is that when I summoned the demon I only lit four candles, I didn't draw a pentagram, and my candles were cheap paraffin, not beeswax. According to this, it shouldn't have worked."

"But when you reversed what you did, nothing happened. Maybe your summoning was a weird fluke."

Alex snorted. "Clearly it was, since I wasn't trying to do anything except calm a terrified dog."

"But maybe we need to learn the proper banishment in order to send this demon back. It's obviously not as simple as lighting a couple of candles and reading the spell backwards."

Obviously. "You said you also learned that the location and atmospheric conditions are important. If we have to wait for a thunderstorm—"

"No. I don't think we have to wait for a storm. But there's something about the flickering candles that's critical—they can't burn too steadily."

"Well they sure as hell were flickering last night—I could barely keep them lit."

"So maybe they were flickering too much. And anyway, you only used four. If we can get the right candles and figure out what sort of breeze we need to get them to flicker just right—"

His enthusiasm was irritating. She was too tired to relish the idea of figuring out flicker patterns. She was certain they'd spend days ordering candles, checking weather forecasts, studying flames, only to have the spell fail again. She just wanted to finish dealing with Gran's stuff and get back to her normal life. "Maybe we *should* just kill her." Not that killing a demon sounded easy, either, but banishment seemed impossible.

Shel stared at her, mouth agape. "We can't do that—I know we can send her back. These people do it all the time." He waved at the online conversation on his screen.

"These people are crackpots." And Mr *We need to kill it* believed them? "I'm already going to have to extend my leave for a week, because I haven't yet managed to wrap up all the business with Gran. I need to focus on that. I—"

"I thought you said you had it under control?"

"That was before I read that the brand and colour of the candles matters. Where the hell am I going to get the right candles? I've never even heard of Colonial Crafts—sounds like an American company—who else celebrates being a British colony two hundred years after they fought a war of independence?" She was ranting. She heard the exhaustion in her voice. Covering her face with her hands, she took a shaky breath and said in a small voice, "I just want to be sad for Gran's passing, and not have all this other shit to deal with."

She heard Shel close the laptop and set it on the coffee table. He wrapped an arm around her shoulder and pulled her closer to him. "I'm sorry about your gran. I wish my grandfather hadn't ever given her that book. And I'm sorry you've had to deal with all this at once." He squeezed her shoulder. "But I'm not sorry you summoned the demon."

Alex uncovered her face and frowned at Shel, who met her eyes. "Why?"

Shel withdrew his arm from her shoulder. "Centipede. I can say that now without freaking out. I looked up some information about them online yesterday and learned that they're quite maternal. Take care of their young and all, and they eat lots of bugs that are pests. I think I'd even like to see one—a regular-sized one—in real life someday."

Alex laughed, the tension in her chest easing a little. "You're cured of your phobia."

"Yeah. Of the little ones, at least. And also … the other reason I'm not sorry you summoned the demon …" he focused on his hands in his lap, "is because if you hadn't, I wouldn't have met you."

Shocked into stillness, Alex stared at Shel's profile, suddenly aware of how close they sat to one another.

He raised his eyes to meet hers, a shy smile tugging at his lips. He shrugged. "Yeah, crazy, eh? So, can we work as a team to send this girl and her eggs back to where they belong?"

Alex smiled. He really was a nice guy. Even if he was a computer geek. "Yeah. That sounds good. Welcome to the team." She stuck out her hand and Shel took it in his. But the handshake was more than that, and lasted for quite some time as Alex searched his face, wondering what exactly he was thinking.

Chapter Twenty

The Perfect Candle

They both agreed that Alex needed a nap before tackling anything.

After that, she would source the candles and buy more meat for the materpoda.

Shel would dig around on the witchcraft forum to find more details about the conditions needed for the right level of flickering, and what it meant to cast your circle clockwise and counterclockwise.

They'd meet again at dusk.

Alex tried to sleep, but the effort was doomed. She'd never been good at falling asleep during the day, and in spite of being physically exhausted, her brain was spinning.

First, there was the question of the materpoda—it didn't make sense that she'd been able to summon the demon, and she kept replaying the storm in her head, trying to remember every detail of what she'd done and said, with the hope that it would give her a clue how to reverse it.

And then there was Shel. That alone could have kept her

from dozing off. He was glad she'd summoned the demon because it's how he met her? What exactly did that mean? What did she want it to mean?

He was a dumpy computer geek, right? Socially inept, and living with his parents. She shouldn't care what he thought of her. She shouldn't have melted into him when he put his arm around her earlier. She shouldn't have liked the way his skin felt against hers when they'd shaken hands. He didn't even like animals, for God's sake!

And yet … warmth suffused her when she replayed his words. He wasn't socially inept, by any means. In fact, he was probably more kind than her last two boyfriends. And he wasn't a loser—he had a job that allowed him to do good with his talents. He was … nice.

She sighed and rolled over, punching the pillow for good measure. She needed to rest, otherwise she wouldn't be able to do anything this evening.

A knock sounded on the door, making her jump. Who could be here? Not Shel—he knew she was trying to sleep. Must be Linda. Maybe she could ignore her.

The knock sounded again, louder this time. Alex huffed and rolled out of bed, grumbling about Gran's nosey neighbour.

When she opened the door, it wasn't Linda. The woman in front of her was middle-aged, with hair dyed a hideous shade of russet, and lashes gummy with mascara. Her polyester pant suit reminded Alex of 1980s sitcoms. As Alex's gaze lifted to the woman's signwritten car, she sucked in a horrified breath.

She'd forgotten to cancel the realtor's visit.

The call from Gran's lawyer had pushed it out of her mind.

"Hi." The woman smiled. "You must be Alex. I'm Carole

from Goodhouse Realtors." She stuck out her hand. Alex was frozen, unable to respond. Carole's smile faltered. "You *are* Alex?"

"Yes. I ... um ... I forgot you were coming." Alex swallowed. Maybe she could keep the woman out of the back yard. "Please. Come in."

She stepped back, and Carole strode past her into the room, eyes scanning in a practised manner.

"Ah. It is quaint, isn't it?"

The word *quaint* carried a note of disdain that made Alex bristle. Never mind that *she* had called Gran's house an old dump when she was a teen—this stranger had no right to sneer at it after five seconds.

"So, have you decided whether you'd like to sell or rent it?" Carole didn't wait for Alex's response. "I can tell you right now that you'll have a lot of work to do before you can rent it out. A house of this age probably has insufficient insulation. It will almost certainly fail a draught test as well. That'll probably mean new windows and doors, possibly new flooring—these old hardwood floors are shocking." She tapped a high heel on the floor. "And I've never seen a house this age without mould problems; those will have to be dealt with before putting it on the rental market."

Well, Carole was just a bundle of optimism, wasn't she?

As Alex showed Carole around the rooms, she considered her options. She should probably sell the house and be done with it—that was the least work and would give her the most immediate financial gain.

But with Gran's life insurance payout, she didn't need the money. She was surprised to find herself looking with fondness at the familiar creaky floors, rusting clawfoot tub and dated mustard-coloured kitchen cabinetry. Maybe she should fix the place up and rent it out. She could always sell it later, and she liked the idea of the passive income it could provide. With rental income, she could take a long vacation—do the gap year she'd missed out on, spend a year seeing the world.

She was yanked out of her reverie by the sound of the back door opening. *Shit!* She could *not* let Carole go out there.

She lurched toward the door, but it was too late. Carole had already stepped through onto the back deck, glancing around and smiling appreciatively for the first time. "Well, this is nice. It will be a good selling point." Then she frowned. "Did your grandmother own a large dog?"

"Ah …" Alex frantically scanned the cage, heart pounding. She could just make out the materpoda's eggs under the shelter she'd built for them. She silently begged the demon to remain still and invisible. "Yeah, she had a pair of Dobermans," she lied as she edged between Carole and the cage, hoping to block her view. "She loved to garden. Over there's her vegetable garden." She pointed to the opposite side of the yard. While Carole was distracted, she spun around to be sure the materpoda was still invisible.

Her movement must have disturbed it, because it rushed out from the shelter, directly toward Alex. She stifled a yelp and whirled back toward Carole as the materpoda hit the side of the cage, rattling it.

Carole turned toward the sound and Alex felt the blood drain from her face. There was no hiding the materpoda now. By the sound of it, the demon was clinging to the side of the cage right behind Alex's head. How was she going to explain *that* to the real estate agent?

Carole's eyes widened. "Are you okay? You look pale."

What? Did she not see the giant centipede? Alex glanced over her shoulder. The demon was invisible. "I … uh … just need to sit down. Come inside and tell me more about what

I would need to do to bring the house up to standard for a rental." She practically shoved Carole through the door and slammed it behind them. She heard the cage rattle as they made their way to the living room.

After she'd finally bundled Carole back into her car and waved her off, Alex sat down at the computer to find a store selling hand-dipped organic beeswax candles … in blue, if possible.

She found soy candles, paraffin candles, and eco-candles made from waste kitchen fat (yuck!). She found tea candles, pillar candles, scented candles, candles in jars and candles in cans. She found cheap candles for a few dollars a dozen and candles costing sixty dollars each.

But the only places she found hand-dipped beeswax candles were online specialty shops. None of them advertised organic beeswax candles, and none of them offered their hand-dipped candles in blue. All of them were mail-order only.

As far as she could tell, there were no hand-dipped beeswax candles to be had on a Friday afternoon within an hour's drive.

Now what?

She googled *how to hand dip candles*.

It didn't look difficult. All she needed was beeswax, wicking string, and a blue crayon. Gran had all those things, but Alex had tossed them out last week. Frustration boiled in her chest.

Well, nothing to do about it now. All those things were available at craft stores, right? A quick search confirmed they were, but she'd have to hurry, because the nearest craft store closed in an hour.

The forty-minute drive to Christchurch seemed to take longer than usual. Then she got stuck in traffic through a construction zone. She had only ten minutes by the time she pulled into the car park at the craft store.

She raced through the doors, muttering to herself, "Beeswax, wicking, and a crayon." Glancing around inside, her stomach sank. The place was huge. She wasn't a crafty sort of person. Who knew there were so many different crafts? How did anyone find what they wanted among aisles and aisles of beads, string, clay, paper, scissors, wool and other items? She scanned hopelessly, keeping an eye out for an employee who could direct her to the right aisle.

"Ah! Kids' crafts!" Crayons would be in that section. She raced down the aisle and snatched up a 24-crayon box.

Three quarters of the way through the store, a harsh voice came over the loudspeakers. "Attention shoppers: we'll be closing in five minutes. All customers should make their way to the checkout now."

Dammit! Where were the candle-making supplies? She began to jog, scanning shelves frantically as she moved. She passed a rack full of rubber stamps, specialty paper sold by the sheet, and dismembered doll body parts in cellophane bags. *Ugh! Disgusting.* She passed colourful squares of modelling clay, a gazillion types of glue, and a rainbow of dyed chicken feathers.

There. She skidded to a halt, panting, in front of a display of little bags of wax pellets and braided string. "Beeswax … beeswax …" *Damn.* There were four different size bags of soy wax pellets, but the hook advertising beeswax was empty.

Would soy candles work? She gritted her teeth.

"We're now closing. All customers should be at the checkout."

She'd find beeswax somewhere else. Her hand hovered

over the selection of wicking in different thicknesses. There were different sizes of wick? Did it matter which one she used? She nearly growled in frustration. Too many choices and too many unknowns. She grabbed the middle-sized wicking and dashed to the checkout.

Ignoring the stink-eye the checkout clerk gave her, she quickly paid and headed back to her car in the now empty car park.

Where could she buy beeswax at five o'clock on a Friday afternoon? The other craft shops in town had already closed.

Beekeepers. That's where the wax came from in the first place. Surely she could find someone to sell her some wax.

She started making phone calls.

Just before six o'clock, she pulled into the rutted gravel drive marked by a sign proclaiming it to be Babette's Bees. Wincing every time the rental car bottomed out in a pothole, she eased her way down the long drive to a beautiful old farmhouse surrounded by gardens overflowing with flowers. Babette clearly enjoyed the quaint, old-fashioned look. Intricate gingerbread framed the eaves, and a freshly painted white picket fence enclosed a small yard full of fancy chicken breeds. She wouldn't have been surprised to learn that Babette made her own beeswax candles while wearing a mob cap and a frilly apron.

The little farm stand where they sold honey was locked up tight—the woman she'd talked to had told her it would be, and that she should come to the door.

There was no doorbell, so she knocked on the door, admiring the leaded glass in it, backed by a lace curtain.

The door swung open. "You must be Alex."

Alex blinked up at a bear of a man. His arms were dark with tattoos, his head was shaved clean, and a row of gold studs framed his left eyebrow. "Babette?"

He laughed, a high giggle perfectly matching the voice on the phone. "Bob. Babette was my mum." He handed over a paper bag. "There's about three hundred grams there."

Alex recovered from her shock and paid for the wax. Could her life get any more surreal?

An hour later, with wax drips splattered across Gran's cooktop and four short, lumpy candles hanging from the cupboard handles to cool, Alex decided life *could* get more surreal.

She began dipping another pair of candles as a knock sounded on the door. "Come in!" she yelled.

Shel stepped in, his laptop under his arm. Thor trotted out and rubbed against his ankles. He bent to scratch the cat's ears. When he straightened, he asked, "What are you doing?"

"Making candles. What does it look like?"

"I thought you were going to buy candles."

"There's not a single hand-dipped beeswax candle for sale in Canterbury."

He fingered one of the dangling candles she'd already finished. "Are they *supposed* to look like this?"

"I'm a biologist, not Martha Stewart. Have you learned anything new? I'll have five candles ready soon."

Thor hopped onto the kitchen bench next to the pot of melted wax. He sat and watched Alex as she dipped the growing candle into the wax and held it above the pot to cool for a moment before dipping it again.

"I don't need your criticism either, cat," she growled.

Shel set his laptop on the dining table. "I did find out that casting your circle clockwise and counterclockwise means the direction you light the candles."

"Oh. So what direction are we supposed to go?"

Shel sighed. "Well, that's unclear. Apparently you're supposed to cast the circle in a clockwise direction, and remove it in a counterclockwise direction. Unless you're doing a banishment, in which case some people do it the opposite way."

"So we do it counterclockwise?"

"Maybe … I read something else that said those directions are only for the northern hemisphere, and you should do it the opposite way in the southern hemisphere. And then there's the issue that most modern witches apparently use only four candles, set at the cardinal directions, and most information says they don't summon demons at all. Apparently it's considered too dangerous these days. So whether any modern guidelines are useful is questionable."

"Well, that's not very helpful." She dipped the candle again, adding an almost invisibly thin layer of wax. Who decided that this was a good way to make candles anyway? It took forever. "Anything else?"

"I'm not sure. There's something important about the flickering. I've been trying to nail it down, but no one seems to entirely understand it." He typed something and lapsed into silence, frowning at the screen.

Another dip, wait, dip again … Alex began humming the tune that was on repeat in her head—the one she'd unconsciously been dipping in time to, each phrase of the song followed by a dip of the candle.

Shel chuckled and a moment later, the song she'd been humming emanated from his laptop. He cranked the volume up and they both started singing along. The stress that had been twisting her stomach all week lifted. Shel grabbed the torch sitting on the bench and used it like a microphone.

Listening to him sing a song about having a mad crush on someone made her blush.

He's just singing the lyrics, Alex. It's not for you. She focused on the rhythm instead, tapping her feet and dipping her candle in time with it and ignoring the lyrics.

Alex admired her lumpy candle. Not pretty, but big enough to call it finished.

As the final chords of the song faded, another sound caught Alex's attention. Shel heard it too, and they both fell silent, listening.

The materpoda's cage was rattling.

Shel's eyes widened. "It's the same song."

"That's why the song was in my head in the first place— she rattled the cage like that the other day, and ..." She frowned in concentration, thinking back to the realtor's visit. "She did it this morning while the realtor was here."

"What does it mean?"

Alex shrugged. "No idea. But it reminds me ... I read an article the other night about bioluminescence, and there are animals that use flashing lights to communicate—insects and some marine organisms. The clicking is just like flashing— it's got to be some form of communication."

"Wish we understood it."

Alex held up her candle. "I think we're ready. Shall we send this girl home?"

Chapter Twenty-One

The Rhythm of the Light

They arranged the lumpy candles—five of them, because what little information they'd found regarding demons suggested five was the right number—around the materpoda's cage while the demon clicked at them and rocketed up the walls and around the ceiling. Alex kept a close eye on Shel, but after his initial startle when the materpoda rushed out from her shelter, he managed to control his fear. She noticed he never looked directly at it, though, and insisted on the candles being at least two metres from the cage. "Are you sure we don't need to draw the pentagram?" Alex asked.

"According to the discussion forum, the pentagram is just a way to ensure the candles are equidistant around your circle."

"Which is why I ask, are you sure we don't need to draw it?"

"I'm certain. I'm good with geometry." He eyeballed the candle Alex had just placed. "That one needs to go a little to the left. Yeah. Right there."

She rolled her eyes at him, certain that little move had been for show. He missed the gesture in the dark. "Are we ready then?" she asked.

Shel scanned the candles once more and nodded. Alex struck a match and then handed him the box. Together they lit all five candles, moving clockwise around the circle. The tapers burned strongly, unwavering in the still night air. "Not a lot of flickering tonight. Is that going to be a problem?"

"Only way to know is to give it a go." He gestured for her to begin.

Alex took a deep breath and stepped into the circle of candles.

"*Thrall and command*," she began, reading by the light of one of the candles. The materpoda stilled, vanishing from sight. "*Voyc my wish. Call my witness and now me find. Fawn and fox loveth materpod. Dawn and dusk 'twixt firelight be gone.*"

She held her breath, waiting. For what, she wasn't certain. The materpoda wasn't visible.

"Is it gone?" Shel whispered.

"I don't—"

The demon burst into view in a flurry of motion, rattling the cage as it hung from the ceiling.

"Damn." Another failure.

Shel stepped closer. "That's the same rhythm. The one from the song."

"What is she trying to tell us?"

The materpoda raced down the wall, clicking angrily, and skittered under the shelter to wrap herself around her eggs.

Shel snorted. "Sounds like swearing to me. Do we try again the same way? Maybe we should put the candles out and then try lighting them counterclockwise."

Alex barely heard him. She'd watched the materpoda go to her eggs, but something didn't look right under there. She fished Gran's torch out of her pocket and crouched to shine it into the shelter. "Do the eggs look odd to you?"

"You mean other than that they're giant centipede eggs?"

"Just look at them and tell me if you think they look different than they did before." Her stomach twisted. Maybe she was seeing things. Maybe the eggs didn't look darker, as though the shells were almost transparent.

Shel swore. "I can see the babies inside. Do you think—"

"That they're about to hatch? Yeah."

"When do you reckon?"

She shrugged. "No idea. Soon."

He swore again, and his voice shook. Even in the dim light, Alex could tell he was pale. His new-found bravery when it came to centipedes obviously didn't extend to clutches of twenty-one giant demon centipedes. She couldn't blame him. She felt pale, too, just thinking about the possibility of those eggs hatching.

She took a fortifying breath and stood. "Well, the sooner we get them all out of here, the better. Let's give it another go. Counterclockwise this time." She began snuffing out the candles. When she'd extinguished them all and returned to the beginning of the circle, Shel still hadn't moved. "You okay?" She placed a hand on his shoulder. He was shaking.

"Not sure."

"Look. Why don't you go inside? I can handle this. Maybe you can do some more research into the flickering."

He didn't move.

"Shel?" She squeezed his shoulder.

He shook himself out of his stupor. "Yeah. Okay. Good idea. I'll just ... do some research."

Alex watched him stagger into the house, then turned her attention to her task. She lit the candles, counterclockwise. The materpoda watched. Did the demon know what they were trying to do? Did she want to go back to wherever she'd come from? Once the candles were lit, Alex paused to gaze at the demon, crooning to her eggs. A different clicking rhythm than the one she made at Shel and Alex. Gentle. Maternal. Were monsters maternal?

The demon paused, as if she'd noticed Alex looking at her. Slowly, she unwound herself from her eggs and flowed on rippling legs toward Alex. The motion was smooth and nonaggressive. When she reached the wall of the cage, she poked her antennae through the mesh, questing toward Alex and clicking softly.

Alex tentatively reached out a hand toward the cage. It shook, but she held it as steady as she could as the materpoda's antennae found it and tapped a gentle beat across her palm. A thrill ran through her.

"Hi," she whispered, afraid to spook the creature. "We'll get you home as soon as possible."

A dark form hurtled from the shadows and threw itself at the materpoda with a hiss. The materpoda jerked backward, clicking furiously.

"Thor! Stop it!"

The cat arched its back, tail puffed out like a bottle brush, and hissed at the demon. Alex scooped him up and shoved him through the back door. He growled his displeasure, but didn't bite or scratch.

When she returned to the circle, the materpoda was back with her eggs. Alex took out the book and read the summoning backwards again. She barely needed the book anymore— she practically had it memorised by now.

She finished the incantation and held her breath. Nothing happened. Had she expected it to work? Not really. The candles still burned steadily, with only the occasional flicker as a moth flitted too close.

She sat down on the edge of the porch, putting her head into her hands.

What were they doing wrong? It could be anything or everything.

She was saying the incantation backwards. That was right … wasn't it?

What had the book said? Demons could only be banished by someone born to magic. How could you tell if someone was born to it? Did magic run in families? And if so, was Shel born to magic? Couldn't hurt to try.

She poked her head in the door and called Shel out.

"I need you to try the incantation," she said, thrusting the book into his hands.

"Why?"

"Maybe you're born to magic, like I suggested before."

"I'm not a witch." He pushed the book back to her.

"Humour me. Give it a go."

"Do I have to go inside the circle?"

She nodded. "That's what you told me I had to do." No way was she going to let him give this anything less than his best shot.

He opened the book and sucked in a breath.

Before he could start, Thor leapt to his shoulder. How had he gotten out again?

Shel seemed to take strength from the presence of the cat. Straightening his back, he stepped forward.

He began the incantation, his voice unsteady. Alex fisted her hands, eyes darting from Shel to the materpoda to the candles.

On the final syllable, the materpoda burst from the shelter, straight toward Shel. He shrieked and lurched backward, tripping over his own feet and tumbling to the ground.

The materpoda raced up the cage to the ceiling, her

vicious clicking keeping time with the rhythm she tapped out with her feet.

The same rhythm she'd tapped out again and again.

What was she trying to tell them?

What had that one post said? *You must learn to feel the rhythm of the light.* The rhythm of the light. The rhythm. The flickering of the light. Light that could communicate.

"Shel!"

An already terrified Shel yelped at the sound of her voice. "What?"

"The candles need to flicker to the rhythm the materpoda is making. The *rhythm of the light.* She's been trying to tell us that!"

"What?" He pulled himself to his feet. "How would an animal know that?"

"She's more than an animal, Shel." She turned to Thor, who was unconcernedly licking his paws on the porch. "Just like you, sir, are more than a cat."

Thor paused in his toilette. *Meow!* Alex swore it sounded like *damn straight.*

"How could candles flicker to a particular rhythm?" Shel rolled to his feet and brushed himself off.

"I don't know. Maybe that's why they say the conditions under which you do a summoning or banishment are critical. Do you think different animals require different flicker rhythms? The book mentioned that some need to be summoned outdoors and some indoors. Maybe that has to do with how candles behave outdoors versus indoors."

Shel's eyes widened. "You summoned the materpoda inside the house. Are we going to have to banish it inside the house, too?"

The thought had already crossed Alex's mind. She'd dismissed it then, but it seemed more plausible now. "Surely there's some other way to get the flickering right." There had to be. No way did she want to let the materpoda out of the cage, let alone into the house.

A breeze picked up, and the candles wavered for the first time that evening. Were they flickering in the *right* way?

Shel saw it too. He shoved the book at her. "Go on. Try it again."

"I think you should try it again." She pushed the book back at him.

"That beast doesn't like me. You saw what it did when I read the incantation."

Alex sighed. He was right; the materpoda *had* been agitated when Shel tried it. Was she trying to tell them he wasn't the right person for the job? She pulled the book from Shel's grip. "We're both going to try while the candles are flickering. I'll go first."

She stepped into the circle and began the incantation. She'd only gotten three words out when the materpoda rushed at her, just as she'd done to Shel. Alex faltered, but then carried on, finishing the incantation while the materpoda raced around the cage.

The demon remained stubbornly present.

They were doing something wrong. The materpoda knew it, and was trying to tell them so.

But what was it?

Maybe she should try relighting the candles in the other direction … again.

One of the candles guttered and went out. *Shit.* Her stubby little candles had burned down to nothing. As she watched, a second candle snuffed itself out in a little puddle of wax. Her shoulders slumped.

"Guess you won't be trying it again. Not until I make some more candles."

A third candle winked out. Alex grumbled as she snuffed out what was left of the two remaining candles.

In the dark, the materpoda's clicking increased in intensity.

"Alex?" Shel's voice wavered. He shone the light from his phone at the materpoda's nest.

The darkened eggs pulsed, and the baby demons were visible squirming inside them. One of the eggs split with a wet tearing sound like the peeling of an unripe banana.

"They're hatching," Shel squeaked.

Out of the egg crawled a centipede that could only be called small in relation to its mother. Half a metre long and armed with the same sickle-shaped jaws of the adult, it was a terror in its own right.

Another egg split, disgorging an identical baby demon. The materpoda clicked and fussed over them, but as more and more babies emerged, the writhing mass of bodies and legs made even Alex's skin crawl.

Shel grabbed Alex's wrist and hauled her into the house, slamming the door behind them.

Chapter Twenty-Two

Multiplying Materpodas

Running inside was the last coherent thing Shel did for a long time. He sank to the floor, back against the door, face drained of colour.

Alex's heart hammered. They had no time to muck around. They needed to get the banishment to work *now*. She hurried to the kitchen and set the beeswax back on the hob to melt. Then she paced the kitchen, considering the situation.

The cage was never going to contain those babies. Their rope-like bodies could easily slip through the mesh. Would they stay near their mother? What did the babies eat? Surely they couldn't take out a dog or cat. How fast did they grow? How much did they eat?

She swore under her breath. She'd forgotten to get more meat for the materpoda today. Her quest to find beeswax had consumed the entire afternoon. They'd all be hungry—babies and mother.

What would a swarm of giant, hungry centipedes do?

Eat mice and rats? Snatch birds out of their nests at night? They'd probably hang out under houses and in walls, picking off rodents. She imagined them skittering through Gran's attic, snacking on the sparrows that nested there each spring. What would people say when they found one of those babies in the bathtub? The thought made her laugh—a grim, gallows laugh of the sort she imagined condemned prisoners of war made.

The wax was finally melting. She cut the remainder of her wicking into candle-sized lengths—she had just enough for another batch. She hoped there was enough wax.

She checked on Shel. He was still slumped by the back door. She brought him a glass of water and set it on the floor next to him, touching him lightly on the shoulder. "Let me know if you need anything."

His head bobbed in acknowledgement, but he didn't look up at her.

So much for his chilopodophobia being gone. And so much for him being glad she'd summoned the demon, she guessed. She'd been relieved to have his help, even though she hadn't asked for it. Now she was going to have to do this alone.

That was okay. She could handle this. It was a matter of casting her circle in the right direction, doing the incantation in the right direction, and making sure the candles flickered properly while she did so.

She was sure of the incantation. The circle casting only had two possibilities, so that was easy to do. It was those damned flickering candles that were causing her grief.

And maybe the fact she wasn't *born to magic*, whatever the hell that meant.

She'd make Shel do it, if she had to.

And what if neither one of you is born to magic?

225

She ignored the flash of fear. She could not fail at this.

Her hands shook as she began the slow process of making another batch of candles. She frowned at their size—even shorter than the first batch, because the wax wasn't as deep. She wouldn't have much time, once she lit them.

What if she had to do a separate banishment for each one of the babies? The thought froze her for a moment. Her pathetic candles would never last that long.

And she still hadn't figured out how to make the candles flicker in the right rhythm.

Think, Alex! Think! She gave her candle another dip.

Wind made candles flicker. Could she create a wind that caused them to flicker in the right way? Maybe with a fan?

Except she'd hauled Gran's old oscillating fan to the Salvation Army last week. She dipped the candle and called back to Shel, still curled on the floor. "Shel, do you have a fan?"

He didn't answer. She dipped the candle again, and walked down the hallway toward him, candle dangling from her fingers.

"Shel?"

His only response was a huff. Alex gritted her teeth. She didn't have time for his weakness.

"Do you have a fan, Shel? I'm thinking we can use a fan to make a breeze that causes the candles to flicker correctly. We're not going to be able to rely on the natural wind—we may have to do a separate banishment for each baby."

He whimpered. "I don't have a fan. And I can't go out there again. Those things are *hatching*." His voice rose with hysteria.

Alex swore—she was doing that a lot more than usual since she arrived here. She stomped back to the kitchen to finish her candles.

226

Half an hour later, she frowned at her handiwork. They were possibly the ugliest, most pathetic candles ever—lumpy, misshapen, and squat. They made her first batch look great. She squeezed her eyes shut against the despair that threatened to well up inside her chest.

This would work.

It had to.

She gathered up the candles and let herself out the front door. Before circling around to the back yard, she stopped by the recycling bin and fished out a flattened cardboard box she'd deposited there two days ago.

Approaching the materpoda cage, she shone a light at the nest. Her stomach squirmed in concert with the squirming bodies of baby demons. It was hard to tell if all the eggs had hatched yet or not amidst the roiling mass of legs and armoured bodies, all clicking like a basket of analogue watches.

Or a basket of ticking time bombs.

She took a fortifying breath. She could do this. She *had* to do this.

She set up the candles on the remains of the first batch. The matches rattled as she drew the box from her pocket.

Clockwise. She'd start with a clockwise casting, then try counterclockwise. She struck a match with shaking hands, and then touched the flame to the first candle.

She worked her way around the circle, annoyed when she had to light a second match and struggled with it. One, two, three times she swiped the tip against the side of the box before it lit. She didn't have time for this.

With all five candles finally lit, she picked up the cardboard and gave a few exploratory up and down waves with it in the air. If she directed the wave at a candle, it wavered a moment later when the puff of air hit it. But she could only direct the air at one candle at a time. She frowned, thinking.

What if she waved the cardboard sideways, sweeping it around the circle? She tried it, watching the candles carefully.

Yes! She was able to make them all flicker. Not entirely in sync, because of the time it took to sweep the cardboard around the circle. But they all flickered.

Time to give this a shot. Good thing she had the incantation memorised, because her hands were busy with the cardboard.

"Here goes nothing." She began flapping the cardboard, trying to recreate the beat of the song still on repeat in her head.

"Thrall and command, voyc my wish. Call my witness and now me find. Fawn and fox loveth materpod. Dawn and dusk 'twixt firelight be gone." She gave the final word extra force, punctuating it with a fierce swoosh of the cardboard. The candle flames danced in the darkness.

Click, click, click, click.

Alex dropped the cardboard and shone her light on the nest. The mother materpoda was still there. Were any babies missing? It was impossible to tell—they all blended together in a mass.

Her gut told her nothing had happened.

She snuffed out the candles, dismayed to see how much they'd shrunk in the short time they'd been lit. Then she relit them in a counterclockwise direction, pushing her dismay aside and focusing on the task at hand.

Cardboard in hand, she began the incantation again.

"Thrall and command, voyc my wish. Call my witness and now me find. Fawn and fox loveth materpod. Dawn and dusk 'twixt firelight be gone." She held her breath, listening and staring at the dim shapes inside the cage.

Click, click, click. The time bomb kept ticking.

She tried it again.

And again.

And again.

She was breathless from waving the cardboard. Her movements became frantic.

The materpoda and her babies kept clicking.

When the first of her candles guttered and died, she sank to her knees, dropping the cardboard to her side. She buried her face in her hands, heart racing, mind numb.

What the hell was she going to do now?

She counted breaths to try to calm herself. One, exhale. Two, exhale.

The clicking in the cage grew louder and more chaotic. She raised her head. In the light spilling from the windows, she watched a nightmare unfold.

Twenty-one leggy bodies oozed from the mass before her. Each was as long as her arm and flowed across the ground on rapidly moving legs. The baby demons swarmed around the nest, exploring the cage. The mother materpoda tapped gently on their backs, as though assuring herself they were all there and accounted for.

Like a puddle of oil, the mass of bodies spread further, until it reached the wall of the cage. Alex held her breath, heart pounding in her ears as she waited and watched.

The first baby to reach the fence flowed out as though the mesh didn't exist. A second followed, and Alex staggered to her feet, a stream of curses flowing through her head just like the materpodas through the cage wall. She turned and bolted into the house, slamming the door behind her.

Chapter Twenty-Three

Bright Ideas

It was a moment before she realised Shel had moved. She considered taking his place, slumped against the back door.

She'd failed. And now there were another twenty-one demons stalking the neighbourhood.

How fast did they grow? How long until there were twenty-one dog-eating materpodas snatching pets off the streets at night? How long before someone else noticed the giant centipedes in their midst?

How long before the babies reproduced too? An invasion of demons would make New Zealand's stoat and possum problems look like nothing by comparison. She grimly laughed at the thought that materpodas would probably eat stoats and possums, too.

She was about to sink to the floor when the front door opened and closed.

"Alex! You in here?" Excitement laced Shel's voice. Where had he been?

She pushed herself off the door and followed his voice

to the living room. He set a snarl of fairy lights and his laptop on the coffee table, then looked up at her. "Come here. I want to show you something."

She sat down beside him on the couch. "Shel, you should know—"

"Wait. Let me show you this first." He plugged some sort of adapter into his USB port, then attached the lights to the adapter. "I was thinking about the flickering pattern."

"Shel, we've run out of candles, and I don't have any more wax."

He waved off the problem. "We don't need candles." His fingers danced furiously over his keyboard. Alex glanced at his screen—he was coding something. She'd never been interested in coding, so it was gobbledygook to her. He hit a final key, and then looked up at her with a grin. "Watch this."

Another keystroke, and the sound of 'Call Me Maybe' emanated from his computer. At the same time, the fairy lights began to flash in perfect time to the music.

"That's cute, but how does that help us make the candles flicker? And we have no more candles anyway."

He shook his head. "I don't think it matters what we make flickering light with. Think about it—what did they have back in the days when that book was written? Candles. And maybe lamps. Those were their only tools. But today, we have all sorts of ways to make light—and ways to control the flickering precisely."

"But that woman on the forum—she was using candles, and she had very specific views about which candles worked and which didn't."

"Yeah, and have you read those forums? Those people are all *Ooh, the olden days! Back when we were one with nature.*" He said the words in a breathy, mocking voice. "They'd never even consider the possibility of using modern technology.

They're Luddites."

He had a point. "But—" Suddenly she remembered. "Wait! When I accidentally summoned the demon, the electric lights were flickering. Do you think it was the electric lights, not the candles that did it?"

"I bet it was. And I don't think it matters if we have four lights, five lights, or fifty lights—they just need to be flashing correctly."

"Like a combination to a lock—the flashing unlocks the portal."

"Exactly!" Shel's eyes were alight with excitement, and he stood abruptly. "We should go out and do it right now before the—"

"It's too late." Alex swallowed. "The babies have all hatched and they've … they've escaped from the cage."

Shelby's face lost all colour and he sat down heavily. "What?"

Alex nodded. "I have no idea where they'll be by now."

Shel's breathing picked up, and Alex was beginning to worry he would hyperventilate when he said, "Fine. Let's get rid of the mother first. The babies … they are smaller, right?"

Again Alex nodded. "I don't think they'll be eating pets yet. Maybe mice or rats."

Shel gathered the fairy lights and his computer with shaking hands. "Do you have the book?"

"It's still out there. I sort of … ran inside when the babies started escaping." She was embarrassed by her reaction. If Shel had done the same thing, she might have rolled her eyes at him.

Shel nodded grimly. "Right. Let's go then."

Alex cracked the back door open just enough to shine a light to scan for baby demons. She wasn't too worried about

232

them herself—having had time to consider it, she decided they weren't likely to be aggressive, and they were too small to inflict too much damage, even if they did attack—but she was worried that if Shel caught sight of one, he'd flee indoors and refuse to ever step foot outside again.

None of the babies were visible. Alex was simultaneously thankful and terrified by that fact. How would she ever find twenty-one nocturnal demons able to squeeze into small spaces and make themselves invisible? She pushed aside that worry. *Focus on getting rid of the one you have first.*

"Should we spread out the lights in a circle around the cage?" she asked.

"I don't think it matters, but it can't hurt."

"Everyone else makes circles, so I think we should make a circle." She paused. "Clockwise or counterclockwise?"

"Again, I don't think it matters. None of the modern witches can agree on which way it should be done in the southern hemisphere, so I'm inclined to believe it makes no difference. Besides, all the lights will turn on at the same time, regardless of which way we run the cord."

Alex frowned. "After all that discussion of direction, you think it doesn't matter?"

"Humour me. Come on. Let's get this over with." Unease coloured his voice, and she knew he was nervous about the baby demons lurking somewhere in the darkness.

Alex stretched the string of lights around the cage. It was just long enough, and Shel crouched where the two ends met, laptop on his knee. When Alex stepped into the circle of lights, he looked up at her. "Ready?"

She nodded.

Shel started the music, and Alex frowned. "I don't think we can have the music playing—won't that interfere with the incantation?" Shel turned the volume down.

She watched the lights flicker, and in her head she could hear the music playing. The materpoda, alone in her cage, lifted her head and tapped her antennae. She raised herself onto her feet and rippled smoothly out from the shelter. The movement wasn't aggressive, it was more inquisitive.

With her eyes on the materpoda, Alex recited the backwards incantation. What would happen to the babies if they sent the mother back? Did materpodas care for their young after they hatched? Might she refuse to go because her babies weren't with her? The closer she came to the end of the incantation, the more her stomach churned.

The lights continued to flash their silent tune as Alex said the final words. The materpoda's antennae waved in the air, questing for something. Was she waiting for the portal to open? Alex held her breath, afraid to blink and miss anything. Would the materpoda just vanish? Would a visible door open?

Or would nothing happen at all?

As the seconds ticked by with no change, Alex's hope withered. Finally, she let out her breath in a whoosh. "Well. That was a fail."

Chapter Twenty-Four

Satan's Voice

Over the next hour, they tried every permutation of their spell they could think of—winding the lights in the other direction, having Shel read it, reading it more loudly, whispering it, slowing down the song, speeding the song up—nothing worked.

It was nearly one in the morning. "We're obviously missing something," Alex said.

Shel yawned. "Yeah. Coffee."

They headed inside for a pick-me-up. Shel retired to the couch with his laptop and dove into research. Thor and Thunder leapt up with him. Alex filled Gran's little stovetop espresso maker and set it on a burner.

After depositing two mugs of strong coffee on the coffee table, Alex picked up her own laptop and sat on the other end of the couch from Shel, with the cats between them.

"Any ideas of where to start?"

Shel frowned. "No. I have no idea what we've gotten wrong. Could be anything."

"Or everything." Alex shut her eyes, thinking. "The materpoda seems to know what's necessary for the banishment."

"At least it seems to have a preference for flash patterns."

Alex nodded. "I'm going to give her the benefit of the doubt and say that she knows—and has shown us—the flickering pattern we need to use for the lights. So let's say we have that correct. What other variables are there?"

"There's the number of lights and the direction they're lit from—but I'm convinced those don't actually matter. Why did witches switch from five to four candles if the number mattered?"

"Maybe modern witches don't summon demons."

Shel shook his head. "Some at least think they're summoning demons."

Alex shuddered. "I can't believe there are people *deliberately* doing this."

"There are some sick people out there."

"Right. So assuming the lights are correct, and the number and direction don't matter. That leaves us with what?"

"The words of the incantation."

"We must have that right. The book clearly indicated that the banishment was a *reverse summoning*. What else could it be but a backwards reading of the summoning?"

"I don't know."

"I'm actually worried about how the book said banishments could only be done by people born to magic. What if neither one of us is born to magic? What does that even mean?"

"Are you thinking we might have to get someone else to do it?"

"I don't know. I just—if we've got everything else right, which we seem to, what else could it be?"

"Okay. Well, that's where we start, then." He took a sip of his coffee. "Oh! That's good."

They both focused on their computers then, searching for any clues to what they were doing wrong.

A dull ka-thunk startled Alex awake. She blinked at the ceiling, trying to piece together what was wrong with her current situation.

She wasn't in bed. She turned her head to the side. The living room. She was on the couch. Her gaze fell on a mostly full coffee cup, then to the floor where her laptop lay. That explained the ka-thunk. And it reminded her why she was here. She sat up, easing a painful kink out of her neck. She'd fallen asleep leaning against the arm of the couch, her legs outstretched next to Shel's. Her movement woke him and the two cats who were draped across their legs.

He groaned, opened his eyes, and then lurched upright. "What time is it?"

She glanced out the window at the morning light. "Seven? Our coffee didn't do us much good, did it?"

He rubbed his face. "Sorry. I didn't mean to spend the night."

She laughed as she stood and stretched. "No. You meant to be rid of the demons, get back to your real life, and never have to deal with me again." It was nice to have him there first thing in the morning, but she wasn't going to tell him that.

"Yes. And no." He smiled at her.

What did that mean? Her stomach growled. Had she eaten dinner last night? She couldn't remember. The fridge was empty—she was supposed to be leaving tomorrow, so hadn't restocked her food.

"I'm going to brush my teeth and change. Then let's go to the bakery for breakfast." She hurried down the hall.

"What, and I've got to go like this?"

She peered back around the corner at him. "I thought you computer geeks didn't care what you wore."

He gave her an exaggerated look of offence. "I very carefully choose whatever is on top of the pile every day."

"Well, we can swing by your place on the way if you want to put on a tie."

He snorted. "No need, though if I can steal some toothpaste from you …"

"No worries. I'll be just a minute."

Ten minutes later they were standing in line at the bakery behind half a dozen tradies in high-vis jackets and scuffed boots. The heady smell of yeast, cinnamon and coffee revived Alex. "What's your favourite?" she asked. Everyone within twenty kilometres of Mansfield Bakery had a favourite.

"Lemon curd muffin," Shel answered without hesitation.

"Cinnamon scroll for me."

They ordered two large coffees to accompany their decadent breakfast and claimed a small table in the corner.

Alex took a big bite of her scroll and moaned her appreciation. "I've missed these things. Nobody in Wellington makes cinnamon scrolls this good. I know. I've checked them all."

Shel laughed and bit into his muffin.

After swallowing and taking a sip of coffee, Alex sighed and sat back. "So, I take it you didn't find any critical information before you fell asleep last night?"

He shook his head, mouth full of muffin.

"I'm beginning to think you were right from the start. Maybe we should have killed it."

Shel swallowed. "We tried, remember? The fly spray? The cricket bat? The knife?"

"Maybe we should have tried harder. We didn't try anything magical, and both the book and Mrs Walker said magic was the way to do it." She lowered her voice. "What happens if these things start breeding here? What if they start taking out any animal smaller than a Labrador retriever? What are they going to do to our pets, our wildlife?" The full scale of the horror she might have unleashed on the country was mind-boggling.

And worse, she could imagine the paperwork piling up on her desk already—the reports, the studies, the policies.

Shel paled, but then shrugged. "Well, it's too late now. Besides, I hit that thing twice with a cricket bat, and it hardly flinched. I don't think we could kill it, no matter what we tried."

Alex nodded, taking another bite and chewing thoughtfully. "How many demons do you think there are on Earth? You know, ones summoned by other idiots like me, or by witches who didn't know what they were getting into?"

"Well I wouldn't believe all the crazy shit we read on those forums. If you believe the crazies on the internet, then the world is flat and the moon landing was faked."

Alex snorted. "Yeah, but Mrs Walker is a pretty normal person. And Gran was a bit weird, but not ... *raving*. We *know* there's a demon in Gran's back yard. And I watched Thor miraculously heal my arm with spit, and I'm convinced the garden group was responsible for him. Maybe some of the crazies are telling the truth."

"Maybe." He took a deep breath, and Alex could feel the stress rolling off him in waves. No doubt she was giving off the same vibes. It was ruining her enjoyment of what was a spectacular breakfast.

The door of the cafe opened, and in blew a gust of wind, carrying with it Mrs Walker and four other women. Alex leaned forward and nudged Shel.

"That's the garden group."

Gumboot lady—who had removed her boots when she walked in—saw Alex and nodded to her. Then she whispered something to Mrs Walker.

As soon as the women had ordered, they descended upon Alex and Shel like a flock of birds, Mrs Walker at the head of the group.

"Alex! Just the person we wanted to see." Mrs Walker pulled out a chair and sat down. "And who's this?"

"This is Shelby."

"Shelby? You look familiar. Did I teach you?"

"He's Dex Saunders' grandson."

Mrs Walker's eyebrows rose. "Oh! That explains it. You look remarkably like Dex."

The other women nodded and exclaimed over the likeness. When they introduced themselves to Shel, Alex tried to pay attention and learn their names this time. Ellen, Margaret, Pauline—that was Gumboot Lady—and Sharon. They all pulled up chairs, until Alex felt surrounded.

"So ... you wanted to talk to me?" she asked.

"Yes, but ... ah ... maybe this isn't a good time?" She glanced at Shel. "It's about matters related to the book."

"Shel knows."

"In that case—" Mrs Walker turned. "Margaret? Do you want to tell her what Leo said?"

Margaret scooted her chair closer and leaned in. "I mentioned your problem to Leo, and he said—"

Shel raised his hand. "Who's Leo?"

"My familiar. We prefer the term over demon, or angel, for that matter. It's more ... friendly."

"You mean you have a demon living with you?" Alex asked.

Margaret nodded. "Same as you—Thor was your gran's familiar. She summoned him to—" She glanced at the other women. "Should I tell her this?"

At the nods of the others, she continued. "She summoned Thor to look after you and let her know how you were doing once you left home."

What? Gran spied on her? Alex's outrage was momentary, replaced by guilt that Gran had to resort to such measures.

Margaret went on. "Thunder is more mysterious. We're certain he's also a familiar, but we don't know whose. He came home with Thor one day and never left. But that's irrelevant. My Leo—also *Felis daemonicus*—said that—"

Shel's hand went up again. "Your demon—familiar—can talk?"

"Because I summoned him, I can understand him."

Alex frowned. "Is that true of all demons? If so, why can't I understand when the materpoda talks?" It would have made things much easier the past week if she'd been able to communicate with the demon.

Margaret shrugged. "I don't know. We're all just amateur witches. We dabble a little, and usually only when we absolutely have to."

Alex sighed. Did anyone understand witchcraft? "Go on. Leo said …"

"Leo said that he didn't know how to open a portal. Apparently, few demons are capable of that. But the lore among his kind is that portals are one-way—you can either pass through them into this world or out of this world—and that not every witch who can open a portal in one direction is able to open one in the opposite direction."

"Great. So even if we do get the process right, we still might fail?" Alex asked.

Margaret nodded. "I'm afraid so. But Leo's been back and forth more than once, so he's experienced a banishment."

"And?" Why hadn't she mentioned this first?

"They didn't speak English for the banishment."

Alex's shoulders slumped. "Didn't speak English?"

"Or any other language he knows—Leo speaks quite a few. In fact, he said the incantation was full of strange sounds and unusual stresses. He said it reminded him of the language of some of the more powerful demons."

"But it wasn't their language?"

"No. He didn't understand a word."

"Is that all he could tell you?"

"I'm afraid so."

The barista called out, "Twenty-three."

"Oh! That's us," Mrs Walker said. "We've got to go. I'm so glad we ran into you."

Margaret patted Alex on the arm as she stood. "Good luck. Let us know how you get on."

The women bustled out, picking up their coffees and scones on their way.

Shel rubbed his face. "How are we going to figure out the incantation if we don't even know what language it's supposed to be in?"

"No idea." Alex's delicious cinnamon scroll tasted like dust. It was hopeless. They'd never get rid of the materpoda. What the hell were they supposed to do now? She squeezed her eyes shut.

"Hey." Shel rested his fingers on the back of her hand. "We'll figure this out. But we can't do it on empty stomachs. Let's not think about it for the next fifteen minutes. Let's pretend we've simply gone out for breakfast. We both need a break."

Alex nodded. "Yeah. Okay." What would they talk about if they'd simply gone out for breakfast? If they didn't have the problem of a potential national biosecurity disaster on their hands? "Did you play D&D in high school? You seem like the kind of guy who would have."

Shel smiled. "Yep. D&D was my favourite, but I played any RPG, really. I was the definition of that stereotype. Still am, if the truth be told."

"Do you still play D&D?" Alex had known a few guys in high school who played, but she didn't know any adults who still did.

"Now and again. Well, not since Covid, but before— when we travelled to conferences and whatnot—I'd play whenever my uni mates and I were at a conference together."

"What did your parents think of all the gaming? Did they get on your case about it? Gran never let me play any of those online RPGs."

"They didn't mind too much. I think Dad thought the computer games were good training for flying—all those reflexes, and the ability to make quick decisions under stress. He gave me a flight simulator game once for my birthday."

"Consider yourself lucky then. Gran thought computer games were a waste of time, and apparently the minister of her church once commented that D&D was akin to satanic worship." Alex rolled her eyes. "Not that I ever asked to play D&D, but it was among her list of 'thou shalt nots' when I was a teen."

Shel frowned. "Hm. I wonder if the D&D crowd would have any information on demons."

The attempt to avoid thoughts of demons hadn't lasted long, had it? "You're in the D&D crowd. Wouldn't you know if they were worshipping Satan and summoning demons?"

"I'm a casual player of D&D. I'm not obsessive like some of those guys. Might be worth having a look."

Fair enough. "What else is supposed to be devil worship—are there other groups of people who might know something about summoning demons?"

"Let's see … witches, D&D players …"

"Heavy metal bands."

"Politicians!"

Alex giggled. "Bagpipe players?"

"Nah. Ukulele players."

"Aw, come on! I love the uke." It was good to laugh. It was good to have someone with her as she muddled through this bizarre situation.

Back at Gran's house, with a second coffee, they sat down with their computers on their laps to continue their search for information. They had a little more to go on now—depressing information, but it was something.

Getting away to somewhere normal for breakfast and not thinking about the demon in Gran's back yard for at least a few minutes had eased Alex's nerves. Sitting next to Shel on the couch, elbows brushing occasionally as they typed, was even better. His presence was distracting, in fact, and she had to force herself to ignore him and focus on her web search.

Alex was most worried about the idea that, even if they got the incantation right, they might still fail because some people couldn't do a banishment. It must have something to do with the comment in the book about people 'born to magic'. She googled *born to magic*. Nothing. She tried variations: *native magic user*, *natural magic user*, *untrained magic user*, and others. No joy.

Okay, how about finding some Satan worshippers. They might know something. She typed in a new search.

She was in the middle of a long article about why D&D was a gateway drug to devil worship when there was a knock at the door.

Linda.

Alex suppressed a sigh and put on a smile. "Morning, Linda. How are you today?"

"Well, I haven't lost any more chickens. And I haven't heard of any more pets going missing. But I read this article on the internet while I was having breakfast and I thought you should know about it. Although, I warn you it might be upsetting. Apparently, there's some sort of cult that makes animal sacrifices. It's a ritual to raise the dead or something."

"Are you thinking the missing pets have something to do with this cult? Are these people even in New Zealand?"

"Well, the article didn't say where they were, but it would explain the pets."

She supposed it didn't sound any more far-fetched than the truth. Still … "I'm not sure you should believe everything you read on the internet."

"Alex, awful people exist. You're not old enough to remember, but back in the nineteen eighties there were musicians who embedded messages from Satan in their music and bit the heads off live animals during their concerts."

Alex couldn't suppress her laugh. "I'm sure that was all a hoax—a marketing ploy to sell more records."

"It's true! When you played the records backwards, you could hear the devil's voice."

Oh boy. Linda had gone off the deep end. "Well, thanks for letting me know about this cult."

"Be sure to google it. You don't want them to steal

Alice's cats, after what they've done to Benji and the other animals in the neighbourhood. You need to be prepared. And be careful."

With assurances that she'd learn more about the cult and keep Gran's cats safe, Alex managed to bundle Linda out the door ten minutes later.

When the door clicked shut, Shel cried out, "That's it!"

"What is? What did you find?"

"Not me. Linda."

"Huh?"

"Play the record backwards and hear Satan's voice."

"So … this is relevant to us how?"

Shel looked up. "Leo said the incantation sounded like the language of some of the more powerful demons—what's Satan but the most powerful demon?"

Alex sucked in a breath as realisation dawned. "A banishment is a reverse summoning. Not word-for-word backwards, but completely reversed."

She snatched up the summoning book and opened it to the incantation page. "I'll need to write this out backwards if I'm going to be able to say it that way."

Grabbing a piece of scrap paper from the recycling bin, she began to transcribe the incantation:

Llarht dna dnammoc cyov ym hsiw. Llac ym ssentiw dna, won em dnif. Nwaf dna xof htevol dopretam. Nwad dna ksud txiwt' thgilerif eb enog.

Finished, she tried reading it. "*Lart dna dnamoc seeyov eem* … Damn, this is hard. How am I supposed to pronounce things like h-s? Or y-m—is it *eem* or *yim*?"

"Or is it pronounced like *I'm*?"

"Why would it be pronounced like that?"

"Because forward, it's *my*—the y sounds like a long i."

"Oh! I hadn't thought about that. In that case h-s should

246

probably be pronounced *sh*—not actually backwards." She swore. "Which way do you reckon is right?"

Shel shrugged. "Your guess is as good as mine."

Alex rubbed her face and groaned. "Just what we need. More variables." She took a sip of her coffee and grimaced—it was cold. Then she turned back to the page. "*Larth dna dnammoc soiv im shiw*," she slowly read out. "Does it matter how fast I say this?" She couldn't imagine ever being able to recite the incantation quickly this way. And forget memorising it.

He shrugged again, his expression less than hopeful.

"Too bad we can't …" An idea struck her, and she did a quick internet search.

"Too bad we can't what?"

Bingo! "Ha! We *can!*" She looked up at Shel with a grin. "I can't believe Mr Computer Geek didn't think of that first."

"Think of what?"

"We're going to record it forwards and use an app to reverse it."

Shel blinked at her for a moment. "You're right. I can't believe I didn't think of that first."

Chapter Twenty-Five

Listen to the Cat

Alex pressed record and began to read the incantation forward. Halfway through, Shel slapped the book. "What if you accidentally summon another?"

Alex suppressed a curse and thought about it. "Without the flickering lights, it shouldn't happen."

Shel frowned. "I'm not willing to take the chance."

"Well how else are we going to record it forward in order to play it backward?"

"We'll record it in parts. Not the whole thing at once. Then we can stitch the two files together before reversing it, so that it's seamless."

It seemed like unnecessary extra work, but … "I suppose it's better to be safe than sorry."

It wasn't as difficult as she expected, thanks to Shel's computer skills. He had the two halves of the incantation combined in minutes, and then it was simply a matter of loading the file onto the app to reverse it. Alex played it backwards, intrigued by the odd cadences and stresses. "I never could have done that myself."

"Yeah, I'm not sure it's going to work, for exactly that reason. Who *could* do that before technology could do it for us? You think they managed that in the eighteenth century?"

"Maybe. The book *did* say it was difficult, and Leo said some witches couldn't do it. Maybe it took a lot of practice."

"Well, we've tried saying it word-for-word backwards, and that didn't work."

"Assuming we had everything else correct ..."

Alex growled in frustration. "I wish we could try it now rather than waiting until dark." She grabbed both their coffee cups and took them to the kitchen, wondering if she should pick up sandwiches for them when she went out to buy more meat for the materpoda. She glanced at the clock, and then dropped the cups with a scream as she saw movement out of the corner of her eye.

One of the baby materpodas was curled in the bottom of the sink. It streaked out onto the kitchen bench as the mugs tumbled toward it, and then dropped to the floor. It shot between Alex's feet as she danced out of its way. There was a loud hiss, and then Thor dashed across the kitchen floor after it. The materpoda raced into the living room, cat close behind in a fury of black fur. It skittered up the wall and Thor leapt, knocking it back to the floor. Shel screamed and jumped onto the couch.

The materpoda rocketed across the floor and made a beeline for the front door. It hit the cat flap with a thunk, pushing it open and flowing out. Thor followed in a leap, and the flap banged shut as the tip of his tail vanished.

Alex's heart was racing, adrenaline pumping through her body. "I should have taped up the cat flap again."

"Do it now, before that thing comes back in." Shel's voice was shaky.

"What if that wasn't the only one inside?"

A moment later, Thor leapt back through the cat flap, calm and cool, as though he hadn't just chased a small demon out of the house. He strolled over to Shel and wound himself around his ankles, purring.

"Good kitty," Shel said, bending down to pet Thor. "Now go get any others in the house. Go on. Go get 'em!" He sang the words like you would tell a dog to go fetch a ball.

Thor turned tail on him and sauntered away.

Alex snorted. "He's giving you the cat salute—bum in your face. I think it means *fuck off, I don't work for you.*"

Shel laughed. It was shaky, but the colour was returning to his face.

Maybe there was only one materpoda baby inside. "I'm going to go check the cage—see if any of the babies are there. Then let's get some lunch." She headed out the back door and immediately heard the clicking that told her there was more than one materpoda in the cage. Peering under the shelter, she saw a mass of legs and segmented bodies. It was impossible to tell if all the babies were there, nestled in the coils of their mother's body, but the shelter was practically overflowing. She shuddered, glad that Shel hadn't come out with her.

The afternoon was uneventful. They continued to research every aspect of the incantation, not coming up with much more useful information. They both ended up falling asleep on the couch again, and Alex smiled when she woke to the warmth of Shel's leg pressed against hers, his left hand resting on her ankle.

As dusk fell, they once again ventured out to the materpoda cage and set up the lights.

"Wind them around clockwise first," said Alex. "If that doesn't work, we'll do them counterclockwise next."

While Shel trailed the lights out, Alex checked the shelter. The mother materpoda was there, and at least some of the babies. Alex wasn't sure there were as many babies there now as there had been earlier. She opened a bag of chicken drumsticks she'd picked up at the butcher's in the afternoon. The moment the bag was open, the materpodas grew restless. Antennae waved and bodies wriggled. Alex pushed several drumsticks through the mesh of the cage, and then staggered back as the mother materpoda and several babies skittered over for them.

"Ew! Gross!" Shel wrinkled his nose as the materpodas crunched bone and gristle with wet smacking sounds.

"Yeah. Don't think about it too hard," Alex said as she stepped to another part of the cage and shoved a few more drumsticks in. With luck, this would be the last time she had to feed demons.

The sun sank further in the west, and the shadows in the yard deepened. "Well, shall we do this?" Alex asked with little hope of success.

"I'm ready when you are." Shel turned on the flashing lights.

Alex stepped into the circle of lights and hit play on her phone. The strange-sounding backward words of the incantation emanated from the speaker. The mother materpoda froze, as if listening, and Alex's hope kindled. The materpoda was paying attention—the first time she'd done that and not flown into a frenzy of cage rattling. Her antennae began waving slowly in the air. Did she sense a portal opening up?

The incantation ended and both Shel and Alex waited in silence.

Nothing happened.

Shel turned off the flashing lights.

Still nothing happened.

Finally, Alex let out a huff of annoyance. "Okay. Let's restring the circle counterclockwise." She tried to keep her voice light and upbeat, but the words were said through gritted teeth, and she was certain she'd failed at *upbeat*.

Shel relaid the string of lights, and his desultory movements told Alex he felt the same way she did about this endeavour—it was going to fail again.

They didn't speak. As soon as the lights were ready, Shel turned them on, and then Alex started the incantation playing. Again, during the incantation, the materpoda was attentive, questing with her antennae. She seemed to expect something to happen.

Halfway through the incantation, teeth sank into Alex's ankle. She jerked her foot up. "Ow! Thor, what are you doing?"

The cat had bitten her! And now he strolled to Shel and rubbed against him, purring.

Shel looked down at the cat, mistrust in his eyes. "What was that all about?"

"Who knows?" Alex sighed. "Let's try that one again. I can't imagine that me interrupting the incantation like that helped."

She restarted the recording, and this time Thor didn't wait for it to be half over. He launched himself at the phone in Alex's hand, batting it to the ground. When he landed, he again went to Shel and rubbed himself around his ankles.

"Okay. I'm not an animal person, but that cat's trying to tell us something," Shel said. "And if he is a demon, like Margaret said, then we should listen to what he has to say."

Alex nodded. "But what is he saying?"

They both frowned at the cat for a moment.

"He doesn't want you to play the incantation," Shel reasoned.

"Yes. But the materpoda is clearly interested in it, so I'm inclined to think we got that part right." Alex watched Thor twine around Shel's ankles. "Does he want *you* to play the incantation?"

"What difference would that make?"

"No idea. Should we try it?"

"It's no more ridiculous than any other idea we've tried. Let's give it a go." He held out his hand and Alex gave him her phone as they switched places.

Alex turned on the flashing lights. "Whenever you're ready."

Shel hit play, and instantly, Thor was knocking the phone from his hand.

"Okaaay," he said. "That wasn't it."

Thor resumed his purring and rubbing around Shel's ankles. Alex considered his particular attention to Shel. "Shel, I think you are born to magic. I think you need to read the incantation."

Shel frowned. "I am not a witch. I know nothing about magic or witchcraft except what I've read on the internet in the past couple of days."

"Thor adores you. And he's clearly trying to tell us something here. He doesn't want me to read the incantation. He wants *you* to."

"He's a cat! What does it matter what he wants?"

At this, Thor bit Shel's ankle, then glared at him.

"Okay. Not a cat." Shel returned Thor's glare.

"Humour me. What do we have to lose—this isn't working."

Shel sighed. "I'll need to go inside where I can read the

incantation—I don't have it memorised like you do."

A few minutes later, they were back outdoors with a new recording. Alex's nerves hummed with tension. She didn't want to hope this would work—nothing else had—but she couldn't help believing it might. Both the materpoda and Thor seemed to approve of what they were doing. If a demonic cat and a giant centipede thought it was right … She shook her head. Clearly she was going nuts—too much stress and too little sleep.

"Okay. Here goes nothing," Shel said. He nodded to Alex and she turned on the flashing fairy lights. Then he started the backwards incantation.

"*Llarht dna dnammoc cyov ym hsiw.*" The incantation sounded no different in Shel's voice than it had in Alex's. Well, his voice was deeper, but that was it, as far as Alex could tell.

"*Llac ym ssentiw dna, won em dnif.*" The materpoda quivered, as if in anticipation.

"*Nwaf dna xof htevol dopretam.*" Thor was a statue with glittering eyes trained on the demon in the cage.

"*Nwad dna ksud txiwt' thgilerif eb enog.*" A thunderclap tore through the air, accompanied by a bright flash of light, as though lightning had struck out of the clear sky above. Alex flinched, and then blinked rapidly to try to clear her vision. She sucked in a breath.

Smoke curled up from each fairy light, and small flames arose here and there along the string. The lights had been obliterated.

The materpoda flew into a frenzy. She hurled herself at the side of the cage. Then she ricocheted around the walls, clicking wildly.

Dammit! Of course it didn't work. And now their lights were destroyed.

Shel lunged for the door, fumbling with the latch. The materpoda crashed against the door.

What the hell? Alex grabbed his upper arm and hauled him away. "What are you doing?"

He shook himself loose from her grip. "It wants to get out—to go home!" Shel pointed at the back yard.

"What are you talking about? We can't let her out. What has gotten into you?"

"The portal! It opened *outside* the cage." Again he pointed at nothing.

"What portal?" Alex squinted into the darkness.

"You can't see it?"

"No. All I see in the direction you're pointing is Gran's compost pile."

"You don't see the big ... rip ... in the air? And the turquoise trees? Purple moss?"

"Are you sure you're okay? That sounds like some sort of magic mushroom trip."

Shel huffed. "I'm not on drugs. There's a portal right there and the materpoda wants to get to it." He turned toward the supposed portal and swore. "Shit! It's closing." Again he lunged at the cage door, releasing the latch and pulling the door wide open. The materpoda surged out, and Shel screeched and ducked as she barrelled past him.

The materpoda skittered to what had been the edge of the circle, and then stopped. She clicked loudly, urgently, pacing back and forth.

A stream of baby materpodas scurried out from under the shelter in the cage. Alex counted as they followed their mother. One, two, three, four ... they kept coming. She glanced toward the mother, still clicking and pacing. As the first baby reached her, she shoved it with her head toward the edge of the circle. As it crossed the line of still-smoking lights, it vanished. Alex sucked in a breath of surprise, then darted her eyes back to the babies streaming from the shelter. Seventeen, eighteen, nineteen …

"Shit. They're not going to make it," Shel muttered. "Go, go, go, go!" He jumped toward the spot where the materpoda babies were vanishing one by one.

"Shel! What are you doing?" Alex's heart raced as she watched in disbelief.

Shel stumbled as he drew near to the materpoda. She ignored him, chittering to her babies and shoving each of them forward when they got to the edge of the circle. A strong wind seemed to be blowing Shel toward the portal. His shirt flapped in the wind, though Alex felt nothing but a mild breeze.

"Alex!" Panic laced his voice, spurring her to action.

She sprinted toward him and he held out his hand, eyes wide. She had no idea what was going on, but she grabbed hold of his hand and pulled.

"Wait!" He hooked his free hand against some invisible object in the air. "Now pull!"

She pulled. She could feel Shel being tugged in the opposite direction. By what, she couldn't tell. His clothing still flapped as though whipped by a gale, while she felt no wind at all.

"It's working! Keep pulling!" Shel said breathlessly.

"What is working? What are you doing?" she asked.

"Holding the portal open." He grunted as Alex felt a sudden tug on him and staggered to resist it.

The last of the babies vanished, but the materpoda was still agitated, clicking loudly and skittering back and forth.

"What's going on? Why doesn't she go?" Alex asked.

"I don't know, but I don't think I can hold the portal much longer." Shel's hand slipped in hers, and she gasped, readjusting her grip, hands slick with sweat.

Then Thunder bounded into view, a wriggling materpoda baby in his mouth. He dropped the baby at the mother's feet, and it skittered forward, vanishing like the others. An instant later, Thunder leapt after it and vanished too.

"Thunder!"

The materpoda turned toward Shel and Alex, drawing Alex's attention away from where Gran's cat had disappeared. The demon's clicking changed. Was she saying goodbye? If only Alex could say something back. Then the demon turned and vanished too.

Shel lost his grip on the side of the portal, but the pull on him didn't stop. If anything, it grew stronger. His hand slipped a little in Alex's grip, and she squeezed tighter.

"What's happening?" She hated that she couldn't see what he saw.

"The portal's not closing. It's ... I think it's trying to suck me in!"

Alex adjusted her grip, walking it up Shel's arm until she was right next to him. She felt no sucking herself, and it was a bit surreal to feel the tension in his body. As soon as he was able, he reached for her with his other hand. His arm shook as he moved it, like he was pulling against a giant rubber band. She had no idea how this force worked, but maybe if she could put herself between him and the portal, she could free him from its grip. Since she felt nothing, she wasn't worried about being sucked in herself.

"Grab hold of me and hang on," she told him. Shel wrapped both arms around her, locking his hands together behind her back. She grabbed his shoulders and turned them both so her back was to the portal, shielding him from its pull. She hoped.

Then she pushed. Whatever had hold of Shel didn't let

go. She felt him pulling against it as well, and they began to stagger away, toward the house.

One step, two steps, three … their progress was slow, and Alex's muscles were beginning to ache with the strain. How far did they have to go to get away from the pull?

And then the force vanished, as though someone had flipped a switch. Still pushing and pulling with all their might, Alex and Shel staggered and fell in a heap on the ground.

Neither of them moved for a long, stunned moment. Alex recovered first. She lay on top of Shel, her chest pressed against his, his arms still locked tightly around her.

"Alex! Alex, are you okay?" Linda appeared around the corner of the house. She ran toward them, and then stopped, stepping back. "Oh! I'm sorry … I … I heard noises and shouting. I thought … I … I'll just go now."

Oh, if only it weren't so dark, and Alex could see her face.

Linda scurried away, and Alex dissolved into laughter. She pushed away from Shel. "Um. You can let go now," she said when Shel didn't immediately release her.

"Oh. Yeah. I don't know if my hands will unclench." But he released her with a chuckle. "Twenty bucks says Linda's already on the phone, telling stories about us."

"No doubt. At least she didn't show up five minutes ago." Alex rolled off him and they both sat up. She squinted toward where the materpodas had vanished. "Is the portal gone?"

"Yeah. It's gone." He blew out a breath. "They're all gone."

"Thunder too." Had he been waiting for a portal to open so he could go home? How long had he been here?

The tension that had kept Alex strung taut for weeks suddenly released, and she slumped where she sat on the ground. Then a sense of euphoria washed over her. "We did it. We did it!" She flung herself at Shel, hugging him and laughing. "I can't believe we did it!"

Before she knew it, her laughter had turned to tears, the emotional tumult of the past weeks catching up to her. Grief, fear, relief—it all poured out in salty rivulets.

Shel tightened his grip on her and held her.

Chapter Twenty-Six

Homeward Bound

"I wish you could have seen it." Shel took a sip of wine. They'd come inside after the storm of Alex's emotions had calmed. He'd grown thoughtful as they sat on the couch in Gran's living room, drinking wine from coffee cups—all that remained of Gran's dishes after Alex's clear-out. "There was another materpoda there—on the other side of the portal."

Alex sat up. "You're kidding!"

Shel shook his head. "No. It was there, waiting. The babies ... when they got through, the materpoda on the other side went to each one and tapped it with its antennae. And then when the mother went through, they ... they embraced. Like, wrapped themselves around each other."

Alex tried to imagine it. "Do you think they were—"

"Yeah. It was daddy materpoda." He huffed out a laugh and shook his head. "You know, you hear the word demon and you think ravening beast or something. And you have to admit, that thing was fucking terrifying. It ate *dogs*! But ..."

"But she was also a mother and ... somebody's mate?"

"And that world beyond the portal! It was unreal. What else do you think lives there?" His voice held little fear, and spoke of awe and curiosity.

"I think," Alex said, "that there are cats there. Or things that look like cats." She stroked Thor's ears.

Shel nodded. "Thunder made a beeline for that portal, didn't he. It was like he knew exactly what he was doing. You think there are more demonic cats out there?"

Alex looked at him and smiled. "We know how to open the portal now. We could find out."

He blanched. "No way."

It was long past midnight, but neither of them were tired. They had polished off a bottle of wine, alternately talking over the events of the evening and sitting in contemplative silence.

They were both stretched along the couch, sitting up against the arms, their legs tucked beside one another's, Thor draped over their knees. Alex sighed and rubbed her face. "I can't believe I have to go back to Wellington tomorrow."

"Today," Shel corrected. "It's two in the morning. What time's your flight?"

"Ten-thirty." She sighed. "I never did figure out what I'm doing with this house or the cats. Cat. Nor have I managed to sell the furniture. I'm going to have to make another trip down, I suppose. And beg Linda to take care of Thor for a while longer."

Shel smiled. "Or I could just move in here."

"Huh?"

"I could pay rent. I wouldn't ask you to let me stay here for free."

"But you've got a place to live."

Shel raised his eyebrows. "With my parents."

"Okay, you have a point. But look, this place isn't legal to rent out right now. It needs insulation and probably new windows, and—"

"It'd just be temporary. Until you sort things out."

A wave of relief hit Alex. She'd been stressing about all she hadn't managed to accomplish over the past two weeks. This would take the pressure off. But … "I couldn't ask you to do that. I dragged you into this drama with the materpoda, and you've been kind and patient about the whole mess. You don't need to help me sort out my shit with Gran."

"I'm happy to do it. I actually wouldn't mind a break from living with my folks."

Alex shook her head. "I won't take advantage of you that way. You should get back to your normal drama-free life."

"What if I don't want to go back to my normal drama-free life?" Shel met her eyes across the couch.

"Don't try to tell me you *enjoyed* the past two weeks dealing with a giant dog-eating centipede, because I know you didn't."

Shel laughed and dropped his eyes to the sleeping cat. "No. But I kinda had fun, too. I enjoyed dealing with you. I don't want to …"

Alex scratched Thor's ears, unable to meet Shel's gaze either. "I can't say I'm excited to go back to my flat in Wellington and the usual stream of boring paperwork at work. Seems even more dull after … whatever this was."

"When do you think you'll be back again? To deal with everything else."

Alex sighed. "I don't know. I probably can't take any more time off work. And I wouldn't be surprised if my boss expects me to make up work this weekend. Maybe next weekend?"

"Let me at least take care of Thor for you. Then you don't have to deal with Linda." He stroked Thor's back, and the cat stirred and began to purr. "And in the meantime, call me maybe?"

Alex laughed at the reference to the song they'd used to banish the materpoda. "Yes. I would like to keep in touch with you, Shel." She raised her eyes to his, and he smiled back.

They parted several hours later. She handed Shel the key to Gran's house and dropped her bag into the boot of her rental car. For a moment they stood in awkward silence. Alex wasn't entirely sure what to say. She wasn't entirely sure what Shel was to her yet—unwitting magical accomplice? Friend? More? Then he opened his arms and leaned toward her. She responded in kind, and they hugged.

"Thank you," she whispered.

"My pleasure," he responded, his breath tickling her ear. "See you soon."

"Definitely." She broke the embrace. "You have to text me if you find out what Linda is saying about us."

He laughed. "Of course. His eyes flicked over her shoulder toward Linda's house. "Do you think she's watching now?"

"I'm sure she is." Alex laughed. "Now I need to get moving or I'll miss my plane.

She opened the car door and slid into the driver's seat. As she pulled out of the driveway, movement caught her eye. A dark form disappeared from sight and the cat door swung on its hinges. She smiled. She was happy Shel was caring for Thor. Maybe by next week, she'd find a flat that allowed her to have pets. She couldn't imagine giving the cat ... or whatever he was ... to someone else.

She was also glad she hadn't managed to finish everything while she was here. It gave her an excuse to come back. She'd like to get to know Shel better while not also trying to banish a demon.

Turning onto the street, she flicked the radio on. The strains of 'Call Me Maybe' emanated from the speakers. Alex laughed and turned the volume up.

Acknowledgements

This story began during the first Covid-19 lockdown in 2020 on the many long walks my family and I took to pass the time and remain sane. Thanks to my husband for spinning wild perambulatory tales with me.

Additional thanks goes to my early readers: Cage, Grace, Ian, Peyton, Rachel and RG.

And special thanks to my editor, Belinda, and cover designer, Jenn, for all those critical final touches.

About the Author

Robinne is an entomologist and educator by training, but she has never been able to control her writing habit. She has been publishing her writing since the 1970s, and has been known to answer entomology exam questions in verse. Unlike her exam answers, which were met with awkward silence by her Very Serious Professors, her short stories have won multiple awards.

Her fantasy books for children include the four-book Dragon Defence League series and other books infested by unusual animals. For more mature audiences, she's written the urban fantasy, Squelched, and the YA epic fantasy series, Fatecarver. She's also published two non-fiction books about insects.

Robinne believes adventures are the key to writing. The list of her own adventures is long, and includes teaching with a live two-metre-long Burmese python, living in a mud house in rural Panama, and delivering a pair of goat kids in the middle of a dinner party.

She writes and blogs from her office in rural New Zealand, where adventures can be found around every corner.

Visit her at robinneweiss.com.

Other Books by Robinne Weiss

Fantasy for adults
Squelched

Fantasy for ages 13-18
Fatecarver
Fatewalker

Fantasy for ages 8-13
The Dragon Slayer's Son
The Dragon Slayer's Daughter
The Dragon Defence League
Dragon Homecoming
The Ipswich Witch
A Glint of Exoskeleton

Non-fiction
Insects in the Classroom
Backyard Bugwatcher

Poetry
Pandemic Poetry: Across the Fence

Want more stories from Robinne Weiss?

Subscribe to my newsletter and get an exclusive story!

Be the first to know about new releases (including the next book in the Rifton Chronicles).

Enjoy special deals and promotions exclusive to newsletter subscribers.

Subscribe now at https://robinneweiss.com